BLOOD BATH

BLOOD BATH

A Matt McCall Mystery

C.C. RISENHOOVER

PaperJacks LTD.

TORONTO NEW YORK

PaperJacks

BLOOD BATH

PaperJacks LTD
330 STEELCASE RD. E., MARKHAM, ONT. L3R 2M1
210 FIFTH AVE., NEW YORK, N.Y. 10010

McLennan Publishing, Inc. edition published 1987
PaperJacks edition published July 1988

This is a work of fiction in its entirety. Any resemblance to actual people, places or events is purely coincidental.

10 9 8 7 6 5 4 3 2 1

ISBN 0-7701-0798-2

Printed in the USA

To Bill

Chapter 1

Tuesday, June 2, 2:30 a.m.

Velda Rose Caldwell was tired and angry. The past evening and early morning hours had been *memorable,* but not in the classic sense of the word.

The customers at the *Cactus Bar and Restaurant* had been rowdier than usual, bolder than in the past in their sexual overtures toward her. She couldn't remember any previous time when she had been touched so much, or any other time when she had been subject to so many lewd suggestions.

For once, at least, she was glad that Texas law prohibited a bar from serving drinks past two a.m.

"The sonofabitches," she said to Annie Cossey, another cocktail waitress. "The no good sonofabitches."

The two women were sitting at a table in the rear of the now almost empty bar, each sucking on a cigarette, pausing between puffs to sip their drinks. Fred Razo, one of the bartenders, was busy checking the liquor stock. And some of the Mexican help was going through the motions of cleaning up the dimly-lit room.

Annie laughed at her companion's anger. "Maybe it's because we had a full moon tonight," she opined. "The crazies always come out when the moon's full."

But Velda Rose wasn't buying her colleague's explanation. "I'm not blaming the moon for the assholes we had in here tonight," she said.

Annie teased, "Well, it's just another night in the life of a cocktail waitress. You should know by now that you're nothing but a potential piece of ass to the guys who come in here."

She was spirited, more accepting of her role than was the younger woman. But then, she was a shade past thirty-one, whereas Velda Rose was only twenty. And she had worked in bars for several years. The younger woman's first experience was the *Cactus*, and she had been there only three months.

Annie knocked the ash from her cigarette, took a healthy swig from her glass and said, "If you can get away from this bullshit job, the more power to you, kid. I wouldn't wish the life of a cocktail waitress on my worst enemy."

You've been doing it a long time," Velda Rose responded. "Why haven't you left?"

The older woman laughed. "Money, pure and simple. The men who come in here might say things you don't want to hear, might touch you in places where you don't want to be touched, but they pay for the privilege. I just accept the shitheads for what they are, take their money and smile.

"Besides, where else am I going to make any decent money? I'm not educated, can't even type. And even if I could, I don't think there's a secretary in San Antonio who makes the kind of money I do hustling drinks. And if there is one making as much, it's because she's fuckin' the boss.

"It may not be the greatest job in the world, but I need the kind of bread I make here to pay the freight on a couple of kids."

Annie's story was not unlike Velda Rose's. She, too, was born and raised in a small Texas town. And like Velda Rose, she had come to San Antonio to be near her high school sweetheart, who was going through Air Force basic training.

They had graduated from high school together, both offspring of poor parents who had other children to feed and clothe. But, together, they had determined to find a better life for themselves. So, the plan was for him to go into the Air Force and for Annie to go to San Antonio and find work. After he received his permanent duty assignment, they would be married and live happily ever after.

At least part of the plan worked. Annie did go to San Antonio, worked in a drugstore, and they did get married after he received a permanent duty assignment. But the marriage was not one made in Heaven, definitely not what either anticipated. In fact, for Annie it became a living hell.

While Annie and her husband were the same age, there was a tremendous gap in maturity. She was quite content to be wifely and supportive of his work in the Air Force. But he preferred gambling and drinking with his buddies to spending time with a wife, especially one who had gotten pregnant shortly after they were married. He seemed to hold her accountable for the pregnancy, as though he had nothing to do with it.

The problems of the couple were compounded by the fact that there was so little money. His Air Force pay provided only for the bare necessities, which he didn't seem to understand. Annie worked at a variety of poor paying jobs to help supplement the family income, but she felt that her efforts were for the most part unappreciated. He continued to spend any extra money, and some committed for bills, on gambling and drinking.

She even tried to make excuses to herself for his actions, figuring it was just a matter of a small town boy discovering a whole new world that he didn't know existed. But she had to wonder when it would end.

Determined to save the marriage at all costs, and not knowing what else to do, she became pregnant again. She thought the additional responsibility might curb some of his carousing. Instead, it worsened. He was angry with her for the pregnancy, said he didn't want the baby.

She had the child, of course, believing that her husband would love it when he saw it. She had been wrong. He cared no more for his new daughter than for his firstborn son.

The straw that broke the camel's back came when Annie learned that her husband had spent some of their money in the company of a prostitute. That's when she loaded the kids in the ragged car they had pinched pennies to buy, and headed for San Antonio.

As to why she returned to San Antonio, she could only surmise that it was because it was the only large city where she had ever lived, and it offered the prospect of work. Also, her parents lived in nearby Boerne. She knew that her parents could not provide financial assistance, but they could offer moral support. And at the time, she needed moral support as much as money.

Annie had ratholed a little money, so she was able to find a modest furnished apartment. And she immediately got a job as a clerk in one of the city's largest department stores. It didn't take long, however, to discover that what she earned at the department store wouldn't pay the rent, buy groceries, provide for childcare and transportation.

So, she got a night job as a cocktail waitress. She didn't like it, didn't even like the idea of it. But since she was a very pretty young woman, extremely well-proportioned, men drooled and gave her good tips. As for the women, she was lucky to get a hello from them.

Her work as a cocktail waitress was soon paying her five

times more a week than was the department store, so she quit the day job. She had been hanging onto it primarily because of her parents. They considered her work at the store decent, her work in the bar as being of the devil.

At the time, she also had some hangups about working in a bar. She liked the department store job because she considered it respectable. Back then, she craved respectability and parental approval.

Because she was working two jobs, though, she didn't have much time for the children. And when it came right down to it, they were the most important thing in her life. Since they were both preschoolers, working at the bar actually gave her more time with them.

Her husband had attempted a half-hearted reconciliation and, because she loved him, she was tempted. But common sense prevailed, and she told him no. She thought he seemed relieved by her rejection.

Anyway, she had continued working at various bars and had done rather well. She had bought a nice home and car, and her children, now eleven and twelve, had never wanted for anything. She had a substantial savings account and considerable financial security. Fellow workers thought her somewhat of a tightwad, because she never wasted money, never did any partying with them.

How people perceived her didn't bother Annie in the least. When she had first started work she had been insecure, sought approval. But all that was behind her.

She couldn't deny that she still hoped *Mr. Right* would come along, that he would swoop her up and take her to a big house, that together with the kids they would start living the American dream. But the dream was fading a bit each day. After all, what *Mr. Right* would want to take on a cocktail waitress and two kids?

It had taken Annie a long time to get to where she was emotionally, so she felt considerable empathy for Velda Rose. She knew that the younger woman had a rough row to hoe, and she only hoped that Velda Rose would come out of the ordeal with her kind of resolve. It hadn't been a rose garden, but it could be worse.

Velda Rose's man hadn't married her. He had suggested that she come to San Antonio, but when he received a permanent duty assignment, he didn't bother to tell her where he would be stationed. She had called his folks, but their son had instructed them to tell her nothing.

So, she had been stuck in San Antonio, with no money and not really knowing what to do. She had wandered into the *Cactus* looking for work and, as fate would have it, met Annie.

Annie was as good an interrogator as she was a barmaid, so, even though Velda Rose was reluctant to talk, she got the full story from the young woman. Annie not only talked the manager into giving Velda Rose a job, but also took her home and gave her a place to stay until she could get on her feet. Velda Rose stayed with Annie and the children a month, then got her own apartment.

"I can't complain about the money," Velda Rose said. "It's more a week than I ever made before. My father doesn't even make as much as I do, but I just can't stand some of the people."

"Look, Velda, I know it's tough," Annie sympathized, "but just remember that there are a whole lot of people out there who don't have a pot to piss in. If you're smart you can do alright here, save your money and go on to something else. You could even enroll in the community college and start learning a trade."

"I've thought about that."

"It's a damn good opportunity," Annie said. "If it hadn't been for the kids, I think I would have gone on to school. Sometimes I think I might still do it."

"There are a lot of people as old as you going to the community college," Velda Rose encouraged.

Annie laughed. "Hell, Velda, I'm not ancient. I'm just

thirty-one going on sixty-five. I'm supposed to be at my sexual peak. The only trouble is that I can't find anyone to peak with."

Velda Rose smiled for the first time since they had sat down. "Annie, I just wish I had your disposition."

"Why? According to most of the people who know me, it stinks."

"That's because they don't really know you."

"Well, don't tell 'em, kid. I can't afford to ruin my image.

Listen, are you ready to blow this joint? My ass is tired."

Velda Rose rode to and from work with Annie.

"I'm ready, and next week you won't have to give me a ride."

"Really," Annie said. "What happens next week?"

"I'm getting a new car."

"See, things aren't all that bad, are they?"

"I guess not," Velda Rose admitted. "I've got my own place now, and I'm getting a car. When I started work here, I didn't have anything. I have you to thank, Annie."

"Hell, don't thank me. What you've done, you've done on your own."

"But I couldn't have done it without you."

"Yes, you could."

"Well, I'm not going to argue with you," Velda Rose said, "but I do want to thank you."

Annie laughed. "Damn it, Velda, you thank me every day. I'm getting tired of it."

Velda Rose laughed at the response, and it made Annie feel good. She wanted her young friend to lighten up a bit, to quit dwelling on the dark side of life. Velda Rose was a beautiful woman, one who was naive but with considerable native intelligence. She just needed to be channeled in the right direction, and Annie was unselfish in wanting her to find that direction.

The two women got their purses, left the *Cactus* and walked the short distance to where Annie's car was parked. It was cool for a June morning, and exactly three o'clock. The sky was alive with stars, and a bright orange moon was in its zenith. It was an awe inspiring morning.

As they drove toward Velda Rose's apartment, Annie asked, "Have you met any good-looking hunks in that place where you live?" As soon as she asked the question, she regretted it.

"I'm not ready for that yet," was the melancholy reply.

"No, I guess not," Annie said. "It took me a long time to get over my man, too."

"Did you ever really get over it?"

Annie pondered the question, then answered, "No, not really. But maybe there are some things in life that you shouldn't get over. Maybe memory keeps you from making the same mistake twice."

"I sure haven't met anyone in the bar that I want to try to forget with," Velda Rose said.

"You're not likely to," Annie replied. "I've made my share of mistakes with jokers who were full of promises. It seems that every man I meet who interests me is already married."

"You don't date much, do you?"

"Hardly ever," Annie answered. "Hell, when normal people are out on a date, I'm working. That's probably good, though. It keeps me out of mischief."

Velda Rose laughed. "Well, as far as I'm concerned, I'll just join you in keeping out of mischief for the time being."

Annie brought the car to a halt in the parking spot adjacent to the stairs leading to Velda Rose's second floor apartment.

"Do you want me to go up with you?" she asked.

"No need, I'm fine."

"Well, I'll pick you up tomorrow."

"I'll be ready."

Annie waited until Velda Rose began walking up the stairs before backing out of the parking spot and leaving.

As Velda Rose walked up the stairs, she fumbled through her purse in search of her apartment key. The light on the second floor landing was out, and she made a mental note that she would mention it to the manager.

By the time she reached her door, she had found the key. She was so engrossed in inserting it in the lock that she never noticed the figure standing in the darkness. As the door opened, the figure moved quickly and grasped her. The suddenness of the attack took her by such surprise that she was unable to cry out. She could only whimper.

Chapter 2

Tuesday, 4 p.m.

Annie pulled her car into the parking spot where she had stopped earlier that morning to let Velda Rose out. She gave the customary two honks on the car's horn and waited, the motor running. She was used to Velda Rose bouncing out of her door on the second honk. In the weeks that she had been transporting Velda to work, she never had to wait for her. She had been impressed with her punctuality.

But after what Annie estimated as three or four minutes, Velda Rose had not appeared. The day was too beautiful for Annie to be irritated. She honked again.

A minute or two passed and nothing happened.

Oh, well, she thought. No telling what the kid's doing. With that thought, Annie cut the engine and got out of the car. She then hurried up the stairs to the door of Velda Rose's apartment.

She rang the doorbell, but there was no answer. Nothing. Annie figured that if Velda Rose had her stereo on, it might explain her not hearing the car horn or doorbell, but there was no music coming from inside the apartment. There was no noise of any kind.

However, in putting her ear against the door, it pushed open a bit. Strange, she thought. Velda Rose always kept her door locked. Annie had warned her that San Antonio was not like some small town where people took for granted that their neighbors were honest and trustworthy. And Velda Rose had heeded her warning. At least until now.

Annie pushed the door open and called out, "Velda, it's me, Annie."

There was no response.

Reluctantly, Annie entered the apartment. It was a small place, so the entry took her immediately into the living area. There was a small kitchen and dining nook to her left.

Maybe, she thought, Velda is in the shower. She walked quickly to the door of the bedroom and looked inside. The bath was just off the bedroom, but she didn't hear the shower running, so she called out again. Still, no answer.

Though she heard nothing, the bathroom called her like a magnet. She moved to the door of the bathroom and looked inside.

A scream lodged in her throat.

Chapter 3

Tuesday, 9 p.m.

Matt McCall and Bill Haloran were sitting in the *Thunderbird Restaurant* at Hillsboro, Texas, both attacking chicken-fried steaks covered in cream gravy. McCall, an investigative reporter for the *San Antonio Tribune,* and Haloran, a San Antonio police detective, had just completed a second day of fishing in the Brazos River below the Lake Whitney Dam.

For McCall, an avid canoeist and angler, such fishing trips were old hat. But for Haloran, fishing a river by canoe was a new experience. In fact, just going fishing was unusual.

"By god, I can't get over what that big bass did to me today," Haloran said.

"You stupid shit," McCall grumbled. "If you'd paid attention to me, you would have landed him."

"Well, asshole, if you had kept the canoe straight, I could have landed him."

McCall shook his head in mock disgust. "You had about as much chance of landing that fish as you've got of getting into Debbie's pants." Debbie was their waitress, a local eighteen-year-old who, among other things, had a good looking ass and big tits. Her body expressed in its own language her many virtues. She had told them her life story while waiting on them the night before. She was a very talkative young woman, but really didn't have anything to say.

"I imagine I've got about as good a shot at Debbie as you do."

"Take your best shot, Bill, because you're not going to get any competition from me. I'd be more interested in her if she couldn't talk."

Haloran was glad to hear his friend joking about females again. It had been only a few weeks since the girl McCall had been living with had been murdered. She had been killed in an explosion meant for the reporter.

After her death, McCall had stalked the murderer until he, in desperation, had come after the reporter. The killer had ambushed McCall and Haloran on a street in San Antonio, wounding both. But a gunshot wound had not stopped McCall from blowing the ambusher's brains out with the detective's revolver.

They had each spent time in the hospital recuperating from their wounds, then more time convalescing at their individual homes. Haloran knew that McCall was okay physically, but he still worried about the mental state of his friend.

Theirs was a strange friendship, born out of an adversary relationship. It was, however, a friendship based on mutual respect and a genuine liking for each other. McCall respected Haloran's performance and competence as a policeman, and Haloran respected McCall's journalistic attitude that *"the people have a right to know."* McCall took his watchdog role very seriously, and at times it had caused Haloran some problems. His superiors were not quite so respectful of McCall and his constant prying.

Haloran figured McCall's physical appearance matched his personality. He was what some might call ruggedly handsome, with the facial coloring of a man who had spent considerable time in the outdoors. His face was ruddy and showed a few lines, but no wrinkles. A prominent nose, high cheekbones and strong chin were granite-like in visage. There was a small cleft in the chin that went virtually unnoticed, which Haloran thought was because McCall's piercing brown eyes discouraged too close an observation.

The detective had noted that his friend looked taller than his six feet, possibly as a result of his seemingly always windblown salt and pepper colored hair. And, too, McCall always carried his one-hundred-eighty pounds in an erect fashion, much like a soldier on parade.

But the latter description was somewhat of a contradiction, since McCall always seemed to be laid-back and relaxed. Haloran knew from experience, though, that such a reading of the man was erroneous. The reporter was, in truth, tense and quick-tempered. While he operated under control, he had a short fuse that was easily ignited. And when a consuming anger possessed him, he was an altogether different person.

McCall's anger was never all that visible, but more like a controlled fire. He was not adverse, however, to settling an argument with his fists instead of by reason, especially when he was on one of his *righteous indignation* kicks.

And Haloran figured that it was a rare day when McCall wasn't on one of those kicks.

One of the things the detective liked most about his reporter friend was that he didn't claim to be objective, that he was subjective and involved in everything he did. He was never detached from the stories he was covering, and he never allowed his ego to become bigger than a story.

That might explain, Haloran thought, why McCall had won a *Pulitzer* and numerous other prestigious journalism awards. And the awards were why the editors of the *Tribune* were forced to suffer McCall's insults, wrath and undisciplined method of operation. His reputation was such that the city's other paper would pay dearly for his services, since his byline would greatly aid in its circulation battle with the *Tribune.*

McCall's past was the subject of much speculation by all who knew him, including Haloran. The detective, at the order of the police chief, had attempted to run a check on him. But Haloran knew that what he had received in the way of information from Washington was contrived. It soon became obvious that someone did not look kindly on inquiries into McCall's background.

Haloran did know that McCall had served with some elite group in Vietnam, which he suspected was CIA connected. He had never been able to confirm his suspicions. He only knew that McCall had served three tours in Vietnam, then spent additional time in the country as a reporter. It was his reporting on the war that won him the *Pulitzer.*

Though McCall would not discuss his role in the war, he didn't hesitate to express bitterness about America not winning it; crediting politicians for the *no-win* policy and all the body bags containing dead American soldiers.

Unlike most journalists, McCall was a political conservative, which was another plus in his favor as far as Haloran was concerned.

Haloran was now a detective lieutenant with San Antonio PD, having worked his way up through the ranks. He had joined the force after several years in the Marine Corps, where he had attained the rank of sergeant. Now in his forties, and with a midriff and graying hair, he was a far cry from the lean Marine that he had once been. But he was still considered one of the city's toughest cops.

"Are you sure you're not interested in Debbie?" Haloran asked teasingly.

"More than sure, pal," McCall answered. "She's all yours. Unless you think you can't handle her. She is pretty fiesty for a man your age."

"Fuck you, McCall. I'm not the ancient mariner."

"Hell, you're not a mariner at all. I spent most of the day trying to keep the canoe balanced, trying to keep you from turning us over."

Haloran grinnned. "I thought I did pretty well today. We didn't turn over one single time."

"Which is more than we can say for yesterday," McCall injected. "I've got only myself to blame, though. When you put a lard-ass in a canoe, you're asking for trouble."

Anyone hearing them talk might think that the twosome were at odds, but jibes and sarcasm comprised an integral part of all their less serious conversation. They were both experts at verbal warfare, though Haloran considered McCall better at the game. He often grew weary in his attempts to match McCall's verbal shots.

But both men were self-assured, able to take it as well as dish it out.

"Are you going to eat the rest of those french fries?" Haloran asked, eyeing a practically untouched pile of potatoes on the reporter's plate.

"No, you can have them," McCall said. "I just want another cup of coffee. That is, if I can get Debbie's attention. She might not be able to see us if she tries to look down at us over those mountainous boobs."

Haloran laughed and shoveled the potatoes off McCall's plate onto his own. "Do you want cream in your coffee?" he asked.

"Well, I don't normally use cream," McCall answered, "but in Debbie's case, I might make an exception."

Haloran doused the french fries with catsup, then raked what was left of his gravy on them. Before he could get the first bite in his mouth, McCall said with disgust, "That's the first plate I ever saw that looked like it was having a period."

"Shit, McCall, you just don't know how to eat."

"I don't have to. You do enough of it for both of us. And I might add that you're getting to be a real porker."

The detective grinned. "And I might add that you are the consummate asshole."

McCall shrugged his shoulders. "What concerns me is that if I accidentally got gravy on my asshole, you'd try to eat it. If you don't quit eating, you're not going to be able to get into your suit."

McCall was always accusing Haloran of having just one baggy, ill-fitting suit. The detective didn't pay much attention to his appearance, whereas McCall normally wore expensive tailored clothing.

"There you go giving me shit about my clothes again," Haloran said with mock resignation. "Not all of us have the bread to spend on clothes like you do, moneybags."

Though it didn't bother Haloran, the fact that McCall was seemingly well-off financially bothered many San Antonio officials and politicians. After all, here was a man who drove a new Porsche, owned an expensive condominium, wore the finest clothes and traveled extensively. He was a man whose financial independence made him impossible to control. What's more, no one could get a handle on the source of McCall's money, though many had tried.

There were, of course, rumors. Haloran had even heard officers in his own department discuss the possibility that McCall might have been one of the CIA's paid assassins. But knowing McCall as he did, the detective didn't put any stock in such supposition. He believed that if McCall had killed, it was because he thought it a patriotic duty, not for money.

To Haloran's way of thinking, where McCall's money came from was the man's own business. He knew beyond a shadow of a doubt that it didn't come from any type of illegal activity.

"I should give you shit about your clothes," McCall said. "You're the only man I know who wears suit pants and a dress shirt on a fishing trip."

"Hell, they're old."

"You don't have to tell me that. I give better stuff than you wear to the Salvation Army."

"You're not going to piss me off, McCall, so you might as well give up."

Debbie had arrived at their table with the coffee pot. "Y'all want some coffee?"

McCall laughed. "I don't know whether y'all does, but I sure do."

Debbie giggled. "Are you making fun of my accent, Mr. McCall?"

"Of course not, dumplin'. And you ought to start calling me Matt, even if I am old enough to be your father."

"Oh, you're not that old," she said, filling his cup.

McCall doctored his coffee with a half pack of Sweet 'n Low and replied, "Well, I'm damn sure not going to argue with you."

"Don't I get any coffee?" Haloran asked. "And believe me, Debbie, the man's old enough to be your father. Hell, he's old enough to be your grandfather."

While the waitress was filling Haloran's cup, McCall said, "Now, you don't want to be listening to this asshole, Debbie. He spends most of his waking hours wishing he was as young and good-looking as I am. But look at the gut on the man. Isn't it disgusting?"

"You guys are crazy," the girl said. "The way you talk to each other, it's hard to believe that you're friends."

"Who told you we were friends?" Haloran asked. "This

guy's no friend of mine."

"And I've got enough burdens without having an asshole cop for a friend," McCall said.

Debbie chuckled. "Do y'all want anything else?"

"What kind of pie do you have?" Haloran asked

"Apple, chocolate, coconut and pineapple," was the reply.

"I'll have a piece of apple with a scoop of ice cream," Haloran said.

"Hell, why not just have a pie with a quart of ice cream on top of it?" McCall asked. "Bring y'all here a whole pie."

"Do you want your pie heated?" Debbie asked with a laugh.

Haloran smiled. "Will it take long?"

"No," she said, "we have a microwave."

"Damn, what'll they think of next?" McCall joked. "I guess y'all have a leg up on every other restaurant here in Hillsboro. I'll bet Kentucky Fried doesn't have a microwave."

"I wouldn't know," Debbie responded. "And don't be so sarcastic, Mr. McCall. Hillsboro happens to be a pretty nice town."

"Damn it, Debbie, call me Matt. And I'm sorry if I implied that Hillsboro was anything short of a mecca on Interstate Thirty-five."

"What does that mean?" she asked.

"It means that I'd rather be in Hillsboro right now than just about any other place in the world."

"You're really hard to understand, you know that?"

Haloran grunted. "Don't try to understand him, Debbie. I'd rather you had something nicer to think about in that pretty little head of yours."

"He's right," McCall agreed. "It's understandable that you don't understand me, but I think we'll all have a better understanding of our misunderstanding of me after a good night's sleep. So, go get *Chubby's* pie so he can finish pigging out, and then we'll all get some sleep."

She laughed again and trotted off to get the pie.

"She does have a nice ass," Haloran reiterated.

"And nice tits," McCall added.

"I think she likes you, McCall."

"So?"

"So, you ought to take her out while we're here."

"Why don't you take her out?"

"Hey, I'm a happily married man."

"What you mean is that you're afraid that your wife would find out."

"You're right, but Debbie wouldn't go out with me if I asked her."

"You don't know until you ask."

"You're wrong, I do know."

When Debbie returned with the pie, Haloran said, "I guess a girl as pretty as you has a steady boyfriend."

"Not really," she replied. "The pickings aren't that great around here."

"Whoa," McCall said. "I'll not tolerate you making such remarks about Hillsboro, my adopted homeland."

Debbie laughed. "Boy, I can't say anything around you but what you jump on it."

Haloran mumbled. "He's been known to jump on damn near anything."

McCall looked at the detective in mock disbelief. "What, pray tell, do you mean by that remark?"

"Only that you're a superb wordsmith," Haloran replied with a straight face.

"Well, Debbie might not have taken it that way."

"I didn't take it any particular way," Debbie said.

McCall asked, "Do you want to take it a particular way, Debbie?"

She shrugged her shoulders. "I don't have any idea what you guys are talking about."

McCall looked accusingly at Haloran. "Don't you realize

what you've done, Bill? You've confused this young lady to the point where she doesn't even understand what I'm saying."

"I'm sorry," Haloran responded. "I guess I just wasn't thinking."

"Aha," McCall said. "Therein lies the very essence of the problem. Not thinking. Not thinking, indeed. I just don't understand how you can so casually dismiss what you've done."

Debbie looked puzzled as Haloran responded with, "Look, I've already said I'm sorry. What do you want me to do, suck the girl's toes?"

"If she wants you to, yes. I don't think that's too much to ask under the circumstances. Tell me, Debbie, do you want Detective Haloran to suck your toes?"

She giggled. "Like I said, you guys are crazy."

"Since I am certifiably crazy, I don't suppose you'd consider having a drink with me after you get off work," McCall said.

"I don't get off until ten."

"According to my watch, that's only twenty minutes from now."

"I don't know where we can get a drink around here."

"We'll search for a place. But hey, no pressure. If you don't want to go, it's understandable, since you don't understand me."

"I want to go, but I do have to get in fairly early," she said. "I have a class in the morning."

"Wait a minute now," McCall said. "Are you still in high school?"

Debbie laughed, "No, I go to junior college."

"Don't get me wrong," McCall said. "I'm not opposed to dating high school girls, even those in junior high. But I do draw the line at elementary school women."

Between bites of pie Haloran injected, "That's a change in attitude, isn't it? New Year's resolution, huh?"

"There is no substance to the rumors you've heard about me and elementary school girls," McCall said. "It may come as a surprise to you, but I've been cleared of all child molesting charges in San Antonio."

"I never thought there was anything to those allegations," Haloran said. "I've always maintained they were started by a jealous junior high cheerleader."

"You know about her, huh?"

"You guys aren't just hard to understand," Debbie said with a laugh. "You're also weird."

"Thanks," they replied in unison.

McCall told Debbie he would pick her up at ten, but she said, "I might be a little late getting off, so I'll just come by your room and knock. Which one is it?"

"Number nine," he said. "And I can see why you might be late with all the customers that you have in here." Other than Haloran and McCall, there were four customers in the restaurant. "Hurry up and get rid of these yoyos, and we'll go find that drink."

"I won't be long," she said.

They were staying at the *Thunderbird Motel*, adjacent to the restaurant. Since both restaurant and motel carried the same name, McCall had figured they were both owned by the same person, or group. But on questioning the desk clerk shortly after their arrival, he discovered there was no connection.

"It doesn't make sense," he had told Haloran.

"Don't worry about it," the detective said. "You worry about too much stuff that doesn't make a damn bit of difference."

"I'm not worried about it, but it doesn't make sense," McCall had replied.

On the way to their rooms they stopped by the front desk to see if there were any messages. There was a message for Haloran to call his office, nothing for McCall.

As they walked back in the crisp night air, Haloran said,

"Good luck with Debbie."

"What's with this good luck shit? The kid's a diversion, somebody to have a drink with."

"Yeah, I know," Haloran replied, "but I think a little female companionship will be good for you."

"Leave the fuckin' counseling to the shrinks, Bill. Besides, being a cupid just doesn't fit you."

Haloran laughed. "You don't think I'd look good in a diaper carrying a little bow and arrow?"

"Hell, you don't look good in anything."

They laughed together.

"Well, all I can say is that I appreciate you bringing me on this vacation, McCall. It's the best one I've ever had. But you might have created a monster by teaching me to do this river fishing. I don't know if I'm ever going to get my fill of it."

McCall chuckled. "You've only been doing it a couple of days. When I start letting you sit in the back where you have to paddle the canoe, you might get your fill real quick."

"Why don't you let me do some paddling tomorrow?"

"Because I like being dry." They had reached their rooms. Haloran was in number eight. "I'll bang on your door at six," McCall said. "Are you going to call your office now?"

"Yeah, I guess so."

"If it's something interesting, let me know. I just hope you don't have to head back to San Antonio."

"It's probably just something routine," Haloran said.

In his room, Haloran gave some thought to what had transpired during the evening, in particular to the fact that McCall was going to be seeing Debbie a little later. There was no doubt that the girl was too young, in addition to being a real bimbo. But he was glad McCall was going to see her. He needed to spend some time with women, to do something to offset the memory of Cele's death.

Of course, there's no way he can ever forget what happened, Haloran thought, but he's got to start living again sometime.

He got the motel night clerk on the line and placed a call to San Antonio PD. Moments later, he had all the details on Velda Rose Caldwell's murder. Remembering his promise to McCall, he then rang room nine.

McCall answered with a "Hello."

"Thought I'd let you in on what my call was about," Haloran said.

"Shoot."

"Cocktail waitress named Velda Rose Caldwell got herself killed."

"People getting murdered isn't exactly big news in San Antonio, unless it's one of the city fathers."

"Probably not much to this one either, except the way the girl was killed."

"I'm listening."

"Throat cut, pretty good job of body mutilation. She was found in her bathtub."

"Psycho?"

"Who knows? I'd guess, though, that anybody who would cut up a victim is a psycho."

"Do you need to get back to San Antonio?"

"Naw, it's being handled routinely. If I cut my vacation short everytime somebody got their lights put out, I'd never get in any fishing."

"Need I remind you that this is the first time you've ever been fishing?"

"It is not," Haloran protested. "I went a couple of times when I was a kid."

"You can remember back that far?"

"Goodnight, asshole. I'll see you at six."

"You got it."

By the time Debbie knocked on McCall's door, he was regretting that he had asked her to have a drink. The memory of Cele was still vividly etched in his mind, and, in a way, he felt that he was betraying her memory by being with another woman.

"Come in, Deb."

She entered the room and took the only chair, so he plopped down on the bed.

"Well, where do you want to go for that drink?" she asked.

"This is your town," he answered. "I figured you'd know a place."

"The only place I know that's open is the Hoot Owl."

"Where's that?"

"It's about fifteen miles down Interstate Thirty-five."

"Is that where you want to go?"

"I don't care where we go, or even if we go anywhere. I see you have a bottle right here."

"That's true. If you like scotch, we're in business."

"I like anything."

"A real connoisseur, huh?"

She laughed. "I guess those big city girls are more particular about what they drink."

"Most of those so-called big city girls come from small towns like Hillsboro," he said. "And I haven't taken a survey to see if all of them are particular about what they drink."

"It's all the same to me," she said. "Gin, whiskey, beer, scotch, it all gets you drunk."

"Is that why you drink, to get drunk?"

"Is there some other reason?"

"Hell if I know. I'll go get some ice, and we'll philosophize on the matter over this bottle of scotch."

McCall took the ice bucket supplied by the motel, left the room and walked down near the office where the ice machine was located. He filled the bucket and started back, a bit irritated that a girl who didn't differentiate between Lone Star Beer and expensive scotch would soon be slurping his Chivas Regal.

When McCall got back to the room, he noted that she had taken off her shoes and pantyhose. He also couldn't help but notice something he had been trying to ignore. She was a damn beautiful woman, built like the proverbial brick shithouse. The legs were shapely, the ass perfectly proportioned, the tits luscious and alive. Silky blond hair framed a uniquely pretty face that looked like it had been tanned by a kiss from the sun.

Maybe she was just eighteen, but the five-foot six-inch body was the body of a woman.

"Before going for the ice, I should have asked if you wanted it straight up or on the rocks."

"How are you going to have it?"

"I'm going to have it with water on the rocks."

"I'll have the same."

He fixed the drinks, handed her one and asked, "What are you majoring in at college?"

"Nothing in particular. I'm just taking basic stuff."

"What do you want to do when you get out?"

"I don't know."

"Well, is there anything in particular that you'd like to do if you were given the opportunity."

"I can't think of anything. I like people, so I might try to do something in public relations."

Oh, shit, McCall thought. Another woman who thinks that liking people is the sole criteria for being in public relations. Maybe it is. For all the flak p.r. types put out about their communications skills, he couldn't think of a single bastard among them who could even write good graffiti. Of course, he had to admit that good graffiti required thought beyond the realm of most newspaper types. So, a p.r. type couldn't be expected to master such prose.

"What are you thinking?" she asked.

"Nothing much," he replied. "About how beautiful you are, for one thing."

"That's very nice of you to say."

"Occasionally, I break down and tell the truth. I even get serious on occasion."

She laughed. "You're never serious with Mr. Haloran."

"Surprisingly, I am at times. We're just laid back this week, trying to forget the day-to-day grind."

"Mr. Haloran told me you were a great writer, that you've won all kinds of awards. He said you even won a Pulitzer Prize."

"Yeah, and when did Mr. Haloran tell you all this bullshit?"

"Last night, when you were in the restroom."

"Mr. Haloran talks too much."

"He also said you were in Vietnam two or three times, that you were wounded twice."

"I was there." He was beginning to wish Debbie was one of the Vietnamese girls he had known, one who didn't know English but knew how to please a man.

"My glass is empty," she informed. "I probably shouldn't drink over one more. Have to drive home, you know."

"Do you still live with your parents?" he asked while fixing her another drink.

"Yes."

"What does your dad do?"

"He's a trucker."

"And your mother?"

"She works at the bank."

They continued to talk about nothing of any consequence. She had another drink, matching his intake. They became very comfortable with one another, so it seemed very appropriate for him to kiss her when taking her empty glass. She didn't resist. And when he handed her a fresh drink and sat down on the bed again, she abandoned the chair and joined him.

"It would probably be a good idea if you went home, Debbie."

"Probably," she agreed, "but I really don't want to

right now."

"Well, I can't be responsible for your safety."

"And I can't be responsible for yours."

For some time, he had known it was inevitable. He pulled her close and began kissing her passionately, and she responded in kind. When the kissing was no longer enough, he removed her blouse and bra and sucked on the nipples of her breasts. He then removed her skirt and panties, took off his own clothes and took her in his arms. After a wild melee of passionate kissing, he penetrated her, started moving rhythmically inside her.

She was ecstasy, a fulfillment of life that he had been missing.

Chapter 4

Tuesday, 11:54 p.m.

Registered nurse Maggie Burleson made note of the clock and asked, "Do you remember the last time we got off when we were supposed to?"

"I can't remember that far back." The answer came from Carolyn Bell, another nurse at San Antonio General Hospital. Both women worked the second shift in the hospital's emergency room. The schedule called for them to get off at eleven p.m.

"I know if I keep this up," Carolyn continued, "I'm not going to have a husband to go home to."

Maggie laughed. "And I'm never going to find one."

The single one of the pair had reached the ripe old age of twenty-three, and she had for a year after college graduation been subjected to the constant inquiries of a mother who wondered if she was ever going to be a grandmother.

"Take your time," Carolyn advised, "or you'll end up like me, an old woman before your time." She was a shade under twenty-eight, but with three children.

"You're not old," Maggie argued. "And I'll bet your kids keep you young for a long time."

Carolyn looked at the other nurse in mock disbelief. "Are you kidding? Those damn kids are going to be the death of me. And Roger's not exactly what you would call a prize." The reference was to her husband, a salesman for a pharmaceutical company.

"I thought you and Roger were happy."

"Relatively," was the reply. "Everything is relative."

The two women were sitting in the hospital cafeteria, each having a cup of coffee before making their respective journeys home.

"Well, I think you're lucky anyway," Maggie said. "You're going home to a nice house, children and a husband, and I'm going home to a one bedroom apartment."

"That nice house," Carolyn grumbled, "is the reason I'm having to bust my butt working."

"I thought Roger made a good salary."

"He does, but you can't buy a house like we've got, two new cars and all the other shit on one salary. We just live from paycheck to paycheck, and I'm talking about his and mine."

Roger and Carolyn Bell's four bedroom home, complete with swimming pool, was in one of San Antonio's upper middle class neighborhoods. Their children, ages six, seven and nine, went to a private school.

"Well, I really enjoyed my visit at your house last Sunday," Maggie said. "Your kids are neat."

"Hell, I don't mean to complain," Carolyn said, "but it all seems so ridiculous. Here we've got a thirty-year mortgage on the house, two cars that will wear out before they're paid for, utility bills that get higher every month, big furniture payments and three kids to send to college. There's just no relief in sight.

"That's why I tell you to enjoy life a little before getting married, because there's certainly not much enjoyment afterward."

Maggie laughed. "I don't think it's quite as bad as you picture it."

"It's worse," Carolyn lamented.

"Well, I'd certainly settle for what you have. It's cold and lonely out there."

"Maybe it would be okay if I hadn't gotten married right out of high school," Carolyn admitted. "But Roger and I both worked our way through college, had kids when we didn't have enough money to put decent food on the table, and I just got tired along the way.

"Don't get me wrong. I wouldn't take anything for the kids, but a little planning wouldn't have hurt anything, either.

"Now we're busting our asses for material possessions and that's about all we've got going for us."

"It seems pretty obvious to me that Roger loves you," Maggie said.

"Believe me, it's just conditioned response on Roger's part," Carolyn replied. "He's doing what he thinks he's supposed to do, including going to church. But the romance all went out of our marriage when we swapped the so-called hard times for what we have now. At least we were working toward something back then. Now, what we were working for owns us."

"It's a good thing I'm in a good mood," Maggie responded with a laugh. "Listening to you tonight is such a downer that if I was in a bad mood, I'd probably go out and kill myself."

Carolyn gave a tired smile. "I think I'm in this mood because I paid bills before coming to work today. There just doesn't seem to be any light at the end of the tunnel."

Trying to change the subject, Maggie said, "How do you

like your new maid?"

"She's okay, but I really miss Theresa. The kids like the new girl, though."

"You're lucky to live in San Antonio, where you can get good help for a reasonable price."

"Don't I know it. As it is now, there's not much left out of my check after I pay the maid and for the kids' private school and clothes."

"But if you couldn't afford a maid to stay with the kids while you're working, you'd be up the creek."

"Hell, with Roger being on the road so much, I wouldn't be able to work. Which, I might add, wouldn't be all bad."

"C'mon, you know that you like your work."

Carolyn laughed. "Compared to what?"

They talked awhile longer before Carolyn said, "I don't know about you, but my ass is tired. I've got to get home."

"Is Roger home tonight?"

"Nope, just the maid and kids."

Out in the employee parking lot, Maggie observed, "Isn't it a beautiful night?"

"I hate to tell you this, honey, but officially it's morning."

"Whatever, it's still beautiful."

Their cars were parked side-by-side, so, after goodnight pleasantries, they each drove off toward their respective destinations.

For some reason she couldn't explain, Maggie wasn't the least bit tired. She was a bit antsy, though, wanting to do something other than going straight to her apartment. So, she headed her car in the direction of *The Plum,* one of San Antonio's livelier bars and restaurants.

On arrival, she went directly to the bar section of the building. It was a large room with soft lights, decorated with old-fashioned posters and pictures. The music, however, was loud and modern.

Rather than take a table, she positioned herself on a tall

chair at the bar and ordered a gin and tonic. In the mirror that ran the length of the wall behind the bar, she could observe the entire room.

She made a mental note that, while the music was loud as always, the makeup of the crowd was far different at this hour than it was shortly after five p.m. On her days off, that was the time she normally visited *The Plum.* During that time it was filled with three-piece suits, secretaries, guys with silk shirts and gold chains around their necks.

The Plum was a place where a girl or guy could get picked up, which was its reason for existence from five to seven p.m. But at this hour, she could see that there were very few people in the bar area. And just a couple of loners other than herself.

Looking at herself in the bar's mirror she thought, not bad. Nice straight teeth and no teenage acne. The hair could use a little work and the tits aren't monsters, but overall you look pretty good, Maggie Burleson.

In truth, Maggie looked better than just a little good. She had auburn shoulder-length hair, big brown eyes and a very shapely five-foot five-inch body. There was an almost catlike suppleness to the way she moved, which didn't go unnoticed by the males around her. More than one of the hospital's doctors, both young and old, married and unmarried, had fantasies about making it with Maggie.

At Trinity University, she had been selected as a Yearbook Beauty in both her junior and senior years, but such recognition had not affected her. Maggie never thought of herself as beautiful or even pretty. She wasn't into cosmetics, clothes or laudatory comments about her appearance. Instead, she was a person who had dedicated her life to helping others. Being a nurse was not just a job to her, it was a calling.

So, there hadn't been much time for men when in high school or college. She had dated, of course, but quite casually. She found the men her own age, even those a few years older, too childlike and without commitment to any real purpose.

Lately, however, there had been a subtle parental pressure to find a nice young man and settle down. And Maggie herself figured it was time to start thinking in such terms. The problem was, where could she find the right man? She wanted someone she could love, respect and admire, not some clown who thought it was cool to wear a gold necklace and silk shirts. She wanted a man like her father.

Her father had been career military, a man's man. He had retired from the Air Force as a colonel, then settled in San Antonio with Margaret, his wife of thirty years. Maggie's mother. The reason Maggie had gone to Trinity was because her parents lived in San Antonio. She had lived at home while attending college, not wanting to be any more of a financial burden on her parents than necessary. She had gotten her own apartment after graduation and employment at the hospital, though her mother had tried to get her to continue living at home.

Maggie's dilemma was that she didn't know where to find a man like her father; a man who was brave, patriotic, loyal and committed to a cause. She certainly hadn't met any in places like *The Plum*. She figured her best bet was a career military man, though many of the young officers she had met hadn't come up to her standards, either.

I'm probably going to die an old maid, she thought.

She had a couple more drinks in the hope that they would help her sleep, paid the check and went to her car. She took in the beauty of the moon and stars, gulped the freshness of the morning air and thought how beautiful it was to be alive. Maggie felt better than good. She felt wonderful.

The drive to her apartment was easy, relaxed. There was very little traffic on the streets. And because she felt so good, Maggie wasn't even annoyed by the headlights of the car that seemed to be following her. The car even followed her in to the parking lot of her apartment complex, but went by when she pulled into her assigned space.

Walking to the door of her apartment, Maggie again felt exhilarated by the beauty of the morning. She was so captivated by her own thoughts that Maggie didn't sense the presence of anyone else until she had the door of her apartment open. Then the presence was on her, and she felt the coldness of steel against her throat.

Chapter 5

Wednesday, June 3, 7 p.m.

McCall and Haloran arrived back at the *Thunderbird Motel* after another day of fishing the Brazos River. Each went to their respective rooms to shower before going to dinner at the *Thunderbird Restaurant.*

As rivulets of warm water cascaded off his body, McCall thought about the events of the day, how time on the river always seemed to cleanse his soul. No matter how many times he canoed the same stretch, it was always different, always changing. There was always the new, the something that might have been there before but that he couldn't remember ever seeing.

He was glad Haloran had made the trip with him. It was obvious to McCall that the detective was enjoying the canoeing and fishing, and to share the river with someone else gave him a sense of satisfaction.

While Haloran had said nothing during the day about the murder that had taken place in San Antonio, McCall knew that it was on his friend's mind. Haloran was a good cop, a cop that cared.

As for McCall, he pondered the murder, too. He wondered who was covering it for the *Tribune,* whether it was being covered right. The paper hired a lot of kids right out of college, and some of the editors weren't too sharp when it came to deciding who was to cover a story. There would have been no problem, of course, if he had been there. He always covered the bizarre stuff.

After toweling himself off, drying and combing his hair, he applied deodorant and cologne, then dressed. He then exited his room and went to the restaurant to meet Haloran.

And Debbie.

He wondered what he was going to do about Debbie. Here he was, forty-one years old, banging a chick who was only eighteen. She seemed older, though. More womanly, really, than some females he'd known who were twice her age.

Well, maybe last night was it. Maybe after last night, he thought, she will have decided not to mess with an old guy like me again. He figured it was wishful thinking on his part, then came to the shocking realization that he didn't want it to be a one-night stand.

Haloran was already seated at a table looking somberly at the menu.

McCall took a seat and asked, "What's the matter? You look like you lost your best friend."

The detective sighed. "Another murder. It looks like I'm going to have to head back to San Antonio."

"Who was it this time?"

"A twenty-three year old nurse, butchered like the cocktail waitress and dumped in her bathtub."

"Any connection between the two murdered women?"

"None that the department knows of, but there really hasn't been time to do a thorough investigation."

"Well, damn it, Bill, I understand. I know you need this vacation, but I also know you need to be back in San Antonio to handle this thing. We can leave tonight or first thing in the morning."

"You don't have to go back. I've already checked and a bus comes through here for points south at seven a.m." They had made the trip to Hillsboro in McCall's car.

"Forget it, friend. We came together, we go back together. Besides, it's not much fun canoeing and fishing alone."

"Do you want some coffee, Matt?" It was Debbie, smiling and looking even better than she had the night before.

Matt grinned. "You bet, pumpkin. I'm going to need lots of it, because talking to this guy puts me to sleep."

"Brother," Haloran grumbled. "That's the pot calling the kettle black."

"Did you guys catch any fish today?" Debbie asked.

"I caught a lot of fish," McCall said. "We could have loaded the canoe if I'd had any help."

"I caught a few," Haloran protested.

"When you didn't have your lure in a tree. You caught more limbs than fish."

Debbie laughed. "Are y'all ready to order? The boss told me I couldn't stand around here talking to you guys all the time."

"Well, that dirty sonofabitch," McCall said. "You want me to go over there and kick his ass for you?"

She laughed again. "No, I just want you to order."

"What's the most expensive thing you have in this place?" he asked.

"The ribeye steak."

"That's not expensive enough. Bring us four of the damn things, two each."

"You're kidding," she said.

"No, we're just hungry," he replied. "You want yours medium, Bill?"

"Medium's fine," Haloran agreed.

"Then make all four medium," McCall ordered. "And bring us each two baked potatoes and two salads."

Debbie left the table with, "You got it."

"What in the hell are up up to?" Haloran asked after she was out of earshot.

"Nothing, Bill. But we should eat, drink and be merry because tomorrow we may die."

"If I eat all you ordered, I may die of indigestion," Haloran responded.

Later that night, after making love to Debbie, McCall told her he would be leaving the following morning. She expressed hurt that he was leaving before planned, a hurt he suspected would disappear quickly after his departure. But for the moment, she did not want what they had discovered in each other to go away.

"I probably won't see you again," she whimpered.

"Why do you say that?" he asked. "San Antonio's not the end of the earth. It's just a couple of hundred miles or so down the road."

"It doesn't matter, you won't be back."

"That's bullshit. I come back here three or four times a year just to fish the river, and now I've got even more reason for coming. Besides, you could come to San Antonio."

That cheered her. "You mean you'd like me to come there to see you?"

"Why not?"

She smiled, pulled the sheet up over her mountainous tits and said, "Going to see you in San Antonio might be a little hard to explain to my mother and father."

"How do you explain seeing me here?"

She laughed. "I don't. You noticed that I got out of here

by midnight last night, and I've got to do the same tonight."

"Too bad. I was hoping you could stay all night."

"There's nothing I'd like better, but . . ."

"If you need a cover for going to San Antonio, I can set it up with one of the girls who works for the paper."

"What do you mean?"

"I mean, as far as your folks are concerned, she can be the friend you're visiting in San Antonio."

"I guess that would work, but are you really sure that you want to see me again?"

"If I didn't want to see you again, I wouldn't suggest that you come," he replied with slight irritation. Of course, the reply was not entirely true. It was hard to tell a woman lying next to you that you didn't want to see her again, especially if you planned to screw her again momentarily. But in Debbie's case, McCall did want to see her again. At least he did at the moment. Of course, he couldn't be sure what his mood would be the following day, or the next hour for that matter.

"I want to see you, too, Matt," she said. "I want to see you lots and lots."

He smiled. "You won't get any complaints from me."

"Why do you have to go back tomorrow?"

"It's Bill who has to get back," he said. "There's been a couple of unusual murders in San Antonio, and his services are required."

"I was reading something about one of the murders in this morning's paper."

"Yeah, the *Dallas Morning News* had a front page story on it," he confirmed. "The body of the second victim wasn't discovered until this afternoon."

"Murder is hard to understand."

"Lots of weirdos out there in the world, Debbie. That's why a girl can't be too careful."

"Stuff like that doesn't happen in Hillsboro."

"Honey, I don't want to bust your balloon, but stuff like that happens everywhere. But let's get on to something more pleasant than thinking about a gory murder or two. We don't have much time."

She came willingly into his arms and they began to kiss passionately. He glanced at his watch while they were embracing and saw that it was eleven-fifteen. They would have to hurry if she was going to get home by midnight. He didn't want her Chevy to turn into a pumpkin.

Chapter 6

Thursday, June 4, 10 a.m.

McCall's first hour or so in the newsroom was spent drinking coffee and conversing with well-wishers. The very fact that other people acted concerned about his well-being made him uncomfortable. He was by nature a cynic, incapable of thinking that anyone could be concerned about him without some ulterior motive. It was, of course, that type of suspicion about his fellow man that made him such a good investigative reporter. He never accepted things simply for what they seemed.

Ed Parkham, the paper's managing editor, was one of the people who dropped by McCall's desk to chat. Parkham didn't really like McCall, but felt the reporter's writing and investigative skills could help further his career.

Of course, McCall was not exactly fond of the forty-two year old editor. He had often challenged Parkham about his news judgment, which no one else on the staff had the balls to do. McCall was, however, playing with a stacked deck, since management was so afraid he might cross over and join the competition.

"I'm sure you've been keeping tabs on the bathtub murders," Parkham said.

"All I know is what I read in the paper," McCall replied.

Parkham chuckled. "Well, I'd really like for you to take over the story and follow it through."

"I noticed Lisa DiMaggio's byline on today's piece. Who's she?"

"New kid, not much experience. Turner put her on the story because she was handy. You know that he doesn't do a helluva lot of thinking when it comes to something like this."

Parkham's statement about Turner Sipe, the city editor, made McCall smile. Sipe, in his late fifties, was definitely not a McCall fan. It was no secret that McCall considered Sipe a *no talent* editor and writer. In fact, he had nicknamed the man Turnip because he considered him on the mental plane of a vegetable.

It seemed that Sipe had been with the paper forever, though he was absent for a period of years serving as assistant to the president of a Baptist university. The job enabled him to get two slightly-below-normal siblings through college. However, when the president who hired Sipe retired, the successor gave him the boot.

Practically everyone at the paper thought of Sipe as an ass-kisser. He had risen to the position of city editor because of his *good ol' boy* friendship with some of the *Tribune's* oldtimers whose own incompetence had been rewarded with management positions.

"You already know it's the kind of story I like to handle," McCall told Parkham, "but I don't want to cause any dissension among the troops."

One of the reasons McCall was such a favorite among the

younger reporters was that he was so supportive of them. He didn't know the new kid, but he didn't want her to think that he had returned to undercut her.

"Let me worry about that," Parkham said. "The other paper's kicking our ass on this story, so we need you on it. I want some of that McCall magic, because I think this one is going to be a biggie."

McCall replied, "Let's let the new kid work with me on the story. If she's been on top of it, she probably has some information that I can use."

"I doubt it, but if you want to be a nursemaid, it's fine with me. I'll tell Turner to assign her to you."

McCall was always suspicious when Parkham was too agreeable, but he figured a part of it was the man's appearance. The managing editor's orb-like face was flour white, accentuated by deepset pale blue eyes, almost colorless eyebrows, a pug nose and oversized mouth. The hair was thin, brownish and receding.

And though Parkham was not overly fat, his five-foot nine-inch body reeked of softness. He was a man who looked like the sun had never touched his skin.

McCall thought he would probably be suspicious of anyone who looked like the managing editor. But, of course, when he thought about it more , he realized that Parkham was not the Lone Ranger when it came to his suspicions. He had learned long ago not to trust anyone.

A couple of hours and several cups of coffee after Parkham left, McCall looked up from his desk to see a beautiful young woman standing adjacent to his chair.

"I'm Lisa DiMaggio," she said.

He smiled. "Any relation to Joe?"

"He's my uncle."

"You're kidding?"

"You're right."

McCall laughed. "Have a seat, Lisa."

Unsmiling, she seated herself in a chair next to the desk.

"Since Turner probably sent you over here, I don't guess I have to introduce myself," he said.

She came back with, "No, I've heard a lot about you."

"Such as?"

She frowned. "That you've banged everything in San Antonio with a split between its legs."

He gave a half-laugh at the comment, but his mental guard went up. "I assume that what you've heard wasn't all that flattering."

"You assume right," she replied. "At least about that part."

"You mean there's more?"

She answered, "Yes. People say that when it comes to being an investigative reporter, you may be the best there is."

"When you say people, I assume you're talking about our peers at this paper."

"Yes, but I'm also talking about people at the other paper. And about the people in radio and television."

"How long have you been with us, Lisa?"

"Seven weeks."

"And how long have you been in San Antonio?"

"A couple of days more than seven weeks."

"And during this time you've made contact with all these media people who have discussed me?"

"I go to the right bars," she countered.

"And so far you've heard about how wonderful I am?" He wanted her to laugh, smile, do something other than frown.

"The only thing they say is wonderful about you is your writing and investigative ability."

"Well, I certainly appreciate their judgment of my work."

"That's not what I hear."

"What do you hear?"

"That you don't give a rat's ass what anyone thinks about

you or your writing."

"Well, you've certainly heard a lot," he said. "What have you decided about me?"

"I've read some of your stuff, so I know you're a helluva writer. As to what kind of person you are, I'll just have to wait and see for myself."

"That's fair enough. What kind of person are you?"

"Not one who's going to drop her panties just because you're the star around here."

He laughed. "So, what am I going to have to do to get you to drop your panties?" During their conversation, the thought of getting in her pants had crossed his mind. He liked the way she was built, figured her to be about five-feet seven-inches tall. The legs were nice, the tits were a bit larger than average, the lips luscious, the eyes large and dark brown, the facial skin slightly tan and unblemished. Her dark brown hair had not been overwhelmed by some fag hair stylist.

To his jestful question, she sarcastically answered, "If I were you, I wouldn't count on it happening."

"I don't count on anything," he said tersely. "But you assume a helluva lot, kid, in thinking that I'd be interested in you."

His response stymied her, which gave him cause to believe that a lot of younger men had made her the subject of their adoration. Well, he didn't like bitches, no matter what their age.

"My assessment of you, Lisa, is that they may have taught you the *who, what, where, when, why* and *how* in journalism school, but they sure as hell didn't teach you much about being a lady. I like my women soft and feminine, not coarse and foul-mouthed.

"Now, when Parkham told me to handle the bathtub murders story, I suggested to him that you work with me. If you want to work together professionally, fine. But if you don't, you can take your juvenile bullshit back over to the city desk and maybe Turner will let you write obituaries.

"What's it going to be?"

She countered with, "I just don't like the idea of you coming in here and taking over my story."

"Correction. It isn't your story and it isn't my story. It's the story of two women who were murdered, and the lives affected as a result of their deaths. It's the story of a killer who wantonly snuffed out the lives of two people before their time, a killer who's probably going to kill again before he's caught.

"As for me covering the story instead of you, it's because you don't have the experience and skill to do it right. After you've paid your dues, baby, then you'll have a right to complain.

"Now, what's it going to be?"

After he had finished, he noted that her beautifully tanned face was a bit ashen.

"I want to work with you," she acknowledged.

"Good. Fill me in on what you've got."

"What I've got is in the two stories I've written."

"That's it? Have you talked to friends of the victims, parents of the victims, employers?"

"No," she replied. "Everything I have came from the police. Turner told me I could get everything I needed from them."

He groaned. "If you haven't already guessed it, I'll just tell you outright that Turnip is a stupid piece of shit."

"Turnip?"

"That's what I call Turner, though it is a slap in the face to a rather important vegetable."

She finally laughed. "I did want to do more, but I thought I should follow orders."

"Don't get the idea that I'm blaming you, Lisa. Turnip wouldn't know a good news story if it jumped up and bit him in the ass."

She laughed again. "I'm sorry about what I said earlier. If

Mr. Parkham hadn't put you on the story, he would have put someone else on it. He really wasn't satisfied with what I've done."

"Of course, I'm sure Turnip didn't tell Ed how he was tutoring you," McCall said. "Count on him to never take the blame for anything. I can just hear him agreeing with Ed that you weren't doing the job."

"I guess I am a little green."

"Well, I'll guarantee you one thing, Lisa. After you work with me on this story, you'll know how to cover a murder.

"By the way, did you have any experience before coming here?"

"I worked a couple of years for a small daily in Arkansas."

"That's good experience. I guess you did a little bit of everything."

"Almost to sweeping out the newsroom," she replied.

"Where did you go to school?"

"The University of Arkansas."

"I didn't know the University of Arkansas even had a journalism department."

"We had a good journalism department," she replied, defensively.

"Easy," he said with a laugh. "I was only kidding. The chairman of the department is a friend of mine."

That loosened her up a bit, the fact that he knew someone at her alma mater.

He continued by asking, "Have you had lunch yet?"

"I don't usually eat lunch," she said. "I'm getting fat as it is."

He surveyed her figure and reported, "I don't see any of it."

She laughed. "Believe me, it's there."

"Well, why don't you break your luncheon fast today, and we'll grab a bite to eat. It'll give us a chance to talk about how we're going to handle the story."

"Okay, but I can already tell that you're going to be a bad influence on me."

"That's encouraging."

"I'm talking about eating," she said.

He laughed. "I assumed as much."

They took the newspaper's slow elevator down to the lobby and went out on the street. It was such a beautiful day that Lisa suggested walking to wherever they were going to lunch.

"I was planning on taking you to the No-Name diner where Detective Haloran and I eat a lot," he said.

"That's the name of it, No-Name?" she asked.

"It doesn't have a name," he replied. "That's why I call it No-Name."

She laughed. "I guess that's a good name for a restaurant with no name, but how in the world does the owner advertise it?"

"This place doesn't do a lot of advertising."

After they had walked a few blocks and McCall had cursed most of San Antonio's drivers, he said, "That's it up ahead." The diner had once been a dining car of a luxury train, but that had been long in its past.

"Well, I'll say this for you, Matt, you're sure as hell not out to impress me with this luncheon date."

"I didn't realize we were dating," he said. "I thought this was a working lunch."

"Sorry, I didn't mean to imply anything."

"Don't be sorry. I like the idea."

She sighed. "It wasn't an idea, it wasn't anything."

"Regardless," he responded, "this place has the best chili dogs in town."

"Chili dogs? You mean you eat that kind of junk?"

"Whoa," he said with a laugh. "You can insult just about anything about me, but don't insult my favorite food."

She shook her head in mock disbelief. "Maybe I was assigned to work with you, but then again, maybe the paper wanted me to try to protect you from killing yourself with indigestion."

"That indicates what a short-timer you are at the paper," he replied. "There are lots of folks at the *Tribune* who would like me to die of indigestion or anything else. They'd like it to be painful, though."

As they entered the door of the diner she said, "Well, I know you're not loved by all. It sure didn't take me long to pick up on that."

He found a booth and she seated herself across the table from him.

"My, these are beautiful vinyl seats," she said. "I wonder what kind of tape this is that they patched them with?"

He chuckled. "Damn, I brought you to a place decorated in red and white. I thought you would enjoy the atmosphere, your old school's colors and all."

"This place makes me think of a school yell alright. Soohey, pig."

He laughed. "You know, I really can't believe your attitude. This happens to be one of the finest eating establishments in San Antonio, and it's certainly a leg up on anything in Fayetteville, Arkansas."

She smiled. "Leg up? I guess that is pretty good terminology for this place."

The waitress had arrived and gave her usual, "What'll you have?"

"I'll have a chili dog and a coke," Lisa said.

McCall was surprised. "Two chili dogs and a large glass of milk, please." After the waitress had left he continued with, "I thought you didn't like chili dogs."

"I didn't say I didn't like them. They're just not good for you. But as long as you're making me blow my diet, I might as well go all the way."

"Don't ever say that to me unless you really mean it," he teased.

"Get your mind out of the gutter, Matt."

"I assure you, that's not where it is. But I guess we'd better get on to the business at hand."

"I'm all ears."

"Well, Lisa, whether you think your role in covering this story is important or not," he said, "I'm going to be depending on you to do a lot of legwork and to compile a lot of information. The key to covering this thing right is going to depend on the information that the two of us can gather, compile and analyze. You may think you're getting the short end of the stick because of some of the shit work that I'll have you doing, but I think you're going to learn a lot from this experience."

"I'm sure I will," she said. "And just because we sort of got off on the wrong foot, don't think I'm not appreciative of the opportunity to work with a pro."

"It's getting deep in here."

"No, I'm serious," she continued. "Sure, my ego was hurt a bit, but the more I've thought about, it the more I'm sure that putting you in charge of the story was the right thing to do."

"I should warn you," he said, "that I get very passionate toward women who flatter me."

She smiled. "From what I've heard, you get very passionate toward women, period."

He feigned astonishment. "I'm very hurt by such rumors. Surely, you can't believe they're true?"

She laughed. "Of course not."

Their lunch arrived, and they both attacked the chili dogs with forks.

"Not bad," she said after the first bite. Then, in a somber voice she continued, "Back at the office you indicated that you didn't think these two murders would be the last victims of the killer."

"I can't see why they would be," he said. "From what I've been able to find out so far, the killings and mutilations were almost identical. And my guess is that the killer didn't know either woman. I'm further guessing that we've got a pervert who has discovered the joy of killing, and he or she isn't going to be satisfied with just two."

Lisa asked, "Do you think it could be a woman? You said he or she."

"Never rule out any possibility," he advised. "I've known some pretty bad-ass women in my time. A lot of women have been pretty mean to me."

She laughed, "Oh, brother."

"Of course, this could be one of those serial killers," he said. "You know, the kind law enforcement gives a number because they travel the country killing at random for no apparent reason."

"But you don't think our killer is like that, do you?"

"No."

"Why?"

"Just a hunch. Some men have intuition, too."

"Pardon me," Lisa said, "but you don't seem the type to play hunches. I have a feeling that you know more than you're telling."

"I hate to disillusion you, but I play a lot of hunches, Lisa. But I did have Bill Haloran run a nationwide check to see if any murders in the past few months match up with these."

"And?"

"Some women have had their throat cut, and there have been some mutilations. But there's enough uniqueness about the way our victims were killed and butchered for me to believe that our murderer only recently went over the edge."

"So, you think that he . . . or I should say he or she . . . needs psychiatric help."

"No, I think he or she needs their fuckin' brains blown out."

The astonishment showed on her face. "I can't believe you said that."

"What, fucking?" he asked in jest.

"No, that a mentally ill person should have their brains blown out. I don't think that's funny at all."

He turned sober. "I don't think the parents of Velda Rose Caldwell or Maggie Burleson thinks it's funny, either. There's always some bleeding heart who gets so caught up in protecting the rights of the killer that they forget that something was taken from the victim that can't be given back."

"I'm no bleeding heart," she denied, "but if a person is sick, they're sick."

While sliding out of the booth, he said, "C'mon. I want you to meet someone while we're in the neighborhood."

"Who?"

"Bill Haloran."

They left the diner and walked the few blocks to the police station on West Nueva. When they entered the building, a lot of eyes turned and followed Lisa's progress through the maze of desks fronting Haloran's office, which caused McCall to mentally observe that policemen were only human.

Entering Haloran's office, they found him shuffling through a stack of papers and grumbling, "Damn paperwork's about to kill me." He stood when he noticed Lisa.

"Bill, I want to introduce you to Lisa DiMaggio. She's going to be helping me cover the murders."

He smiled and extended a hand, which she accepted. "DiMaggio? Are you any relation to Joe?"

"She's the old Yankee Clipper's niece," McCall said.

Obviously impressed, Haloran asked, "Is that true?"

"No, it's not."

The detective's elation faded. "Damn it, McCall, do you have to lie about everything? I'm certainly glad to meet you, Lisa, but McCall knows that I'm an old *dyed-in-the-wool* baseball fan. And he knows I was a big DiMaggio fan when I was a kid."

"Kid, hell," McCall said. "You're as old as Joe DiMaggio. Besides, I doubt that Lisa even knows who we're talking about. She's probably not a baseball fan."

"I am, too."

"Really," McCall responded with disbelief. "Most of the women I know don't like baseball. They think the game's slow and boring."

"Well, I don't," Lisa protested.

"Well, anyone who understands the game doesn't think it's slow and boring," McCall said, "but I've never found a woman who understands it."

She countered with, "I understand it."

"Hey, I like this one, McCall," Haloran said with approval.

"Glad you approve, asshole, but we're here about something other than baseball," McCall said. "Are the bodies of both victims still at the morgue?"

"Yeah," the detective replied.

"We want to see them."

Lisa tried to act as though she was not shocked by the request.

"Maybe you want to see them," Haloran said, "but I doubt that Lisa does."

"I want to see them," she countered.

McCall said, "She needs to see the victims, because I think she feels sorry for the killer."

"I do not," she argued. "All I said was that if a person is sick, they ought to be helped."

Haloran looked at McCall and asked, "And what did you say, asshole, that the killer ought to be blown away?"

"Something along those lines," the reporter answered.

Haloran sighed. "You have to understand, Lisa, that your friend here thinks psychiatry is a crock of shit. But whether it is or isn't is not the issue. McCall and I have both seen too many animals turned back on the street by psychiatrists who thought they were cured. I guess neither of us are all that confident about the ability of our system to rehabilitate a criminal, but I can't be as verbal about it as McCall."

"You want to know how I feel about it?" McCall asked.

Haloran laughed. "Not really, but you're going to tell us anyway."

"If," the reporter said emphatically, "a psychiatrist had to stand trial for the crime of a *so-called* cured patient, he might not be so quick to let one out of the looney bin."

"Do you think our killer has been under the care of a psychiatrist?" Haloran asked.

"It wouldn't surprise me," McCall answered. "Now, are you going to show us the bodies or not?"

"They're not pretty."

"I've never seen any pretty dead people," McCall responded.

The threesome drove to the morgue in Haloran's car. The detective rolled down the window on the driver's side of the automobile, and they all enjoyed the summer air. It was one of those days when it felt good to be alive.

Just entering the morgue quelled that feeling. The fact that it was what it was made the building depressing.

They were stopped by a smocked young man whose face needed the help of a razor. "Can I help you?" he asked.

"We want to see the Caldwell and Burleson bodies," Haloran replied.

"Do you have authorization?"

Haloran flashed his badge.

"Okay," the man said. "This way." He led them back to the lockers and asked, "Which one do you want to see first?"

"It doesn't matter," Haloran answered.

The man opened a locker and brought out a sheet-draped slab with the explanation, "This is Caldwell." Then, pulling back the sheet, he continued with, "Gruesome, huh?"

One glance at the body and Lisa lost her lunch. Retching, she retreated from the room.

"Sorry," Haloran apologized.

"No problem," the man said. "I have to wash the room down with a hose anyway."

"It's worse than I thought it would be," McCall admitted.

"The Burleson girl's the same," Haloran said. "Do you want to see her?"

"As long as I'm here, I might as well."

The detective nodded, and the guy in the smock opened another locker and pulled out the body of the Burleson girl. McCall inspected the corpse and said, "I don't guess there's much doubt that these murders were committed by the same person."

"I'll give you copies of the coroner's reports," Haloran volunteered. "According to him, the mutilations are identical."

McCall somberly opined, "You know the killer is going to strike again."

"That would be my guess," Haloran agreed.

Outside the storage room, Lisa was leaning against the wall, her face ash-colored.

"You okay?" McCall asked.

"I'm fine," she lied, but without conviction.

On the way out of the building and in the car going back to the station, none of them spoke. There really wasn't anything to say.

Chapter 7

Friday, June 5, 1:30 a.m.

Colette Ramsey was in *The Plum,* having a drink with her best friend, Michelle Sharp. She had spent the early evening hours with her lover, the man for whom she had left her husband. It had been a pleasant, loving, but frustrating time, which had prompted her to call Michelle. They had met at *The Plum* at ten-thirty.

Over several drinks, they had discussed Colette's lover at length. Both were feeling mellow, and Michelle asked, "Is there any chance that you and Clark will go back together?"

The reference was to Colette's husband. She had been formally separated from him for about a month.

"I don't think there's any chance," she replied. "We've just become too incompatible."

Colette was thirty-eight, strikingly beautiful in a cold sort of way. She was five-feet seven-inches tall, with dark black hair that seemed always to be perfectly in place. The nose was classic Roman, the eyes dark and rounded, the mouth and lips like an artist's painting. She was picture-perfect.

But her hour-glass shapeliness, beautiful legs, large and well-defined breasts, were easily overlooked because of her icy sophistication.

"What do you think this is going to do to his political career?" Michelle asked.

"I don't give a damn," was the reply. "I'm at a stage in life when a lot of things are more important to me than maybe being the governor's wife."

Colette's husband was Clark Ramsey, the county's elected district attorney, a man who aspired to higher political office. With a personal fortune of his own, plus the backing of some of the state's wealthiest Democrats, there was a very good chance that he could realize what he thought was his destiny. He had not planned, however, on the wife he had so carefully selected walking out on him.

"I don't think I've ever told you this, Michelle, but Clark denied me children, because he thought they might hinder his political career."

"You've told me," her friend replied, hoping that Colette was not going to start crying. Michelle recalled that on numerous occasions Colette had told her that Clark didn't want children because they might not be controllable, that if a child couldn't be controlled, he or she would be a political liability.

"I have missed so much by not having children," Colette continued, "and now it might be too late."

Michelle was quite aware of how carefully Clark Ramsey had selected his wife. He had searched for a beautiful woman of grace and sophistication, one who was educated and intelligent. It was also important to him that her parents be influential and people of substance. He wanted in-laws who would not be a political liability.

He had found all that he wanted in Colette, the perfect mate for a long-range public relations campaign that would ultimately lead to the governor's mansion, and possibly beyond. Being Governor of Texas had been his goal from the time he entered the University of Texas Law School. And until Colette walked out, it had all seemed so close.

Michelle was aware of the entire situation, because Ramsey had solicited her aid in trying to initiate a reconciliation with Colette. She thought it a bit amusing that he was trying to work through her, because Ramsey had always been opposed to her friendship with Colette.

But Michelle realized Ramsey was a user, that he would use anyone or anything to get what he wanted. So, she wasn't interested in helping him, only Colette. They had been friends since their freshman days at Southern Methodist University. It had been mere chance that they both ended up in San Antonio. Michelle was glad for such circumstance, though, because she thought it important that Colette have her best friend available at this critical time in her life.

And while Michelle was certainly not a Clark Ramsey fan, she thought Colette's new romantic interest offered only the possibility of heartbreak. She hadn't come right out and told Colette how she felt because the time wasn't right.

Choosing her words carefully, Michelle said, "It's not too late for you to have children, Colette. And under the circumstances, I'm sure Clark might even be agreeable."

"It's over between Clark and me," she reiterated. "And besides, you shouldn't have to bargain for children."

Michelle shrugged her shoulders. "That's true. I'm sorry if it sounded like I meant it that way."

"Oh, Michelle, I know that you didn't. You're the only friend that I have, and I know you're only trying to help."

"About the only way I can help is to listen," Michelle said, "to be there when you need me."

"And you have been there, and I'm grateful."

"I just want what's best for you, Colette. I just want you to be sure that you know what you're doing."

"I'm not sure I've ever known that. For me, things have just happened."

"For me, too, but now you have some choices," Michelle replied.

"Funny, I guess it's the first time in my life I've had choices to make. Up until now, they were all made for me."

"If you're not going back to Clark, that's all over."

"I'm not going back," she said emphatically.

As soon as she finished her drink, Colette chimed, "Time to go."

"Are you okay?"

"Of course," she answered.

"Do you want to come over and spend the night with me?"

"Thank you, Michelle, but no. I'm fine, and I'm very comfortable in my new place."

The new place was a very expensive townhouse in the best section of San Antonio. Colette had already furnished it elaborately and tastefully. For Colette, money had never been in short supply.

"I would think that after living so long with Clark, being alone would be difficult."

"Living with Clark was like being alone," she responded, pensively.

They said their final goodnight in the parking lot, Colette driving away in her Mercedes while Michelle was unlocking the door of her car.

Colette was feeling much better than she had earlier in the evening. The drinks had helped, but getting the chance to talk to Michelle had helped more. She appreciated her friend's willingness to listen.

Driving along, she couldn't help but wonder why

Michelle had remained unattached for so long. She knew Michelle had loved Robert deeply, but he had been dead for years, one of the early victims of the Vietnam War. To her knowledge, Michelle didn't even date anyone casually. Anytime Colette had called, Michelle was always available to talk to her, to meet with her.

It's almost like she's waiting for my call, Colette thought.

Traffic was not heavy, so Colette made the drive from *The Plum* to her townhouse in record time. As her car approached the garage, she pushed the button on her electronic opener, and the door began its upward trek. When the door had reached its zenith, she drove the car into the garage and killed the engine. She then pushed the button on the electronic device to close the door.

Had she looked in her rear view mirror while driving into the garage, she might have noticed the figure that emerged from the shrubbery and followed the car into its sanctuary. But she didn't, so when she opened the car door, she came face-to-face with the last person she would ever see.

Chapter 8

Friday, 4 a.m.

McCall was not asleep when the telephone rang. He had been up since three-fifteen, had devoured three cups of instant coffee, and was deeply involved in a book on existentialism. There was no particular reason why he was reading the book, except for the fact that it was handy and dealt with a subject that he knew little about. The very fact that he knew little about it bothered him. His mind demanded that he know everything possible about every subject.

More than one person had brought to his attention that it was impossible for a man to know everything about everything, but he had always been undaunted by unattainable goals.

Bill Haloran began the conversation with, "The killer has struck again."

"I can't say that I'm surprised," McCall replied, matter-of-factly.

"You're probably going to be surprised at the identity of the victim, though."

"Yeah, who was it?"

"Clark Ramsey's wife."

McCall was surprised, as was reflected by a pause before his questioning response, "Colette Ramsey?"

"The one and only," Haloran answered.

The reporter mentally pictured the cold-eyed beauty, whom he had known as the wife of county district attorney Clark Ramsey, a man who aspired to the governor's mansion. Initial surprise had now, however, given way to McCall's analytical mind, and he asked, "Are you sure that it's the same killer? The other two women were single and killed in apartments."

"Well, Mrs. Ramsey was not living with her husband."

"You're kidding?"

"No," Haloran replied. "From what I've been able to gather, they were separated."

"I sure didn't know that."

The detective laughed. "Did you expect Clark Ramsey to call you up and tell you?" The humor on Haloran's part was because McCall and Ramsey were adversaries. In fact, to say they were mere adversaries was an understatement. The reporter was sure that the D.A. was in some way connected with the murders of several persons, including Cele, McCall's fiance.

Any proof of Ramsey's connection, however, had been temporarily stymied when McCall had been wounded by Cele's killer and had, in self-defense, put a bullet in the man's brain.

Even prior to Cele's death, McCall had, in the course of a murder investigation, reopened a case where Ramsey, while serving as a county commissioner, had allegedly swindled a nursing home resident out of some prime land. Ramsey had paid the woman ten thousand dollars for the land. Then, after resigning his county commissioner's post, had sold it to the county for several million.

The victim of the alleged swindle was now dead. And mysterious circumstances also surrounded the death of her son. He had been a career Army man, had tried to do something about his mother being duped.

Though he couldn't prove it, McCall was sure that Ramsey had for all practical purposes stolen the elderly woman's land. And he was sure that the now district attorney had also had something to do with the son's death.

It was obvious to McCall that Ramsey lusted for power, that he would do anything to attain it. He figured that every step toward ultimate power was like an orgasm for his adversary.

McCall didn't like politicians in any shape or form, but detested Ramsey most because he thought the man used the law for his own purposes while claiming to champion justice.

"Anyway," Haloran continued, "she was killed and mutilated in the same way. Identically, in fact."

"Well, based on the way the other two victims were cut up, I don't guess there's any doubt then," McCall acknowledged.

"The only difference is that on this one we got a call."

"Yeah?"

"Yeah," Haloran said. "The desk sergeant got a call with some mumbling about the *bitch* being dead, along with the address."

"Did the caller say who the *bitch* was?"

"No," Haloran replied. "The sergeant said he was lucky to get the address, because the voice was so muffled."

McCall sighed. "I guess you've already ruled Ramsey out as a suspect."

"You know better than that. The husband's always a suspect, but I really don't think this is Ramsey's style."

"I don't either," McCall agreed. "I'd like to think that he at least had it done, though."

The detective laughed. "Damn it, McCall, I admire the fact that you never give up, but what motive could the man have?"

"Maybe he wants his constituency to feel sorry for him, the old bereaved widower routine."

"I sort of doubt that he would want people to know that his wife had left him," Haloran argued.

"Hey, he is a man who has known sorrow," McCall countered, sarcastically. "A man trying to do good and contending with a wife who doesn't understand him. That'll play in Texas."

"You have an unbelievable imagination."

"All you have to do is look at the shit we have down at the state capital, and you know it's not imagination. You don't have any criminals in San Antonio compared to what we have in Austin."

Haloran laughed. "You always amaze me with the confidence you have in your fellow man."

"Fellow man, hell. Those assholes aren't my fellow man."

"Well, anyway, I've got to get my ass in gear, McCall. I just thought you'd want to know about the murder."

"I appreciate it, Bill. Why don't you meet me at the diner at six-thirty and give me more details?"

"I don't see why not. I'm going to be damn hungry, McCall, so bring plenty of money."

"Hungry, huh? What else is new."

"By six-thirty, I'll probably have a little better handle on this mess."

"I'll see you then," McCall said.

After hanging up the phone, he pondered what Haloran had told him, then dialed Lisa's number. He really would have preferred to play this story alone, but felt a certain obligation to the young woman. After all, even though she was green as a gourd, she had been in on the story since its beginning.

It was a sleepy voice that answered after several rings.

"I hope I didn't interrupt anything," he said.

"Only my sleep," she replied. "My god, don't you sleep, Matt? What time is it? Why are you calling me at this hour?"

"To answer all your questions," he said, "there's been another murder."

"Oh." Any surprise on her part was obliterated by grogginess. "You said there would be more."

"Yeah, I'm a real genius at predicting perverts, but I didn't know one of the victims was going to be famous."

"Who was killed?" she asked.

"The D.A.'s wife."

"Colette Ramsey?"

"I see you're already up on San Antonio's more elite social circle," McCall said.

"It's pretty hard not to know about a man who plans to be governor, even if you've only been in town a short while," she responded. "And I even met Mrs. Ramsey right after I got here. I met her at a luncheon. Some bullshit meeting Turner had me covering."

"You can count on Turnip to know what's important," McCall said. "But the reason I called was to see if you wanted to go with me to meet Bill Haloran at six-thirty."

"Sure, I want to go."

"We're going to meet at the diner, so I can just meet you at the paper at six-fifteen, and we can walk over together."

She laughed. "The diner, huh? Are you trying to spoil me, Matt, taking me to such an exotic place all the time?"

"Hey, I can do without your asshole Arkansas sarcasm this time of morning."

"Bullshit, Matt. You thrive on sarcasm."

He sighed. "Whatever. Just get your ass out of bed and I'll see you at the paper."

"It's just a little after four o'clock," she complained.

"I figured it would take you a couple of hours to get your face on."

"Well, thanks a lot."

He laughed. "If you want to play sarcastic games with me in the morning, expect some repercussions. And by the way, if you know what time it is, why did you ask me?"

"I can see my clock radio now."

"Great," he said, "I'm glad your peepers are working. Now, I'm going to shower, shave and go down to the paper. I'll see you about six-fifteen and, please, don't keep me waiting."

McCall couldn't make out what Lisa grumbled before she hung up.

While standing in the shower with warm water cascading over his body, McCall couldn't help but wonder what Lisa would be like in bed. There was a sensuality about her that he had not yet interpreted, but thoughts of her caused his penis to harden.

He laughed inwardly at himself and thought, do you want to screw every pretty bitch you meet, McCall? He knew the answer was yes.

By five-thirty, McCall was at the *Tribune,* drinking coffee and reading the paper. Colette Ramsey's body had not been discovered in time to make the final edition, but there was a recap of the Caldwell and Burleson murders that carried Lisa's byline.

By six, he had gleaned the entire paper and was working on a recent copy of *Sports Illustrated* when Lisa showed up.

"Damn, you're punctual," he said approvingly.

"Not all women are late," she countered, "though I'm sure you had all of us categorized that way."

"You think I'm the kind of guy who lumps all women in the same category, huh?"

"I'd be surprised if you weren't."

"Well, be surprised because I have two categories."

"Just two?"

"Hell, a few minutes ago you were accusing me of having just one."

"Okay, so you've got two. I'm afraid to ask what they are."

"I intend to tell you anyway."

"Fire away."

"Well, I categorize women as either *bimbos* or *bitches*."

She laughed. "I might have known. How do you classify me?"

He chuckled. "Well, I sure as hell don't consider you a bimbo."

"Frankly, I kind of like being a bitch," she said. "And I happen to have a couple of categories for men, too."

"I don't want to hear them."

"Tough shit. I had to listen to your categories, and now you have to listen to mine."

"Must I remind you that I'm a veteran?" McCall asked with a laugh. "I shouldn't have to suffer additional slings and arrows."

"Sorry, Mr. McCall, but I would be untrue to the feminist movement if I didn't tell you that men are either *bastards* or *assholes*."

"And me?"

"I think you have a lock on both categories," she answered.

He feigned hurt. "I can't believe you would say something like that about me."

"You can't, huh? Even after the way you categorized me?"

"I thought I was complimenting you," he said.

She laughed. "You asshole."

They walked to the diner. The air was brisk, and the seemingly always present wind played with their hair. Early morning traffic was light, a situation that would change in another hour.

Haloran was already perched in a booth, a half-empty cup of coffee in front of him. He greeted them with, "Damn, McCall, I didn't know you were going to bring Joe's niece."

Lisa rolled her eyes, did something funny with her lips and said, "Do you mind?"

"Hell no," the detective replied. "I thought I was going to have to look at *Old Ugly* over breakfast."

"Scoot in there, Lisa," McCall said, referring to the seat across from Haloran. "You'll have to sit by me because there's not enough room next to old lard-ass. Not that you'd want to sit there anyway."

"I certainly wouldn't mind sitting next to Detective Haloran," Lisa countered.

"Forget it," McCall said. "I can't play with your legs if you're all the way across the table from me."

She gave a half-chuckle, and her face flushed a bit.

Haloran shook his head in mock dismay and said, "The man has no shame."

"Don't encourage her," McCall said. "She's already called me an asshole and bastard this morning."

The detective laughed. "Both would be compliments for you, my friend."

The waitress came, and they all ordered. Lisa and Haloran ordered ham, eggs and biscuits. McCall chose fried chicken breasts with biscuits and cream gravy.

"You eat funny, McCall," Haloran said.

"You mean what I eat, or the way I eat?"

"Now that you mention it, both."

"Coming from you, I consider that a compliment," the reporter said.

Haloran handed McCall some papers and said, "That's all we have right now on the Ramsey murder. Preliminary stuff."

McCall looked at the material the detective had given

him and replied, "Thanks, Bill. My guess is that this one won't be treated routinely."

"That's for sure. The Chief's already on my ass to get something done fast."

"Anyone talked to Ramsey yet?"

"The Chief. He's the one who called Ramsey and told him about his wife."

"And where did he reach learned counsel?"

"He was at home. From what the Chief said, he was asleep."

"I hope that's not his alibi," McCall said.

"The hell you do," Haloran responded. "I'll bet my telling you he doesn't have an alibi just made your day."

Lisa injected, "Am I missing something here? Are you saying that Clark Ramsey murdered his wife, Matt?"

"It's what he wants to believe," Haloran volunteered. "Maybe he hasn't had time to tell you about his vendetta against Clark Ramsey."

McCall grumbled, "I didn't know you were one of the asshole's fans, Bill."

"I can't say that I care for the man," Haloran said, "but until I get evidence to the contrary, I have to treat him like any other citizen."

"C'mon now. He's not treated like any other citizen."

"Poor choice of words," Haloran agreed. "I guess we do have to treat his office special. And before you say anything else, you know damn well that I don't like it."

"I know, Bill. And I understand your situation, whether you believe it or not."

The waitress brought their food, and they began eating, making small-talk between bites. It was after the waitress removed their empty plates and refilled their coffee cups that they got on to the real purpose of the meeting.

"Okay, Bill," McCall began, "was there any physical evidence at the scene of Mrs. Ramsey's murder?"

"None that we've discovered so far," the detective

answered. "Except for the blood, the place was clean as a pin."

"In other words, just like the scenes at the other two murders."

"Exactly. The killer obviously forced Mrs. Ramsey into the bathroom and killed her there."

"And she was killed in exactly the same way as Velda Rose Caldwell and Maggie Burleson?"

"According to the coroner's preliminary report, there was so little variation in the way the women were killed and mutilated that we're ninety-nine percent sure that the same person killed all of them."

"Does the coroner think the killer used the same weapon to cut their throats that was used to mutilate their bodies?"

"He thinks it was the same," the detective said. "It had to be razor-sharp, and the blade had to be strong for the killer to do what was done."

"Like a surgical blade?"

"Probably."

Matt turned to Lisa and said, "In the articles you wrote, did you describe the way the victims were mutilated? Did . . ."

She interrupted with, "I didn't know about the mutilations."

"I know," he continued. "I was going to ask if the other paper mentioned the mutilations?"

"If they did, I'm not aware of it," she replied.

"I can answer your question about that," Haloran injected. "The police department has kept the mutilations under wraps. No one was told."

"A good reporter could have found out," McCall said.

Haloran laughed. "You were out of town, and I don't know of any other reporter who makes out with some of the girls who work in the coroner's office."

McCall grinned. "Cut me some slack, will you? Lisa's

liable to get the wrong idea about me."

The detective countered with, "I haven't known Lisa long, but I'm pretty sure she has the right perception of you, McCall."

"Are you saying the man will do anything for a story?" Lisa asked.

Haloran did a little crawfishing. "I'm not going to say he'll do anything for a story, but he'll do damn near anything to get the information he wants."

"Even to screwing some woman in the coroner's office?" she asked with a smile.

McCall feigned shock. "I'm more than a little concerned about the way you talk, young lady."

She laughed. "I'll bet."

McCall brought them back to the subject. "Okay, so nobody knew about the mutilations, so we can assume the same person killed all three women." He paused, then as an afterthought added, "Of course, police officers knew. And the people in the coroner's office knew."

Haloran sighed. "Unbelievable. With you, everybody is a suspect."

"You have to admit it makes a pretty good scenario," McCall said. "A police officer or coroner investigates a murder, sees how it was committed, then goes out and duplicates the killing."

"That imagination is always getting you into trouble," Haloran said. "Can't you just let the facts speak for themselves?"

"I don't think my imagination is all that far out. Especially when you consider that the women were possibly killed and mutilated with a surgical instrument. Who better than a coroner to do something like that?"

"What bugs me about you, McCall, is that you can take some off-the-wall theory and make it sound logical."

"I do not, of course, think the second and third murders were committed by a police officer or coroner," McCall admitted. "Unless, of course, the first murder was also committed by a police officer or coroner. But I brought all this up to say that someone from the police department or coroner's office could have talked about the mutilations, and probably did.

"However, most copycat killers get their information from the media. And from what I've been able to find out, the media hasn't done a very thorough job of reporting the Caldwell and Burleson killings. So, I'm willing to assume that all three killings were done by the same person."

Haloran laughed. "That's mighty big of you."

"On this report, I was noticing the address where Mrs. Ramsey was killed. She obviously wasn't living in an apartment."

"Townhouse," Haloran said, "and it is posh."

"I'd expect as much," the reporter responded. "Colette Ramsey had plenty of money before she met *Mr. Wonderful*, and her parents could buy and sell our district attorney several times over."

"I don't think she had to buy from Goodwill," Haloran agreed.

"What bothers me," McCall said, "is the difference in the victims. One's a cocktail waitress, one's a nurse, and the other's a social butterfly."

"I don't understand what you're saying," Lisa injected.

"You look for a common denominator," McCall explained. "There needs to be something that ties the three women together. Two of the women lived in apartments, of course, but the third lived in a posh townhouse. There has to be something else."

Haloran nodded agreement and said to Lisa, "He's right."

"I know this sounds a bit squirrely," McCall said, "but suppose the Caldwell and Burleson murders were committed just to set-up the Ramsey murder."

"What you're saying is that maybe the first two murders

were committed to make it look as though a psycho is on a killing rampage," Haloran interpreted.

"Exactly."

"And, of course, you think Clark Ramsey might have been the one to come up with this scheme."

McCall laughed. "Such a thought did cross my mind."

"Well, I think you're way off base," Haloran said. "Of course, all these murders happened so close together that we haven't really even had time to thoroughly investigate the Caldwell and Burleson killings. It's going to take some time to get all the pieces together, and maybe, after we've investigated, we'll even come up with that common denominator that you want."

"Okay, Bill, I know you haven't had time to study the Ramsey murder thoroughly, or the other two for that matter, but why don't you tell us what you know about how the killings took place."

Haloran pondered the request for a few moments before he answered with, "My theory is that the killer had to be a pretty strong individual. I say that because there really wasn't a sign of struggle by any of the victims. He must have taken them by surprise, subdued them quickly.

"Each victim was killed in her bathroom. I think the killer took each victim to the bathroom before cutting her throat, then placed the victim in the bathtub to perform the mutilation.

"We've interviewed everyone in the Caldwell and Burleson apartment buildings and couldn't find anyone who had heard a scream or noise of any kind. As to why one of these women didn't cry out, I don't know. But with the thin walls of apartment buildings, you'd think that someone would have heard them if they had."

McCall interrupted with, "Do you think the killer could have rendered the victims unconscious before taking them to the bathroom?"

"I certainly think that's possible," Haloran replied, "but

we found no evidence of them being dragged across the floor. In fact, no evidence of any kind of foul play, except in the bathtubs."

"The women were totally undressed, right?"

"Yes."

"Were they killed after they were undressed?"

"Evidently. There was no blood at all on any of the clothing. In fact, the clothing that each of the victims was wearing prior to being murdered was laid out neatly on her bed.

"I might add that we haven't verified what Mrs. Ramsey was wearing, but assume it was what we found on the bed."

"The autopsies on Velda Rose Caldwell and Maggie Burleson show that neither was raped," McCall said. "I don't guess you know about Mrs. Ramsey yet?"

"No," Haloran confirmed, "but I'll probably have that information by the time I get back to the station."

"It would seem to me that the killer would have gotten blood all over him," McCall said, "maybe even on his shoes."

"If he did, he didn't get it on the soles or heels," Haloran informed. "We couldn't find a single bloodstain on the carpet at any of the crime scenes. In fact, except for the blood in the bathtubs, each of the bathrooms was spotlessly clean."

"Are you saying that the killer cleaned the bathrooms?"

"Maybe," the detective said. "But I also believe the victims were unconscious when they were placed in their bathtubs. I believe their throats were cut while they were unconscious."

"No indication that any of the victims had their hands or feet tied, were gagged, anything like that?"

"None."

"So the mutilations occurred after the victims were dead," McCall surmised.

"Obviously," Haloran agreed. "Otherwise, I think there would have been some screams that tenants in the Burleson and Caldwell apartments would have heard."

"Bill, would you call and tell me if you get anything else on the Ramsey murder this morning?"

"As long as you didn't hear it from me," the detective answered. "And since when haven't I kept you informed?"

McCall laughed. "Well, you're usually pretty good about it, but sometimes the bureaucracy keeps you from informing me as quickly as you should."

Haloran shook his head in disbelief and said to Lisa, "He is an asshole. You know that, don't you?"

"I know," Lisa agreed.

McCall paid the check, and they all exited the diner at the same time, Haloran on the way back to the police station, he and Lisa on the way back to the *Tribune.* Traffic had picked up dramatically, and the sidewalks had gotten congested.

"I have a hard time believing that a person could kill other human beings the way Mrs. Ramsey and the other women were murdered," Lisa said. "And I especially have a hard time believing another human being could do what was done to their bodies."

"People always get uptight about mutilation," McCall responded. "Especially in this country. But I saw a lot of body mutilation in Vietnam. The Viet Cong and North Vietnamese were specialists at it."

"Doesn't it bother you?"

"Sure," he admitted. "It bothers me a lot more than it bothers the person who's dead. I think that was the whole purpose of mutilation in Vietnam."

"Why do you think the killer mutilated the bodies of his victims?"

McCall shrugged his shoulders. "It beats the hell out of me. I'm sure a psychiatrist could give us an off-the-wall explanation, but only the killer really knows."

They walked the rest of the way to the *Tribune* Building in silence, caught the slow elevator up to the newsroom, then made the journey to McCall's desk.

"What do you want me to do?" Lisa asked.

"Well, we need files on all the players," McCall answered. "You know what I mean. We need a file on each of the victims and everyone connected with them. Like with Velda Rose Caldwell. We need a file on her, her parents, friends, boyfriends, any and all folks connected with her that might give us a lead.

"The same with Maggie Burleson and Colette Ramsey. By the way, I have a pretty good file on Clark Ramsey, but it only goes back a few years. We need to dig up everything we can from that asshole's past."

"Do you really think Clark Ramsey had something to do with killing his wife?"

He laughed. "Bill was right in saying that I'd like for the killer to be Ramsey, but that's not likely. Whoever killed these women knew a lot about surgery."

"You're basing that on the mutilations, of course," she said.

"Yes, and also the way each victim's throat was cut, the way the breasts were removed, and the way the vagina was butchered shows that the killer studied human anatomy."

"So, you weren't kidding when you said a coroner could have committed the murders."

"Well, it's my roundabout way of saying that a doctor could have been involved. Of course, a lot of people know how to cut up an animal or human."

It was about thirty minutes later that Haloran called and told him that evidence indicated that Colette Ramsey had not been raped. The detective also told him that Michelle Sharp had called the police on learning that Mrs. Ramsey was dead.

"She was probably the last person, other than the killer,

to see Mrs. Ramsey alive," Haloran said.

Chapter 9

Friday, 10 a.m.

Ed Parkham had called a ten o'clock meeting in his office to discuss the bathtub murders. More specifically, Colette Ramsey's death and the way the paper should play it. McCall, Lisa, Turner Sipe and Katie Hussey, the metro editor, had answered his summons.

The managing editor directed his first statement to McCall. "This looks like it has turned into all you could ask for."

The reporter, nursing a cup of coffee, stared at Parkham and with disdain replied, "I'm not exactly into people getting themselves killed and butchered so I can have a good story, Ed."

"I didn't mean it that way," Parkham answered, defensively. "I just meant it's the kind of story that you handle well."

McCall laughed. "Well, if I handle it so well, why are we having this meeting?" He hated bullshit meetings. He knew that some of the editors loved them, especially the trio with whom he and Lisa were now cloistered.

Katie chimed in. "We just need an update. We need to know how much space to make available to you, whether the paper can provide any other resources to help you."

McCall didn't respond to Katie, just gave her a glance. Instead, he said to Parkham, "You know that I can't tell you how much space I'm going to need, Ed. It'll depend on how the story develops. As for other resources, Lisa's all I need."

Parkham cleared his throat, then replied, "Do you mind telling us what you have so far?"

"Not at all. We know that Mrs. Ramsey was killed in the exact manner as the other two women. She wasn't raped, either."

"You know that Mrs. Ramsey's murder makes this situation much more sensitive than it was," Katie said.

"No, I don't know that at all," McCall responded. It was hard for him to believe how much he detested Katie Hussey, a former society writer in her early thirties who had selectively screwed her way up through the ranks. She was now Parkham's chief squeeze. McCall couldn't understand how Katie or Parkham could stand each other. He knew that her only interest in the managing editor was to insure her power base, but he couldn't understand why Parkham would be interested in her.

She was maybe five-feet three-inches tall, with a larger than normal ass that drooped a bit. Complimenting the ass were sagging tits, thick ankles and heavy legs. Nice brown eyes were offset by a nose that was too pointed, slightly protruding teeth, a weak chin and small, straight, narrow lips. She had shoulder-length, piss-colored hair.

"Just so you'll know where I stand, Katie," McCall continued, "I plan to give considerable ink to the Caldwell and

Burleson killings, too. I consider their deaths just as tragic as Colette Ramsey's."

Parkham defended his editor with, "I think you may have misunderstood Katie."

"I doubt it."

"Anyway," the managing editor continued, "knowing how you feel about Clark Ramsey, I think you know we have to exercise extreme caution in the way we handle the story."

"You mean the way I handle the story," McCall corrected. "You've got nothing to worry about, Ed. I'm not going to get the paper involved in a libel suit. At this point, I don't even think Ramsey's guilty."

He sensed that all three editors breathed a sigh of relief.

"So, where do you go from here?" Parkham asked.

"Well, there's no doubt that we've got a page one story on Mrs. Ramsey's murder for tomorrow's edition," McCall answered. "The television and radio people will give it plenty of play all day and tonight, but it'll be the typical bullshit. No substance. I plan to have an in-depth story for Saturday, then follow up with a biggie for the Sunday edition.

"At eleven-thirty, I'm having lunch with the last person, other than the killer, who saw Mrs. Ramsey alive."

They all showed surprise, including Lisa. He hadn't told her that he had made contact with Michelle Sharp.

"That's great," Parkham said.

McCall thought there was nothing like the possibility of a journalism award to light up Parkham's eyes. Awards were the criteria by which the managing editor measured his performance. And he smelled one, maybe several, in the stories about the bathtub murders.

"Do you know what length story you'll have for tomorrow?" Sipe asked.

"Not yet," McCall replied, "but you'll be the first to

know, Turnip."

After the meeting broke up, Lisa followed McCall to his desk.

"Am I supposed to go to lunch with you?" she asked.

"I'd better handle this one solo," he answered. "You've got more than enough to do in preparing files on the players."

"I guess you're going to take Michelle Sharp to the diner?"

He laughed. "No, as a matter of fact, we're meeting at The Plum, which is where she last saw Colette Ramsey alive."

"Do you know if she's married?"

"Nope, I don't know." He wondered why she had asked the question, then continued with, "Try to get in touch with someone who worked with Velda Rose Caldwell. I'd like to talk to them sometime this afternoon."

"Do you know what time you'll be back from lunch?"

"No later than two o'clock."

McCall arrived at *The Plum* at eleven-twenty and found Michelle Sharp waiting. He hadn't known what to expect in a friend of Colette Ramsey's, but was immediately impressed with the woman's easy and friendly manner. There was a warmth to her large brown eyes, accentuated by shoulder-length hair that surrounded a cameo face. McCall guessed her to be about five-feet six-inches tall, with a model's figure and the poise to go with it. He thought she was probably about the same age as Colette Ramsey.

And he immediately sensed that he wasn't dealing with a bimbo. She was an intelligent lady.

The Plum was half bar, half restaurant. The hostess led them to a small table beside a window, and they sat down across from each other in oversized chairs.

"I want you to know how much I appreciate you meeting me here," McCall began.

Before she could answer a waiter was standing beside

their table asking if they wanted a drink.

"I'll have a bloody bull," she said.

"Just bring me a Michelob Light," McCall ordered.

"I really don't know if I should be here," Michelle said in reply to his earlier statement, "but I want to do what I can to help find Colette's killer."

It was obvious to McCall that the woman had been crying. Her expressive eyes couldn't hide it.

"Since you've already talked to the police, answering some of my questions might seem like you're covering old ground," McCall said, "but, believe me, it's important. Something you think is totally unimportant might be just the lead we need to find the killer."

"Detective Haloran told me that you are as good an investigator as you are a writer," she informed. "And he said you would dedicate your fulltime efforts to finding the killer.

"Bill may be overly kind in assessing my investigative skills, but you can count on me to do everything in my power to find out who killed Colette Ramsey, and why."

"Well, I'm willing to tell you whatever I can."

The waiter brought their drinks and asked if they were ready to order. McCall deferred to Michelle who said, "I'll just have the taco salad."

"Bring me the chopped sirloin and forget the salad," McCall said.

After the waiter was out of earshot he asked, "Just how long did you know Mrs. Ramsey?"

"We first met when we were freshmen at SMU," she replied. "I hate to say it, but that was twenty years ago."

"Are you from San Antonio?"

"No, I'm a native of Bonham, Texas."

"How did you end up here?"

"I first came here with my husband. He was career Air Force."

"Was?"

"He was a pilot. He was killed in Vietnam."

"I'm sorry."

She didn't acknowledge his sympathy, but continued. "I lived here while he was in Vietnam and just never left after he was killed."

"Where do you work?"

"I own a gift shop."

"I'd think that would be a pretty good business."

"It's okay, but it's time consuming and confining."

He smiled. "I've found practically all work to be that way."

She returned his smile. "I guess it is."

"The way you look, I would have guessed you to be a model," he said. He was trying to put her at ease, not get into Colette Ramsey too quickly.

"I'm flattered, but I'm a bit too short to be a model."

"If modeldom wants someone taller than you, it's their loss. You're a very pretty lady."

"Again, thank you," she said. "But I'm sure you're not all that interested in talking about me. You asked me here to talk about Colette."

"And I will. But I can also assure you that I enjoy the company of a beautiful woman."

"I'm afraid I'm blushing."

If she was blushing, it was not obvious to McCall. But then, she had a nice tan.

"My guess is that you didn't get that tan in San Antonio," he said.

"Maybe I went to a tanning salon here."

"I doubt it."

She laughed. "To be truthful, I got the tan in the Bahamas. In fact, Colette and I were there just last week."

"How long had she and Ramsey been separated?"

"Six weeks."

"The separation was kind of sudden, wasn't it?"

"Not really. She had been planning to leave Clark for some time."

"She told you this?"

"There wasn't much that Colette didn't tell me."

"She was a native of Dallas, right?"

"That's right. Her father's in the oil business."

"Yeah, I guess everyone in the state has heard of Baker Poole. His political influence would certainly be a help to Ramsey's gubernatorial bid."

"Colette thought her father was the only reason Clark married her."

"And what do you think?"

"I think Clark Ramsey is an opportunist."

"Do you think he's capable of murder?"

"Yes, but I don't think he killed Colette."

"Why's that?"

"I don't see how he could benefit from it."

"So, you're saying he's capable of murder, but only when he can benefit from it."

"I guess so," she acknowledged. "And besides, I thought the same person killed Colette that murdered those other girls."

"It does look that way, but maybe the two girls were murdered to set up Colette's death."

"That's a ghastly thought."

"Stranger things have happened."

"You have an unusual mind, Mr. McCall, to even think of such things."

"Please call me Matt. As for the unusual mind, maybe. But over the years I've dealt with the macabre so often that I tend to analyze all the possibilities available to the criminal mind."

She shuddered. "Just thinking about what you suggest causes as chill to run down my spine. Don't most people think the killer is a lunatic?"

"The killer could very well be some irrational psycho,"

McCall agreed, "indiscriminately killing for no apparent reason."

"When you catch him, I guess you'll know."

"We won't have to wait until then."

"Why's that?"

"If the theory I put forth is wrong, then the killer will strike again. He'll kill again and again until he's caught.

"Of course, even if my theory's right, even if the first two murders were committed to set up Colette Ramsey's death, the killer is still an irrational psychopath."

She shuddered again. "Murder, things like that, all seemed so distant until Colette. I could understand my husband's death because he was in a war, but the deaths of Colette and the other two women seem so senseless."

"It is senseless. All murder is senseless."

The waiter brought their food, and they began eating. Between bites, McCall asked, "Would you tell me why Mrs. Ramsey left her husband?"

Michelle pondered the question a few moments, then answered, "They just weren't getting along. I guess you could say they had some irreconcilable differences."

"I can certainly believe that," he responded, "but if I'm going to help find your friend's murderer, I'm going to have to have the whole truth. Was that all you told Bill Haloran, that they had irreconcilable differences?"

"Yes, and I really can't tell you anything more."

"Was she seeing anyone else?" he asked.

She dropped her eyes to her food and answered, "I don't know."

He knew she did know. Her eyes were too expressive to hide a lie. Even her voice gave her away.

"Look, I'm not out to nail the guy," he said, "but I do need to talk to him. It could be very important."

"I'll help you in every way I can, but I won't have Colette's name dragged through the dirt. Her parents have been hurt enough, and I want them to have the best memories possible about their daughter."

"What if the guy's the killer?"

"If there was another man, and you'll note that I said if, there wouldn't be any reason for him to kill her."

"I thought we'd already established that there's no reason for murder."

"I can't argue with you about that, but the police think that Colette was killed by a maniac, someone who didn't even know her."

"And maybe she was, but what's the harm in checking out the possibility that she was killed by someone who knew her. I know the theory I spouted off a while ago is off-the-wall, but let's just suppose that the other two women were killed just to set up Mrs. Ramsey's murder, to make the police think they were dealing with a psycho who kills indiscriminately?"

"That's what we'd be doing, supposing," she argued.

"Of course, but there is a possibility that she knew the killer. That's why we need to check everyone with whom she had contact, to try to find something, anything, that might lead to the killer. Killers like this one are usually someone the victim runs into in the course of their daily routine. It could be a gas station attendant, an appliance repairman, you name it."

"So, you think Colette and the other two girls may have known the killer?"

"It's very possible."

She sighed. "Colette was having an affair. If I tell you the person's name, will you promise to be discreet? If the word gets out, a lot of people are going to be hurt."

"I'm not interested in a banner headline about two people having an affair," he assured her. "I'm just interested in talking to anyone who might give me a lead. Now, who is the guy?"

"Dr. Norris Summerfield."

The name didn't ring a bell with McCall, but the fact that

he was a doctor did. The killer knew a lot about anatomy.

"I don't guess I know the good doctor," he said.

"There's no reason you should, but he's one of the city's leading gynecologists."

"Was he Mrs. Ramsey's doctor?"

"Yes."

"And does Clark Ramsey know he was Colette's lover?"

"I don't think so."

McCall knew Ramsey had the manpower to have had his wife tailed, but figured he wouldn't have done so. He wouldn't have wanted any of his troops to know that Colette was unfaithful, or that he suspected her. It would have made him vulnerable. The way McCall saw it, Ramsey probably didn't know, and probably, because of his ego, even refused to suspect.

"My guess is that Dr. Summerfield is married," McCall said.

"Good guess. The man has a wife and a couple of kids. I didn't like what he and Colette were doing, so I'm not trying to protect him. I just want to protect Colette's memory for her folks and from a lot of sensational gossip that wouldn't do Mrs. Summerfield and her children any good, either."

He knew that Michelle was sincerely concerned for the innocents in the scenario, and it made him like her all the more.

"You can count on my discretion, Michelle."

"I know I can. I can read people pretty well."

He laughed. "I'll have to remember that."

"You know, in a way I'm glad I told you. I hated it when Colette told me about playing house with Norris, and . . ."

"Oh, you know Summerfield, too, huh?"

"He's also my doctor. And as I was saying, I wish Colette hadn't let me in on her little secret. Ever since she told me, it has been like a weight on my shoulders. I've never liked to be involved in stuff like that. The one thing I can say about

Colette, though, is that she took full advantage of a friendship. She was never one to suffer alone."

"Was she having problems with Summerfield?"

"Only the normal problems of a woman in love with a married man."

"Oh, then we're not talking about just a lark?"

"Oh, no," she affirmed. "Colette was very much in love with Norris."

"And what about Norris?"

"As to his feelings, I can't say. I've certainly never discussed Colette with him. As to his relationship with her, I only know what she told me."

"And what was that?"

"That Norris planned to divorce his wife and marry her."

"And do you believe that?"

"I don't know what to believe," she answered. "Colette was a very beautiful woman, and I'm sure a lot of men would also have taken advantage of the situation, slept with her and let it go at that."

"So, you don't actually know what Summerfield's intent was in regard to Mrs. Ramsey?"

"No, but I wouldn't believe him. He's a good doctor, and I respect his medical opinions, but I wouldn't trust him otherwise."

"Has he ever made a move on you?"

"In a subtle kind of way. I think he considers himself a real ladies' man."

McCall laughed. "I guess his profession makes him one."

She smiled. "I hadn't thought of it that way, but you're right."

"Is he a good-looking guy?"

"He's handsome enough. In fact, I'm sure you've seen him before, but just didn't know the name."

"Where?"

"At some of the charity functions around town. I've seen you at some of the same ones he has attended."

"What? And you mean I didn't see you."

She laughed. "Well, I sort of blend into the crowd. And I have to admit that I didn't see you all that much. You came and went pretty quickly, and it was more than obvious that you weren't having a good time."

"If I didn't see you, I probably didn't see Summerfield. And you're right about me not liking those things. I'm not big on crowds of any kind. But that does bring up another question. Does Ramsey know Summerfield?"

"Very well. They play golf together. Colette and Clark socialized a lot with the Summerfields, even went on vacation with them last year."

"That does make it sticky," McCall said. "I guess I never thought about Ramsey hanging around with a doctor."

"Clark has the utmost respect for doctors," Michelle said. "You probably didn't know this, but he was even enrolled in medical school for a while before deciding to go into law."

Chapter 10

When Michelle told McCall about Clark Ramsey studying to be a doctor, his mental processes began computing on all cylinders. Because of the way the women had been murdered and brutalized after death, Ramsey's brush with a possible medical career made him a prime suspect.

McCall knew, of course, that he was assuming a lot by even thinking that the first two women might have been killed to set up Mrs. Ramsey's murder. If the killer struck again, maybe even several times, it would blow the hell out of his theory.

Or maybe not.

Maybe Ramsey was smart enough to kill again in order to better cover his tracks. Maybe the D.A. had gone off the deep end and was now deeply in love with killing. Maybe murder had become his sexual relief.

McCall laughed at his thoughts. He realized that he so badly wanted Ramsey to be the killer that his objectivity could become clouded in investigating the murders. He had to be careful of that.

God knows that Ramsey is capable of murder, he thought, but only if it would benefit him in some way. Just how would he benefit from his wife's death? Could the man think that he would become an object of voter sympathy as a result of such a tragic circumstance?

He had no doubt that Ramsey would sacrifice his wife, anyone else for that matter, for a few votes. The man was the complete politician.

McCall figured, of course, that Ramsey would have preferred to have had the beautiful Colette by his side in his journey toward the governor's mansion. She would definitely have been an asset. Her queenly manner would have awed the voting sheep.

And Colette's father would certainly be an asset Ramsey wouldn't want to lose. He had the money and political power to make his son-in-law's journey a lot easier. And even with Colette being dead, there was every reason to believe that Ramsey might have the support of her father.

All this supposition was running through McCall's mind as he drove toward Annie Cossey's home. Lisa had made an appointment for him to see Velda Rose Caldwell's friend and co-worker.

On arrival, he was impressed with the exterior of the house. The front yard was immaculately manicured, with plants and shrubs perfectly positioned. The neighborhood, he guessed, was one comprised of above-average white-collar workers.

Annie greeted him at the door. She was wearing what looked to be a comfortable, low-neckline sundress that didn't hide an outstanding figure. McCall's eyes never failed to show his appreciation for such beauty, a fact that didn't escape Annie. And though she was not one to be bothered by the gazes of men, his penetrating look caused her to blush a bit.

"Please come in," she said. He followed her to the den, well-furnished and hospital-clean. After he was seated on the couch, she asked, "Can I get you some coffee?"

"If it's no trouble," he answered.

"It's not. I just made a fresh pot. What do you take in yours?"

"Just a half pack of Sweet 'n Low."

A minute later she appeared back in the room with two mugs. She placed them on coasters that were already on the coffee table and seated herself in a chair next to the couch. McCall took an appreciative glance at her tanned and shapely legs.

"I appreciate you taking the time to see me," he said. Her tits were generous and, from what he could see, just as tan as the legs.

"If I can give you any information that will help catch Velda Rose's killer, I want to," she replied.

"Well, you can start by telling me all you knew about Velda Rose. Her past, family, friends, anything."

He listened attentively, took notes, while she talked about the dead girl. But during her discourse, he couldn't help but continue to approve of her beauty. She was not like a touched up *Playboy* photo, but had all the right features to appear on one of the publication's pages. The honey-colored, waist-length straight hair, the mysterious and expressive dark brown eyes; she was a woman who had it all.

After she finished her monologue, he asked, "Did your husband object to Velda Rose living here before getting her apartment?"

"I don't have a husband. I'm divorced, have a couple of kids."

He was glad she was free. "I guess that's good."

"I'm satisfied," she said. "Velda Rose and I had a lot in

common when it came to men."

"What do you mean by that?"

"I mean that neither of us were very lucky in our selection of men. The guy she came here to marry was as big an asshole as my husband."

He laughed. "Do you think Velda Rose's former boyfriend might have had something to do with her death?"

"No way. She didn't even know where the guy was stationed. And from what I understand, he wasn't anxious to see her again."

"He knew where she was though," McCall said. "From what you say, she kept in touch with his folks."

"Yeah, I guess so," she replied. "The girl was carrying a real torch for the sonofabitch. She kept writing to him in care of his folks. And every once in a while, she'd call his parents to see if he was okay. I think she kept hoping that he would send for her."

"But to your knowledge, there was never any contact at all?"

"Zero."

"And to your knowledge, Velda Rose never dated anyone in San Antonio?"

"No one," she answered. "And I would have known. Of course, if you're working as a cocktail waitress, you don't exactly have much time for dating."

"Don't you get a couple of nights off a week?"

"Yeah, but that's not the whole problem. Who in the hell am I going to date? About the only guys I meet are those that come into the bar, and they're usually married men on the make or single guys who think every cocktail waitress is an easy lay."

McCall laughed. "Well, I'm not here to defend my fellow man."

She smiled for the first time since he had met her. "I don't think your defending them would do much good with me. I'm a bit opinionated on the subject."

"How long have you been divorced?"

"Several years."

"What does your ex-husband do?"

"He's on the government tit. He's in the Air Force."

McCall laughed. "So, you're anti-military, too?"

"Not at all. It's just that if it wasn't for the military, my ex-husband couldn't survive. I don't think he could hold a real job."

He laughed again. "You don't consider the Air Force a real job?"

"It may be for some, but it's just a pension for him."

McCall couldn't help but think about the two women he had met for the first time this day, one the widow of an Air Force officer who had been killed in battle and the other the ex-wife of an Air Force enlisted man accused of being worthless.

And Velda Rose Caldwell had been ditched by an Air Force enlisted man. If he hadn't dropped her, she might be alive. He knew that kind of thinking was probably going on inside Annie Cossey's head. Subconsciously, of course.

Blame it on the Air Force, he thought. Blame everything that's wrong in life on the Air Force.

Stupid.

"Did Velda Rose, by any chance, know Maggie Burleson?" McCall asked.

"You mean the second girl who was murdered?"

"Yes."

"You know, it's strange but I think I saw Maggie Burleson in the Cactus," she said. "The reason I think that is because I saw her picture in the paper, and I'm certain that I saw her in the Cactus more than once."

"So, it's possible that Velda Rose knew her?"

"It's possible, I suppose. But only as a customer. Velda Rose didn't socialize with anyone other than me."

"You're sure about that, no dates or anything like that?"

"I'm very sure," she said emphatically, "She just couldn't accept the fact that her boyfriend had dumped her."

"Those times you may have seen Maggie Burleson in the Cactus, was she with anyone else?"

"I'm not all that certain that I saw her," Annie replied. "But if I'm not mistaken, she was with another woman. And I think they were both wearing uniforms."

"Maybe another nurse, huh?"

"Maybe."

"I understand that you discovered Velda Rose's body."

As soon as he mentioned it, McCall could see the memory of the discovery in her face. It became almost ashen.

"Yes, it was horrible. I still dream about it."

"That's understandable."

"I'm scared, too. Just knowing that maniac is still loose keeps me awake at night."

"Do you have any protection?"

"I have a shotgun."

"Do you know how to use it?"

"Are you kidding? I grew up in a small Texas town. I can shoot a shotgun or rifle as well as a man."

He laughed. "Maybe as well as some men."

"Are you going to challenge me to a shooting contest?"

"I wasn't planning to."

"I think you'd be surprised."

"I probably would," he agreed. "Do you know if Velda Rose had a weapon in her apartment."

"She didn't have anything. I told her to keep her door locked."

"Did she?"

"I think she did. I think she was scared enough that she always kept it locked."

"But it wasn't locked the day you discovered her body?"

"That's right. She must have opened it and let the

killer in."

"Didn't you warn her about opening the door to strangers?"

"Yes, but Velda Rose was a bit ignorant about the way things are in the city. She was still a small town girl with small town ways."

"Of course, there's a possibility that she knew the killer. But you tell me that she really didn't know anyone."

"I think the only people she knew were those that worked for the Cactus and her apartment manager."

"What about sales people? Had she bought anything recently?"

"Oh, sure. She bought some clothes and things like that."

"Anything else?"

"Well, she rented all her furniture. Even her stereo and television set."

"Were you with her when she bought the clothes or rented these items?"

"I was with her when she bought clothes and rented all her stuff. She didn't have a car, so I transported her around. She kind of depended on me for everything."

"When she was buying clothes and renting stuff, were you suspicious of any of the people who helped you?"

"Not really. In fact, we were helped by women with everything that Velda Rose bought and rented."

"No men at all."

"Well, there were men in the stores and rental place, but I didn't pay any attention to them. And I don't think they paid any attention to us."

"Where did Velda Rose buy her clothes?"

"Joske's. She bought linens and towels there, too."

"What about the furniture rental?"

"Cort."

"And the stereo and TV?"

"ABC."

"Were any of the women you dealt with strong-looking? You know, healthy and muscular?"

She laughed. "Gosh, I don't know. They were just women."

He made a notation to have Lisa question the clerks who had helped Velda Rose with her clothes purchases and rentals. He was certain they could be traced through receipts Haloran would have confiscated at the dead woman's apartment. The rentals would be easy enough to trace, and even if Velda Rose had thrown away the sales slips on clothing and so forth, there would be no problem tracking down the clerks who had waited on her. It would be a good test for Lisa.

"Women are capable of murder," he said.

"There would be no reason for a woman to kill Velda Rose."

"No reason for a man, either."

"That's true."

"Were you present when the furniture, TV and stereo were delivered?"

"No."

He made a notation. The delivery men would also be easy to check.

"What about when she had her phone put in? Did you see the guy who installed it?"

"There was already an outlet, so nobody came out. We went to one of the company's outlets, and she rented the phone."

"And a woman waited on you?"

"Yes."

"Do you remember how she looked?"

"She was young and healthy."

He made a notation to have Lisa interview the woman at the telephone store. The company would have a record of the person who had helped Velda Rose.

"Do you know the apartment manager?"

"I met the one who leased Velda Rose the apartment. She's young and healthy, too. There's more than one, though."

More people for Lisa to interview, he thought, making a notation.

"What about maintenance people at the apartment?"

"I don't know anything about them."

"And Velda Rose never mentioned a maintenance person?"

"No."

"What about other tenants?"

"She never mentioned any. I don't think she had really met anyone there."

"During the time she lived at the apartment, did she lounge around by the pool?" McCall asked. "Did she play tennis or anything?"

Annie laughed. "Velda Rose wouldn't have known which end of a tennis racket to hold. I told you that she was a country girl. And she spent all her free time inside her apartment, listening to music, writing letters and waiting for the phone to ring. She kept hoping that asshole boyfriend would call her. I happen to know that the first thing she did after she got the phone was to call his parents and give them her number."

"I assume that the two of you went to the grocery store together," McCall said.

"You assume correctly."

"Anything suspicious happen there?"

"Not that I can recall."

"Where did you do your grocery shopping?"

"The Kroger's a couple of blocks from Velda Rose's apartment."

"Ever shop anywhere else?"

"No," she replied. "It's convenient and had everything that either of us needed. But I don't think the killer could have been anyone we saw at the grocery store anyway. No one there knew Velda Rose's address."

"How did she pay for her groceries?"

"With a check."

"And wasn't her address on the check?"

She looked surprised. "That's right, it was. In fact, I helped her set up her checking account."

"What we've established here is that a lot of people had seen Velda Rose and knew her address," McCall said. "Most people don't realize how much they're seen, how exposed they are to some crazy. The crazies have to work somewhere. They work in grocery stores, department stores, for the utility companies, rental places, banks and so on. And someone from any of those places could have known Velda Rose's address."

"I warned her not to give it to anyone at the bar," Annie said.

"But people who work at the Cactus knew her address," he responded. "They might give it to someone who asked."

"They're not supposed to."

"I'm saying that they could have, though. And it's possible that the crazy who killed her might even work at the Cactus."

"That's hard for me to believe," she said.

"Maybe so, but I've found that damn near anything is possible, especially when it comes to murder. By the way, did you ever see Mrs. Ramsey in the Cactus."

"No," Annie answered, "and I would have remembered her."

"I guess I'm looking for some connection between the three women who were murdered," McCall said.

"Does there have to be a connection?"

"Well, I say there's no reason for murder, but there is often a reason why certain people are murdered. It's often some common denominator, even if you're dealing with a psycho. And if we can just find the right pieces, we might be able to keep someone else from becoming a victim."

She asked, "Do you think the murderer is going to kill again?"

"It depends. If this is some maniac on a binge, yes. If it's premeditated murder for reason, maybe not."

"I've just never been involved in anything like this," she said. "I don't know what to think."

"I've investigated a lot of murders, and I don't know what to think, either," he admitted. He got up from the couch and continued with, "Listen, I really appreciate you taking the time to talk to me."

"Glad to," she replied. "If I can do anything to help find Velda Rose's killer, I'm willing." She had gotten up from her chair in order to walk him to the door.

"Right now it's all kind of a puzzle," he said, "but you've given me some pieces. It's just a matter of putting everything together."

Bill Haloran had already interviewed Annie. McCall planned to get the detective's notes, compare them with his own.

At the door she said, "I've read a lot of things you've written. You're good."

"I appreciate the compliment."

"I hope that I see you again."

"Likewise."

During their entire conversation, there had been a magnetism between them. It was like a pressurized balloon, full to the point of exploding. All it took was for him to reach out a hand and touch her arm. Then she was in his arms, and they were embracing.

"What time do you have to go to work?" he asked.

"I wasn't planning to leave until four o'clock," she replied. "We have plenty of time."

Chapter 11

Friday 5 p.m.

McCall returned to the *Tribune* for the purpose of knocking out a story for the Saturday edition. He was greeted by Lisa's cool, "Someone named Debbie Dawson called. She wants you to call her."

He thanked her for the message, then gave her instructions on contacting and interviewing persons who had come in contact with Velda Rose Caldwell.

"Did you learn anything from Sharp or Cossey?" Lisa asked. "And by the way, were either of them married?"

"Cossey's divorced and Sharp's husband was killed in Vietnam," he responded. "And yes, I learned quite a bit from both of them. I put together that list of persons who had contact with Velda Rose Caldwell with the help of Mrs. Cossey. And I got a couple of very good leads through Mrs. Sharp.

"What have you been up to?"

She answered, "I was able to contact Carolyn Bell, who was a good friend to Maggie Burleson. She's also a nurse, worked with the victim."

McCall's mind computed what Annie Cossey had told him, that she thought she had seen Maggie Burleson in the *Cactus* with another woman. If she actually had seen the victim, the woman with her could have been Carolyn Bell.

"Yeah, I remember her name from one of Haloran's reports. Is she willing to talk to me?"

"She said she would do anything she could to help."

McCall teased Lisa with the question, "Is she married?"

"Yes."

There was a tinge of annoyance in her answer. He knew that she was a sharp young lady, knew she realized he was teasing her.

"When does she want to talk?"

"It doesn't matter to her. She works tonight, but said you could talk to her when she's on break."

"When's that?"

"She said she would take a break when it was convenient for you."

"Well, I've got to crank out this story, but I could probably be at the hospital around eight o'clock."

"Do you want me to go with you?"

"Sure, if you want."

"I'll call and see about the time," Lisa volunteered. Then added coyly, "Don't forget to call Debbie."

"Oh, don't worry about that," he came back. "I'll call her right away."

He didn't call Debbie, though. He got busy putting together a vintage McCall story and forgot that she had called. He became so absorbed in writing that he forgot about time, about everything except the bathtub murders. During the time he was working on the story, someone brought him a cup of coffee. He didn't get the identity of the good samaritan, figured it was Lisa.

At seven o'clock, he took his eyes off the video display terminal, looked across the other VDTs to the city desk and yelled out, "Call it up." It was then that he noticed Lisa standing slightly behind him.

"Great story," she complimented.

"Thanks. So you've been reading behind my back, huh?"

"Do you mind?"

"Not at all. Did you get in touch with Carolyn Bell?"

"Yes, and she said eight o'clock was fine with her."

"Good. How are you coming on getting in touch with the people who had contact with Velda Rose Caldwell?"

"I'll be seeing some of them tomorrow. But do you think some of these people are going to be a help?"

"I have no idea. But keep this in mind, Lisa. In the course of doing what you're doing, you might even end up talking to the killer."

Her facial expression indicated that the thought excited her.

"Do you really think so?" she asked.

McCall shrugged his shoulders. "Who knows? The killer has to be somebody, and he could certainly be someone she came in contact with."

"Some of the people I'm interviewing are women," she said. "You don't think a woman's the killer, do you?"

"I think you've asked that before, haven't you?"

"I guess I have."

"Well, a good rule in this business is not to rule out anybody. In a sense, I guess I approach everyone as guilty until proven innocent. If you don't have any concrete leads as to who a killer is, everyone who had contact with the victim is a suspect. Don't take anyone lightly.

"We're dealing with a pretty ruthless person here, one who is obviously capable of damn near anything. And over the years I've come in contact with weak-kneed little bastards and frail-looking bitches who were vicious killers."

"But you have a pretty good idea of the type person who committed these murders, don't you?" she asked.

"Yeah," he admitted, "but I've been wrong before. Just get as good a profile as you can on all the people you interview. I'll have Haloran run a check on them for any priors. The cops are going to be interviewing some of these same people, but I want you to be more thorough than the police."

"I'm looking forward to it."

"It's shit work," he said, "but it's got to be done. Just try to pick up on little things, because it's the little pieces to the puzzle that are often the most needed ones to complete it."

"You like this, don't you?"

He laughed. "Haven't you heard that old line about everyone loving a mystery?"

"What bothers me," she said, "is that the killer is still out there, maybe getting ready to kill again. Unless, of course, your theory is correct about the first two women being killed to make it look like Mrs. Ramsey was killed by a maniac. Do you really think that theory holds water?"

"It's just a theory," he answered. "All I really know is that early Tuesday morning, early Wednesday morning and early this morning, someone killed and mutilated three human beings. The killings and mutilations were identical, so we have to assume they were done by the same person or persons."

"Persons? Up until now I thought we were just talking about the murderer being one person."

"Again, we assume it was one person, but there's always the possibility that more than one were involved. The person or persons who committed the murders could be drug-crazed, not necessarily a maniac, though I'd have to say that a person on drugs is on the verge of being a maniac.

They're sure as hell idiots to let some fuckin' drug have control of their mind."

She laughed. "C'mon, McCall. The next thing you'll tell me is that you've never smoked a joint."

"That's right, baby. Never have, never will."

"That's kind of hard to believe, you being in Vietnam and all."

"Lisa, not everyone who went to Vietnam, became a drug addict. Not everyone who went into battle had to have a crutch."

"Some guys who were there told me they smoked joints all the time."

"Well, good for them," he replied with sarcasm. "They may have been rear echelon troops, especially if they wanted to describe their battle heroics. There were a lot of guys in Vietnam who never saw any action, who spent their time smoking pot.

"I can only tell you that I was scared as hell the entire time I was there. I didn't want anything to screw up my mental faculties, because I was interested in staying alive. A lot of pot smokers came back in body bags."

"Whoa," she said. "I didn't mean to get you on a tirade."

"Well, I have to admit that society's relaxed attitude about drugs pisses me off more than most things." Then he chuckled and continued, "Of course, I tend to get pissed off about a lot of stuff."

"So I hear."

"We have thirty minutes to kill before going to see Mrs. Bell," he said. "Let's spend a little time in the snack bar. My treat."

"You always take me to the nicest places."

"You're an ungrateful wench," he said with a laugh. "I've known you only a short time and I've already taken you to one of my favorite places. And the *Tribune* snack bar might just be my second favorite place."

"Is the diner really your favorite place?"

"It certainly is."

She laughed. "Most of the guys in Arkansas don't have any class. You'd probably like it there."

He smiled. "I'd like to live in Arkansas, but it would raise the intellectual level of the state too much."

"Oh, boy," she challenged. "You sure have a monopoly on IQ here in Texas."

He laughed. "You're not going to find too many geniuses in pick up bars, Lisa."

"I don't go to pick up bars."

"That's good. How about snack bars?"

"Okay," she said with a laugh. "The snack bar it is."

When they arrived at the room that was overwhelmed by vending machines, he asked, "What'll you have?"

"Just a Diet Coke. What are you going to have?

"I'm going to join you with that Diet Coke, but I'm also going to have some microwave popcorn."

"Popcorn sounds good," she said.

"This can be kind of a special time for us," he teased, "sharing a bag of microwave popcorn."

"Anyone ever tell you that you're a real romantic, Matt?"

"Not that I recall."

"I didn't think so."

While the microwave was doing its number on the popcorn, she continued, "What do you expect to learn from Mrs. Bell?"

"I don't know."

"Do you have any particular technique you use to interview someone?"

"Not really. I just play it by ear. I usually ask a few personal questions to get the person to relax, then I get on with the meat and potatoes questions. But it's usually the person's answers that trigger my next question."

"In school, we didn't get much help with interviewing

a subject."

"If you got any help, it would surprise me."

"Why do you say that?"

"Because most journalism professors aren't journalists. They study the field from afar, deal in theory rather than fact. Most of them can't write worth a shit."

"They're not all that way."

"I qualified my statement with the word *most*. I even know some journalism professors who teach it the way it is, and the way it ought to be. There's a guy at SMU named McHam. If you'll give me some time, I might even think of another one."

"Never mind, I think the popcorn's ready."

"So it is," he said. "This moment we share will live in infamy."

"That may be the wrong word."

"I never use the wrong word."

They kidded around while sharing the popcorn and drinking their Cokes, then got in McCall's car and drove to San Antonio General. They arrived five minutes early.

They met Carolyn Bell in the hospital cafeteria. But before the nurse arrived, Lisa commented, "Gee, you're showing me some of San Antonio's finest eating establishments."

"I guess they are a step up from anything in Arkansas," he deadpanned, "but after we leave here I'll take you to an even better place. That is, if you don't have any plans."

"I don't. A single woman who works for a newspaper can't make plans."

"Are you complaining?"

"Of course not."

"Good, because you're better off working than running the streets."

"I don't run the streets."

McCall's observation of Carolyn Bell was that she was no striking beauty, but that she did have an aura of sensuality about her. The woman's shape was certainly worth a second look, and the legs were far above average. But the tits were small, and her face could only be classified as cute. A few freckles ran across the bridge of her nose and accentuated reddish-colored, short-cropped hair that was too butch-looking in McCall's estimation. A couple of other negatives were that her brown eyes were set too close together and her mouth was somewhat larger than it should have been in comparison to the size of the face. McCall guessed that she was about five-feet five-inches tall.

After an initial greeting, they all got a cup of coffee and found a table that provided a degree of privacy.

"Thanks for taking some time to talk to us," McCall began.

"I'm glad to, though I don't know what helpl I can be," she answered.

"Well, it's possible that you might remember something that will help us find Maggie's killer."

"I've already talked to the police."

"Yeah, I know. Bill Haloran's a friend of mine and he said you had been very open and cooperative. I may ask you some of the same questions he asked, but there's always the possibility that you'll remember something that you forgot to tell him."

"I doubt it. He was pretty thorough."

"I'm sure he was, so please bear with me," he said. "Now, it's my understanding that you and Maggie Burleson were good friends."

"Yes, very good friends."

From the time they had first met, Carolyn Bell's voice had bothered McCall. It was not that she hadn't been friendly and responsive, she had. But there was a recognizable hardness and harshness in the tone of her voice, even in friendly overtures. He sensed there was no real compassion in her, which he figured was essential to being a good nurse.

"From what you told Bill Haloran, you and Maggie worked later than usual Tuesday night, then had a cup of coffee before parting company."

"It's not unusual to work late here," she corrected. "But yes, Maggie and I worked until almost midnight. We were supposed to get off at eleven."

"So, after midnight, or early Wednesday a.m., you went home and Maggie went on her way."

"That's right. I told Detective Haloran that I thought Maggie might have gone to The Plum after leaving me. She told me earlier in the evening that she might drop by there for a drink. She asked me if I would join her."

"Any particular reason that you didn't?"

"My husband was out of town, so I figured I needed to get home to the kids."

"I believe Bill told me you had three."

"That's right."

"Well, I talked to Bill Haloran earlier, and he confirmed that Maggie had been by The Plum for a drink. He talked to the bartender who was on duty that night, and he remembered her. In fact, he knew her. She must have gone by The Plum pretty often."

Carolyn shrugged. "I guess. She was free, white and twenty-one."

"Did you ever go with her?"

"Occasionally."

"Please don't take this the wrong way, but did Maggie go to The Plum to try to pick up a man?"

She laughed. "It's easy to see that you didn't know Maggie."

"I know it's a bit late to do so, but I'm trying to get to know her now."

"Maggie wasn't afraid of men," she said, "but she certainly wasn't out to bed down with just any man. She was looking for Jack Armstrong, the All-American boy. She wanted someone like her father."

"An older man?"

"More than that. I don't know how to say it, but in a way she was looking for a hero. She wanted someone with the morals of a saint."

"She was pretty straight then."

"That's an understatement. I don't guess I ever saw her have more than two drinks."

"So, no jilted lovers, no man problems in her life?"

"Not any that I know of. Like I said, she wanted the kind of man I don't think exists."

"From what you say, she must have shared a lot of her feelings with you."

"She did. She spent a lot of weekends at the house. She loved the kids."

"She didn't date?"

"Sometimes, but not all that much. At least, not that I know of. She was usually at the house during the day."

"Did you ever go to the Cactus Bar with Maggie?"

He noted that the question caught her by surprise. "Yes, I've been there with her a few times. It was another place we sometimes stopped for a drink after work."

McCall's mental computer clicked on, remembering that Annie Cossey thought she had seen Maggie Burleson at the *Cactus*. And in the company of another woman dressed like a nurse.

"Do you remember a cocktail waitress named Velda Rose Caldwell?" he asked.

"You're talking about the first girl who was murdered."

"Yes."

"To be honest, I didn't pay that much attention to who waited on us when we were at the Cactus. Men probably notice cocktail waitresses more than women do. They all look alike to me."

The response caused Lisa and McCall to smile. Carolyn noticed, also smiled and continued, "Sorry about that. I guess we all have some prejudices."

"Did you happen to know Colette Ramsey?"

"No," Carolyn answered. "Of course, I've seen her picture in the paper and I saw her on television a few times."

"Did you ever see her in the Cactus or at The Plum?"

"Not that I recall."

"Do you know Dr. Norris Summerfield?"

"Why do you want to know about Nor . . . I mean, Dr. Summerfield?"

It was easy to see that he again had caught her by surprise. "I assume by your response that you do know the doctor."

"Yes, I know him. He uses this hospital, but I don't understand why you would bring his name into this conversation."

"It's just a matter of checking out people who knew the victims," he assured. "Dr. Summerfield was Colette Ramsey's doctor, and I would guess that he's yours, too."

"You're right," she said.

"And he was probably Maggie's doctor, wasn't he?"

"I think you already know that."

"No, it was just a guess on my part. But I would think that a woman would recommend her doctor to a friend, especially if she thought he was good."

"Dr. Summerfield is very good."

"So I've heard."

She looked a bit puzzled by his response, as if searching for a deeper meaning to it. Then she looked at her watch and said, "I really do have to get back to work."

"Carolyn, we certainly appreciate your help," McCall said. "If I think of some additional questions, I hope you won't mind if I contact you."

"I don't know that I've been any help," she replied, "but if you do have other questions, I'll try to answer them."

They all stood to their feet and he said, "Again, Carolyn, many thanks."

"I hope you or the police catch Maggie's killer. I just wish I could have convinced her to take karate lessons with me. If she had, she might have been able to defend herself."

"Oh, you're into karate, huh?" He had always been amused by women who claimed to know karate. He was sure there were a few who did, but it was just more bullshit exercise for most of them, of no value whatsoever.

"I've been taking karate for the past couple of years," she said.

"I'm impressed," he lied.

After Carolyn departed, McCall and Lisa walked down one of the hospital corridors toward an exit. Lisa was smiling when she said, "You may have convinced Mrs. Bell that you were impressed, but you sure as hell didn't fool me."

He laughed and showed mock dismay. "Do you think I would lie to that poor lady about something as important as karate?"

"I take it that you don't think a woman can be adept at the sport."

"I never thought of it as a sport," he answered, "but my guess is that Carolyn Bell is like most women in that regard. She just thinks that she looks cute in a karate outfit."

"There's no hope for you," she said.

When they were in the car, pulling out of the hospital parking lot, Lisa asked, "Where to from here?"

"I thought we might drop by the Cactus."

"Damn it, Matt, I'm really getting hungry. Popcorn, coffee and Diet Coke just doesn't cut it with me."

"Relax, the Cactus serves food."

"What kind of food?"

"All kinds."

"Do you want to tell me why you asked Carolyn Bell about Dr. Norris Summerfield?"

"Like I said, he was Colette Ramsey's gynecologist."

"Bullshit."

"You know, they should have cleaned up that mouth of

yours at the University of Arkansas."

"You could use some truth lessons, too."

"Okay, you need to know this anyway. Summerfield and Colette Ramsey were lovers."

"I figured there was some reason she dumped her husband. I don't know about this Summerfield, but Ramsey's a good-looking man."

"You're kidding. How can you think that piece of shit is good-looking?"

"Just because you don't like him, Matt, doesn't make him ugly."

"As far as I'm concerned, it does."

She laughed. "Boy, I can really see why people in the newsroom laugh at your objectivity."

"What objectivity? I've never been objective, never claimed to be."

"It's a good thing."

When they entered the *Cactus,* McCall told the hostess that they wanted to go to the bar. Also, that he wanted one of Annie Cossey's tables.

Annie was at the table almost by the time they were seated. She gave him a smile, but the lips straightened out when she looked at Lisa. He introduced the two women to each other and asked Lisa what she would like from the bar.

"Just a glass of white wine."

"I'll have a scotch and water."

When Annie left to get the drinks, Lisa said, "She's very pretty, Matt."

"Who?"

"You know damn well who."

"Oh, you mean Annie. I guess I hadn't noticed."

"The hell you hadn't. And I thought you said we were going to eat."

"We will. I just want to ask Annie a couple of questions."

When the waitress returned with the drinks, he asked, "Annie, do you know Dr. Norris Summerfield?"

"Yes, he's my doctor."

"And did Velda Rose know him?"

"I'd forgotten about that. She did go to see him a couple of times at my recommendation."

Bingo, McCall thought.

"Why," Annie continued, "is Dr. Summerfield connected to the murders in some way?"

"Not that I know of," he answered. "He was Colette Ramsey's doctor, too. Has he ever been in here by chance?"

"If he has, I didn't see him."

The place was crowded, so Annie couldn't linger and talk. Besides, McCall could see that she wasn't too enamored with Lisa, a feeling shared by the woman reporter.

"What are you looking for, Matt?" Lisa asked.

"I've found it, the common denominator."

"Dr. Summerfield?"

"Yes," he replied. "All the murdered women were patients of the good doctor. And the way they were mutilated indicates that the killer knew a great deal about human anatomy."

"Like a doctor?"

"Precisely."

"So, you think Dr. Summerfield is the killer?"

"I don't know, but at least we've got a connection now. And I don't think I told you that Clark Ramsey once planned to be a doctor and is a good friend of Summerfield's."

"You're bound and determined to tie him into these murders, aren't you?"

He grinned. "Not unless he's guilty. But hey, let's forget about the murders for a while. You said you were hungry. Would you like anything in particular?"

"I could eat a cow."

"You got it."

McCall settled the tab and they exited the *Cactus* and got in the car.

"Where are we going?" she asked.

"It's a surprise."

It was about a fifteen minute drive through traffic to McCall's condo. On arrival, she said, "Don't tell me, this must be your place."

"You know, you're beginning to catch on to this reporter business."

"I told you I was hungry. I didn't say anything about a tour of your home."

"You said you could eat a cow, and I've got some fantastic cow in the refrigerator. C'mon, get out of the car and I'll fix you one of the best steaks you'll ever eat."

She obeyed and they were soon inside the condo.

"Just make yourself comfortable, watch TV or whatever and I'll get dinner going," he said. He pointed to an area of the room and continued, "The bar's over there. I think you'll find just about anything you could want."

"Your place is beautiful. The furniture's magnificent."

"Thanks."

"I wouldn't have thought you'd be into antiques."

He laughed. "Why not? I'm one."

She laughed. "Can I fix you a drink."

"A scotch and water would be nice. I'm going to get out of this coat and tie, and then I'll get our dinner going."

By the time he got out of the bedroom and into the kitchen, she was there with his drink.

"I see you're sticking with wine."

"I found a bottle open in the bar refrigerator. It's excellent."

"Someone must have given it to me," he teased. "I usually buy the cheap stuff."

He took a couple of porterhouse steaks from the refrigerator and put seasoning salt on them.

"My god, I can't eat a steak that big," she said.

"The rule here is that you don't have to eat everything on your plate." He put the steaks on the Jenn-Air grill that was part of the stove, and they started sizzling. "Now we'll put together a salad and we'll be set. Do you want a baked potato? I can throw one in the microwave."

"A steak and salad will be sufficient."

She watched while he took all the salad fixings from the refrigerator, then observed, "Damn, you've got everything ready."

"I prepare everything right after I buy it. It saves a lot of time and effort in the long run."

While he was watching the steaks, Lisa wandered through the rest of the condo. By the time dinner was ready, she had put away another glass of wine and had lit the candles that were on the table. She also had some good music going on the stereo.

It was a pleasant meal. They ate leisurely, drank wine, and she told him all about her background, about college and her journalistic aspirations.

He refused to let her help with the dishes, so she took a glass of wine and made herself comfortable on the couch. When he joined her ten minutes later, she was asleep. He shook her gently and asked, "Are you ready to go home?"

She grumbled an indiscernable reply, so he decided to let her alone. It had been a long day. If she wanted to nap on the couch, it was okay with him. He would take her home later, but for now he wanted the refreshment of a warm shower.

Moments later he was in the shower, soaping himself, letting rivulets of water cascade down his body. The shower curtain was pulled open slightly and she stepped into the tub with him. There was no voice communication between them. He soaped her entire body, then, while the water rinsed both of them, he pulled her against him and they began to kiss.

Chapter 12

Saturday, 7 a.m.

McCall met Haloran at the diner. He had been up since five-thirty, had left Lisa asleep in his bed. He wasn't quite sure how he felt about her being there. She was the only woman to have occupied the bed since Cele's death.

Over a breakfast of ham, eggs, biscuits and steaming coffee, he told Haloran about Dr. Norris Summerfield.

"I don't know how you do it, McCall," the detective said. "I talked to Mrs. Sharp for I don't know how long, and she didn't tell me about Summerfield."

"Maybe she didn't think it was important."

"Bullshit. You just have a way of prying stuff out of people."

"Well, regardless, we finally have a common denominator."

"As soon as I get back to the station, we'll get Summerfield in for questioning," Haloran said.

"Do me a favor, Bill, and be discreet. I promised Michelle Sharp that we would spare his family the sordid details."

"You mean if he's not guilty."

"Of course. If the bastard's guilty, we nail his ass out for everyone to see."

"Well, we certainly don't have any evidence at this point, only his connection with the three murdered women."

"I agree it's not much, but it's all we have right now. Unless, of course, you've discovered some physical evidence that you haven't told me about."

"We don't have shit."

"It's strange to have three killings by the same person, or persons, without a slip-up somewhere."

Haloran shrugged his shoulders. "I wouldn't know, McCall. I haven't had all that much experience with multiple killers. My favorite homicides are crimes of passion, where we find the killer standing over the victim with a smoking gun in hand."

McCall laughed. "Don't you enjoy using your powers of deduction?"

"What powers of deduction?"

"C'mon asshole, you know what you're doing."

"I have all I can do until retirement just catching up on overdue paperwork."

The reporter laughed again, then said, "Did you get even a sniff of a lead from any of the employees at the Cactus or The Plum?"

"Nothing. We've questioned the neighbors of all three victims, too, and we've come up with a zero. This Summerfield clown you came up with is the closest thing to a break we've had."

"Well, he would certainly know about anatomy, which the killer had to know to mutilate the victims as he did."

Haloran grumbled, "Chances are that he has an airtight alibi."

"That would be my guess."

"Damn, McCall, are you telling me that you don't think he's guilty before we even question him."

McCall chuckled. "Hey, don't get on my ass. You're the one who said he probably has an airtight alibi."

"Fuck, you don't have to agree with me."

"If you want to be a pessimist, I'm not going to argue with you."

"Why do you do this to me?" the detective asked.

"So you'll be a better person."

"Okay, but why do I get the feeling that you don't think Summerfield is guilty?"

"Too neat a package," McCall answered.

"We don't have a conviction yet."

"I know. All Summerfield's guilty of to this point is fucking Clark Ramsey's wife. And that very well could be his only transgression. Michelle doesn't think he had any reason to kill Mrs. Ramsey."

"Michelle, huh? So, you're already on a first name basis with this damsel."

"Cut me a little slack, will you? I call a lot of people by their first name."

"People you've just met?"

"Sure," McCall said. "I started calling you asshole the first day we met, didn't I? That proves I call people by their first names right away."

"Fuck you, McCall." Then Haloran changed the lightness of the conversation with, "Don't you think it's possible that Mrs. Ramsey was going to blow the whistle on Summerfield with his wife, so he had to put her away?"

"Anything's possible, but you'd think that would be a crime of passion directed at one person. Why the other two women?"

"Maybe it's like you said earlier, that he killed the other two to confuse us regarding the person he really wanted to kill."

"You know, we're really overlooking something here."

"What?"

"Well, we just assume that if my theory is correct the killer was after Mrs. Ramsey. What if it was one of the other women? What if the killer was really after Velda Rose Caldwell? What if the other two murders were committed to cover that murder?"

"You love to complicate things, don't you?"

"It's not a matter of complicating something," McCall contended, "it's just a matter of us . . . me really . . . thinking that Colette Ramsey was the real target because she was more important than the other two women."

"And because she's Clark Ramsey's wife?" Haloran asked.

"I guess that has something to do with assuming that she was the target," McCall admitted. "I'm not too stupid to know that my thinking is a little colored where Ramsey is concerned."

"Amen to that," Haloran agreed. "But I guess in this situation, you've at least eliminated him as a suspect."

"No way," McCall said emphatically. "You probably don't know this, but before Ramsey decided to be a lawyer he was studying to be a doctor."

"Holy shit. I might have known you'd find some way to tie Ramsey into this mess. If you had your way, you'd nail him for every crime in Bexar County."

"And," McCall said, "chances are that he'd be guilty of a lot of them."

"You think that because he once studied medicine, he'd have the expertise to carve up three women as precisely as the three victims were cut up?"

"Why not? Hell, he's certainly strong enough to have overpowered them."

"I won't deny that, but maybe Dr. Summerfield is strong enough to have done it, too."

"I don't know. I've never seen Dr. Summerfield."

"Well, McCall, I've got some news that's going to shock the shit out of you."

"I know," McCall said, "Ramsey has an alibi for the time of every murder.

"I don't know about that," the detective responded, "because I've only talked to him briefly, but he asked me to see if you would help him on the case."

McCall allowed enough silence before speaking so that Haloran knew he was surprised. Then he said, "If that sonofabitch wants my help, it's because he's up to something. He detests me as much as I detest him."

Haloran shrugged his shoulders. "All I know is that he said he would like to talk to you, and that he would like to solicit your help."

"The mother fucker's a real con artist."

"Well, are you going to talk to him or not?"

"Of course. I don't turn down any opportunity to let Ramsey trip himself."

"For god's sake, McCall, you may not think the man gives a shit for anything, but he might really be torn up about his wife. I hope you'll be half-ass civil to him."

"Damn, Bill, I'm not without feelings."

"Sometimes, I wonder."

"Well, while we're on the subject of Mr. Ramsey, I should warn you not to say anything to him about Summerfield."

"Yeah, why not? You know he's going to ask me if we have anything, and I was going to tell him about the doctor's connection with the three women."

"I wouldn't do that. Ramsey and Summerfield are close friends, play golf together and all that shit. In fact, the Ramseys and Summerfields socialized together."

"Oh, boy, tapping a friend's wife. Summerfield must be a real dandy."

"Hey, it takes two," McCall said. "If Mrs. Ramsey hadn't wanted to play, the doc couldn't have scored."

"Good point, but this makes questioning Summerfield a bit sticky."

"My suggestion is that you not make it official, not bring him to the station. After all, what we have at this point could be classified as coincidence. The man's not going anywhere. You can reach him anytime."

"You're right about that," Haloran said. "And I think he's going to be more than willing to talk to me, rather than have some sticky situation with his friend the D.A."

"Need I remind you that at this point we can't even prove that he and Mrs. Ramsey were lovers."

"We both know that," Haloran agreed, "but it sure won't hurt to ask him about the truth of that situation. I can at least tell him that we have testimony from a person who said they were lovers."

"He'll know it was Michelle."

"So, what am I supposed to do, not even mention his relationship with Mrs. Ramsey?"

"I wouldn't mention it at this point. I'd just talk to him about the fact that you're talking to everyone with whom the victims had contact. The fact that he was physician to all three is a strong enough link to bring up at this time."

"What you're saying is that you wouldn't put him on the defensive right now."

"Right," McCall agreed. "I'd do a little background work first."

"That makes sense," Haloran said. "I'm a little surprised that you gave him to me before confronting him yourself."

"I've got more than I can say grace over. Besides, I think it will be more effective if I come in behind you."

"Aha, you're going to confront him about Mrs. Ramsey."

"That's right. You can't make wild allegations about his relationship with Mrs. Ramsey, but I can. I can stampede the sonofabitch."

Haloran laughed. "I always get to play the straight man,

and you have all the fun."

McCall grinned. "It's the end result that counts."

"Agreed."

"By the way, when did Clark Ramsey say that he wanted to see me. I was going to try to talk to him anyway, but I was going to be courteous enough to let his wife's body get cold."

Haloran shook his head in mock disbelief. "And people think you're such an uncaring sonofabitch."

"See how wrong people are about me?" McCall deadpanned.

"Ramsey said he would talk to you anytime that was convenient for you. He said he's anxious to track down his wife's killer."

"Where am I supposed to reach him?"

"He said to call him at his house."

"I'll give him a call and try to see him this afternoon."

"Let me know how it goes."

"Glad to, and I'll expect a report on your talk with Summerfield."

"You got it."

McCall drove back to the condo and found that Lisa was up and about, was having a breakfast of bacon, eggs, toast and orange juice.

"I hope you don't mind that I made myself at home," she said. She was wearing one of his shirts, nothing else, and it gave him a good view of her legs.

"As the old country/western song goes, *You Can Eat Crackers In My Bed Anytime, Baby*."

"I guess I'm supposed to interpret that."

"It simply means that you can have the run of the place anytime you choose." He kissed her gently on the lips, and she responded.

"You'd better be careful," she warned. "I might take you up on that."

"You don't know how much that frightens me," he

teased. "Do you want a cup of coffee?"

"All that I could find was instant."

"That's all I have."

"I don't call that coffee."

"Well, I do." He put a kettle of water on and turned the burner on high.

"Did you learn anything from Bill Haloran?"

"No, I just gave him Summerfield."

"Aren't you going to question Dr. Summerfield?"

"Later," he answered. "And by the way, you've got a lot of people to question today, people who came in contact with Velda Rose Caldwell."

"I know. I need to go by my apartment, get dressed and get busy. And you'll need to drop me by the *Tribune* to pick up my car."

He laughed. "Do you think I'm running a taxi service?"

"Well, I would hope our night was worth a ride to the newspaper," she responded with a smile. "Or taxi fare, at least."

"It was worth far more than either," he assured.

The water in the kettle was boiling, so he got up from the table and made himself a cup of coffee. By the time he sat back down, she had finished eating and was polishing off the remains of her orange juice. She got up from her chair, came around the table and sat down in his lap. She began kissing him on the neck and ear. It was obvious to him that she had nothing on under the shirt.

What the hell, he thought. I don't need another cup of coffee anyway.

Chapter 13

Saturday, 10 a.m.

McCall dropped Lisa at her car, which was parked near the *Tribune* Building. A couple of parking tickets were shoved under the windshield wiper on the driver's side.

"Damn it," she complained. "I hate parking meters."

He laughed. "I can't say that I'm all that fond of them. Give the tickets to me, and I'll take care of them."

"I can't have you paying my parking tickets, Matt."

"Who said anything about paying them. I just said I'd take care of them."

After Lisa had sped off toward her place to change clothes, McCall found a parking spot and made the journey to the newsroom. His desk was piled with various and sundry papers, including his mail.

He trashed a couple of pieces of literature he was supposed to send in for the purpose of possibly winning a sweepstakes, then opened a couple of letters that looked personal. One was a letter from Debbie Dawson, the other a card from Celeste Grigg.

He conjured up a mental image of Celeste. She was in her mid-twenties, had superb legs, a sensuous mouth, nice tits, naturally blonde hair and sparkling eyes. She was a truly beautiful woman, one who caused every male head to turn when she entered a room. And she had made it very clear that she was in love with him.

McCall had met Celeste while he was living with Cele. It was before Cele had been killed by a bomb meant for him. Celeste was a legal secretary, and she had provided McCall with some much needed information. She had also provided him with some intimate moments, the kind that she wanted to continue providing.

Of course, he thought he might want those moments on a continuing basis, too. But because of certain events, including Cele's death and his wounds, their timing had been off. There was no reason now, however, not to begin their relationship anew, which is what Celeste had written in the card, along with its trite printed message.

The letter from Debbie was hard to follow, but he was able to ascertain that she wanted to see him again, and right away. He pondered the situation with Debbie while going after a cup of coffee.

He had three cups of coffee while cranking out a story on the murders. The story was full of detail, with just enough speculation to keep readers in suspense regarding its ultimate conclusion.

It was a bit after noon when he finished. He wondered whether or not he should call Clark Ramsey. After all, the man's wife had been dead for such a short time. But Haloran had said Ramsey wanted to talk to him. And McCall figured that if he wanted any substantive information from Ramsey, he would have to get it himself. The cops would be a little paranoid about questioning the D.A. He figured even Bill Haloran would be reluctant to ask the right questions. No, if he wanted answers, he'd have to get them himself.

What the hell, he thought. He had Ramsey's home phone number in his file, so he looked it up and dialed the number. After a couple of rings, a voice answered. Surprisingly, it was the district attorney.

"Clark, this is McCall. I'm sorry to bother you at a time like this, but Bill Haloran said you wanted to talk to me."

"Yes, I do need to talk to you, McCall."

To McCall, the voice sounded subdued, not pompous like the Ramsey he knew. That's why he followed up with, "Look, if it's too tough for you right now, we can talk another time."

"I'm fine," Ramsey said, "and I think we need to talk right away."

"Well, where do you want to meet? I can come there if you like."

"No, I need to get out of here for a while. Maybe I could come down to your office."

"No problem there, but you sound like you need a drink," McCall said. "Why don't we meet at the Cactus?"

Ramsey agreed to the meeting place, suggested they make it about three-thirty because, "I have some things I have to take care of here first."

McCall telephoned the always hungry Haloran and asked if he wanted to meet at the diner for lunch. The detective agreed, and they met thirty minutes later.

Over chili dogs, McCall questioned Haloran as to whether there had been any new developments in their investigation. He replied in the negative. Asked if he had been in contact with Summerfield, Haloran said the doctor had a mid-morning golf game and was supposed to call when he came in off the links.

"Sounds like a cold sonofabitch," McCall observed. "You'd think he'd be a little more broken up over the death of his mistress and the sorrow of his good friend, Clark Ramsey."

Haloran agreed.

Back at the *Tribune,* McCall downed a couple more cups of coffee, then made a few calls to sources to see if they had picked anything up on the street about the murders. It was for the most part a dead-end exercise, but he wasn't one to leave a stone unturned.

At three-ten, he left the *Tribune* Building and headed for the *Cactus.* He arrived at three-twenty.

Ramsey was already occupying a table in the bar area. McCall joined him, and they exchanged greetings.

"I admit to being a little surprised that you wanted to see me," McCall said. "No one has ever accused us of being friends."

Ramsey shrugged his shoulders. "I'm not suggesting that we be friends, McCall. I just know that you move in some circles that are impossible for me, my people or the police to penetrate. I just thought some of the people in those circles might have a clue as to who murdered my wife."

McCall feigned surprise. "Are you accusing me of being involved with elements that are not law abiding?"

"You can cut the bullshit, McCall. I'm not in the mood for your clowning."

"So we'll understand each other, I don't give a fuck what you're in the mood for. And it wouldn't surprise me if you killed your wife or had it done."

"I'm going to ignore that accusation," the D.A. said. "If I had killed my wife, why in the hell would I be talking to you?"

"Because you think you're so fuckin' smart, Clark. You probably even think you can baffle me with your bullshit."

The waitress arrived at the table and asked for their order. It wasn't Annie. She was scheduled to go on duty at five.

"I'll have a J.B. and water," McCall said.

Ramsey followed suit with, "The same." After the waitress left, he continued with, "Look, McCall, I'm not going to make any secret of the fact that I hate your guts, but I'm smart enough to know that you're good at what you do. You've always been able to dig up information that the authorities can't, so I'm not too proud to ask for your help. I want to find the man who murdered my wife."

McCall took a long look at Ramsey. He had never considered the D.A. a truthful man, so he wasn't about to be duped now. He figured there was much more to the man asking for help than was on the table.

Ramsey, the elected district attorney of Bexar County, was in his early fifties. He was tall, imposing, built along the lines of a professional football player. His facial features were granite-like, and his hair gave the illusion of being blue in color. There was some gray at the temples.

"Clark," McCall began, "you know that I don't trust you any more than I would a rattlesnake, but in this case I'm going to be stupid and believe that you mean what you say." He didn't believe Ramsey, of course, but he figured it didn't hurt to say that he did. "But in order for me to do a good job of investigating, I'm going to need your cooperation."

"I thought it was obvious that I would cooperate when I asked for your help and came here," Ramsey said.

"So, you're not going to get pissed and clam up if I ask you some pretty harsh questions, huh?"

"I'm willing to answer any reasonable questions," Ramsey replied.

"Hey, you might not think they're reasonable, but I need the answers anyway."

The waitress arrived with their drinks.

"Damn it, McCall, I told you I'd answer your questions and I will."

"Okay, okay, don't get your ass in an uproar. I don't know

if anyone has ever told you this, Clark, but you have a bad temper."

For a few seconds, Ramsey looked as though he was going to laugh. Instead, he said, "Let's get on with it. Why don't you tell me what you have so far?"

"Whoa," McCall replied. "You answer some questions, then I'll tell you what I have. Your answers will help me better interpret what I've put together so far."

Ramsey sighed. "Your way or no way, huh?"

"That's about the size of it," McCall agreed. "Now, why don't you start by telling me where you were when your wife was murdered?"

"I was home in bed."

"Anyone to vouch for that? Did you have a chick with you, anybody?"

Ramsey's face flushed red. "No, I didn't have anyone with me. I don't have anyone to verify that I was asleep."

"Don't get so testy, Clark. You know that the husband is always the natural suspect when a wife is murdered."

"Not when the wife is murdered by some maniac."

"Husbands can be psychopaths, too."

"Well, I'm not one."

"Well, I don't know that."

"I forget, McCall. You don't operate like those of us in the legal profession do. We assume someone is innocent until proven guilty."

"Cut the rhetorical horseshit, Clark. With you lawyer types, the whole legal system is just a game."

"Alright, alright, I don't want to get into a verbal hassle with you. I'm just interested in having you find my wife's killer."

"Shocking as it may be to you, I would be trying to find your wife's killer even if you hadn't asked for my help," McCall said.

"I know," Ramsey replied with a sigh. "I just thought we could make better headway if we combined our forces and sources."

"You made a rhyme, Clark, but I'm not sure what you mean. What I think you mean, though, is that you'd like for me to give you everything I've got. And, of course, you'll give me nothing in return."

"That's not true. I will order my entire staff to cooperate with you."

"If they don't have anything, cooperation's easy."

McCall could see that Ramsey was becoming frustrated, which pleased him a great deal.

"Damn it, McCall, you really get on my nerves sometimes."

"Just sometimes?" the reporter responded. "When I'm getting on your nerves one hundred percent of the time, then I'll think I'm making headway. But enough, did you know either of the other two murdered women?"

"No," Ramsey answered.

"You're absolutely sure that you never had contact with either of them?"

"Why would I?"

"Well, I assume you've been here for a drink, because you didn't ask me the address."

"I've been here," the D.A. admitted.

"Well, if you were here, you might have run into Velda Rose Caldwell or Maggie Burleson."

"Oh, you think I might have had contact with the Caldwell victim because she was a cocktail waitress here. She might have waited on me sometime, I don't know. I don't pay all that much attention to cocktail waitresses."

There he was, his usual pompous self, which pissed McCall.

"Really, Clark. Hell, I pay all kinds of attention to them. I check out their wheels, their asses, their tits. When I stop checking out the female populace, it'll be when someone with a shovel is tossing dirt in my face."

"I was a happily married man."

"Was Mrs. Ramsey a happily married woman?"

"That's kind of a low blow, McCall."

"Maybe, but let's face facts. If you hadn't been separated, she probably wouldn't have been killed. Unless, of course, you had it in your mind to kill her all along."

"That's kind of a stupid assumption."

"I just want you to know, Clark, that I'm not eliminating you as a suspect."

"I'll reiterate that I don't really care if you consider me a suspect. I know that you're cynical regarding my reasons, McCall, but all I'm interested in is finding my wife's killer. And I'd like to find him before he kills again."

"It's possible that he won't kill again."

"I won't argue with you on that score, but all the evidence points to a homicidal maniac who is going to kill and continue killing until we catch him."

"Would you be interested in my theory?"

"What theory is that?"

"That the first two women were killed in order to set up your wife's murder. That the only reason the first two women were killed was to make it look as though a homicidal maniac was on the loose."

"I can't buy that one, McCall."

"Think about it, Clark. The first two victims were young and lived in apartments. Your wife was older, lived in a townhouse."

"That's pretty thin."

"Maybe."

"You're trying to say the killings weren't random."

"I'm not just trying, I'm saying it. I think this trio of killings were premeditated and that the first two victims were carefully selected, with your wife being the primary target."

"It doesn't hurt to theorize, but it just doesn't hold water."

"Can you think of anything the victims had in common?"

"No, but Maggie Burleson and Colette were last seen alive at The Plum. The fact that they were both there indicates to me that the killer was there or in the vicinity, that he followed both of them home. Since Velda Rose Caldwell wasn't in The Plum the night she was murdered, since she worked here, I'd say that Colette and the Burleson woman had as much in common as the Burleson and Caldwell women."

McCall wanted to tell Ramsey that the three women all had something in common, that being Dr. Norris Summerfield as a physician. But the time wasn't right.

"You make a good case, Clark," the reporter admitted, "but I operate a lot on gut instinct, which I think gives me an edge on the legal system. And in this case, my gut feeling tells me there was method to this maniac's madness."

"Oh, so you're now admitting the killer is a maniac?"

"Anybody who butchers people as neatly as this clown did is crazy, but I still think it's someone with a definite reason, not a serial killer."

"Well, I can't say you're wrong until the killer strikes again. And I think he will."

"That doesn't really make me wrong, Clark. He may kill again to cover his tracks even more."

Ramsey chuckled. "You've got an answer for everything, don't you, McCall?"

"I'm not different than other people in that I don't like to be wrong."

The D.A. shook his head in mock despair. "Okay, are we going to share information or not?"

"I'm not going to hide anything from you or the police, Clark, but we're not talking one-way street here. I give, I get."

"Agreed."

"Now, to continue, do you know whether or not your wife was having an affair?"

"Of course not," Ramsey coldly replied.

"Hey, don't get your dandruff stirred up, Clark. The woman did leave you."

"It was a temporary thing. She just wanted to find herself, then we would be back together."

"That's what she told you, huh?"

"Yes."

"And you believed her?"

"Of course. She was just confused, having a hard time dealing with the pressures of my job."

"And your political aspirations?"

"I'm satisfied to be district attorney of Bexar County."

McCall laughed. "Sure you are. But back to what I was asking you earlier, you're absolutely sure that you had no contact with Maggie Burleson or Velda Rose Caldwell?"

"Not to my knowledge."

"Could Mrs. Ramsey have had contact with either of them?"

"I can't say definitely, but if she did it was probably just in passing. Maybe she had a drink here, and the Caldwell girl waited on her. Maybe the Caldwell girl waited on me. If she did, though, I don't remember it."

"I've never had much of a problem remembering good looking women," McCall said.

"Obviously, I'm not adverse to good looking women either, McCall. My wife was very beautiful."

"That she was," McCall agreed. But in spite of Ramsey's declaration of being attracted to beautiful women, the reporter couldn't help but remember that the D.A. had once had very strong connections with a group of homosexual lawyers. It was one of those lawyers who had killed Cele.

"You've asked me a lot of questions, McCall, but so far you haven't told me anything about your investigation."

"There's nothing to tell. I've told you my theory, which to date is all I've got. I've got my lines out, though, and in a few days I expect to have something."

The waitress was back, viewing their empty glasses.

"Do you want another?" Ramsey asked.

"Sure," McCall answered. "Maybe if we sit here and drink a while, our minds will ponder something significant about these murders."

Ramsey looked at him with disgust, and the waitress went to fill their order.

"What's the matter, Clark?" McCall continued. "Would you rather spend a Saturday afternoon with someone other than your favorite reporter?"

Ramsey grunted. "I can think of people with whom I'd rather spend time."

"Don't you get tired of measuring every word, Clark? Of always trying to speak so precisely?"

"Don't you get tired of ragging people?" Ramsey asked.

"Never."

"You're probably being very truthful about that."

Their conversation over a second drink was not productive, but it gave McCall a chance to continue reading Ramsey, to continue looking for feelings deeper than the D.A. usually revealed. He finally decided, however, that his task was in vain. Ramsey was what he seemed, a cold-blooded and calculating politician, one capable of murder if it would help him get what he wanted. He couldn't find one redeeming feature in the man.

And McCall knew that if he was honest with himself, he was glad. It would make nailing Ramsey all the more pleasurable.

Chapter 14

When Clark Ramsey left the *Cactus*, he was pleased with what had occurred with Matt McCall. He didn't like McCall, even hated him, but he had made a personal vow to win over his old nemesis. He didn't want McCall crusading against him when he ran for governor.

As for his *bitch* wife, he was glad that she was dead. She had, of late, become a pain in the ass, even moreso with her decision to initiate a trial separation. He had tried to keep the situation quiet for a time, but finally decided to hell with it. He had then instructed his public relations people to use the separation problem to elicit sympathy for him. But before the p.r. types could formulate a plan, Colette had bought herself a burial plot.

Ramsey laughed inwardly. It was even better this way. The attempt to elicit sympathy for a separation, even though he was blameless, could have backfired. But for a man's beloved wife to be brutally murdered, that should be worth a lot of votes.

If McCall didn't fuck the thing up. Of all the people in the city, in the whole state for that matter, there was no one Ramsey feared more than the *Tribune* reporter.

He cursed mentally. The sonofabitch, the no good sonofabitch. McCall could be an editor, anything he wanted to be, but the bastard chose to be on the street digging up dirt. A dead McCall would be just as nice as a dead Colette.

Then his thought processes mellowed. I'm smart, he surmised. I should be able to use the sonofabitch to my benefit. I think I made a good start today. The bastard has an ego, and the fact that I asked for help had to make him feel good. It won't hurt me to eat a little humble pie to get what I want. When I'm governor, I can kick him in the ass.

I handled the situation well, didn't act as though I liked him. If I had tried to be buddy-buddy, he would have seen right through it. And I acted remorseful about Colette, but not too sorrowful. He bought it. I know he bought it.

But in spite of trying to reassure himself, Ramsey couldn't help but worry about McCall's reaction. The man's crazy, he thought. He's too fuckin' unpredictable.

Ramsey was obsessed with the idea of power. He had been since his public school days. He had been all-everything in high school, athlete and politician. Everything he had tried to achieve in life had been for the purpose of obtaining power.

Initially, when he had planned to be a physician, it was because of the power a doctor had over human life. He craved such power. It was like a burning fire within him.

Ramsey soon came to realize, however, that a doctor didn't have power over enough human lives to suit him. But a politician, the Governor of Texas or the President of the United States, now that was power.

So, he had gone to law school. And he had excelled. At an early age, he convinced everyone Clark Ramsey was going places.

When it was time to marry, he picked a woman who he thought would be a good governor's wife. Or possibly even a President's wife.

Colette was beautiful, wealthy. She walked in the right circles. More important, her father walked in the right circles. She was the perfect mate, though cold in bed. But that didn't matter to Ramsey. He had more on his mind than sex when he married her.

He figured Colette married him because she saw a chance to get to the Governor's Mansion through him. That would have made her father proud and, if nothing else, Colette was a daddy's girl.

So, even though there was no warmth to their marriage, Ramsey figured it was a good deal for both of them. They were both getting what they wanted from it.

Ramsey did not come into the world with money of his own. He didn't have wealth until he bilked an old woman of her land and sold it for millions. He now realized that his newfound wealth didn't help his relationship with Colette. In fact, it had deepened the chasm between them. When she had money and he had nothing, she felt more in control. And a certain amount of control had been important to her. She had been very much like her father in that respect.

Even though Colette was dead, Ramsey figured he could still muster political support from his father-in-law. After all, he didn't plan on remarrying. He wasn't that interested in women, so he could play the grieving husband role to the hilt.

Ramsey smiled as he herded the car toward home. Other than going to the funeral, he would stay close to home for a few days. There would be continuing sympathy expressed, which he would acknowledge. He would also express righteous indignation for what had happened to Colette and the other two women. His outrage at such heinous crimes would gain considerable public attention through the media. Everything was falling into place beautifully. And he was glad the bitch was not going to be around to share the glory.

The thought crossed his mind that he would again be alone in the big house for the evening. The Mexican servants would be there, of course, but they didn't count. Hell, they could hardly speak English. He didn't like Mexicans, but his p.r. people kept stressing the importance of the Mexican vote. He figured, however, that the minority vote was in his pocket because he would be running as a Democrat. The stupid shits always voted for a Democrat.

Anyway, he liked being in the house alone. He had negated the idea of anyone staying with him during his period of grief, even Colette's parents. They said they understood.

He wondered what would be on television. He would have the cook fix him a good dinner, eat in the master bedroom and watch the tube.

It would be a good evening, better than if the bitch was still with him.

Chapter 15

Sunday, 5 a.m.

McCall woke from a sound sleep, shifted his position in the bed and looked at Lisa lying beside him. She looked good, and he was tempted to wake her. He fought off the temptation. He figured she wouldn't be all that interested in early morning lovemaking. Women who liked it in the morning were unique, and he didn't figure Lisa fit into that category.

McCall thought she was a neat woman alright, but he also thought she worked too hard at lovemaking. It wasn't natural for her. She tended to respond to him in an almost clinical way. He was fairly certain that she had gotten most of her sexual knowledge from books.

Anyway, he decided not to bother her. He decided, instead, to get up and brush his teeth. They had drunk a lot of wine the night before. The taste was still in his mouth.

He got up, put on a robe, and stepped into a pair of houseshoes. He used the guest bathroom to brush his teeth so as not to wake Lisa, then went to the kitchen and put on a kettle of water. Then he went out the front door and got the Sunday paper.

By the time he got back to the kitchen, the water in the kettle was hot. He made himself a cup of instant coffee, added some Sweet 'n Low and sat down at the breakfast table to read the paper.

McCall did a quick check to make sure nothing about his page one story had been changed, then turned to the sports section. Sipping his coffee, he quickly scanned it and found nothing of interest.

He put the paper aside, sipped his coffee and began thinking about the bathtub murders. Obviously, the murderer had not struck during the night. Or if he had struck, the victim had not yet been found. He knew Haloran would call him if there had been another murder. Or the guy at the newspaper who monitored police calls would have called.

The more McCall thought about it, the more certain he was that two of the murders had been committed to set up the other. But he had to admit that it was only a gut hunch, that he didn't have one shred of proof to back up his theory.

Haloran had told him about questioning Summerfield the previous day, and that the doctor had good alibis for the time periods in which all the women had been killed. Haloran said that Summerfield, being a doctor, kept excellent records of his whereabouts at all times.

"He's a pompous sonofabitch," Haloran told McCall, "but I don't believe he's the murderer. If he is, he's the coolest one I've ever known."

"Doctors kill people every day," McCall had said. "They just do it legally."

From Haloran's report on questioning Summerfield, McCall was certain the detective had done an excellent job. However, he wasn't satisfied. He determined to question the doctor himself. He had more freedom to ask certain questions than Haloran did, especially questions about Colette Ramsey.

Clark Ramsey, now there was a cool one, his wife's body not even cold, and he was already calculating how he could turn her murder into a political advantage. Ramsey thought he was so smart, but McCall considered the man one of the most transparent he had ever met.

McCall was quite aware of what Ramsey was doing in soliciting his help, but was determined not to be used. If anyone was going to do any using, he would do it. But he would allow Ramsey to think that he was getting his way.

As for Ramsey being the actual murderer, he figured it wasn't likely. He was capable, of course, but in this case the pieces didn't fit. But even if they did, his gut feeling was that Ramsey was innocent. He couldn't be eliminated as a suspect, but McCall really didn't expect to nail his adversary on a murder charge.

No, Ramsey was innocent. The murder had proved to be a favorable incident in the continuing saga of his political life, but he probably hadn't instigated it. The man was just lucky. A problem had been eliminated, and he would probably even get some pretty good bucks from his wife's estate. McCall doubted that Colette had changed her will, even though they were separated. Her will was something McCall planned to check carefully.

He recalled his conversation with Lisa over a couple of bottles of good wine. She hadn't come close to getting a clue from the persons she had interviewed about Velda Rose Caldwell. Most could not remember having had dealings with the dead woman. Velda Rose had been strictly low-profile.

Haloran had checked with the Air Force regarding her ex-fiance's whereabouts at the time of the murder. He had been in Germany. McCall had never considered him much of a suspect anyway.

The police also hadn't been able to turn up anything when questioning all the employees at the *Cactus*. The consensus was that Velda Rose was well-liked. All of those interviewed guessed that she was just a victim selected at rand)m, that she had been unlucky enough to have been in the wrong place at the wrong time.

It was a theory that McCall could not buy. He couldn't accept the murderer as being a man without a plan. He was sure the man was not a serial killer.

After two more cups of coffee, McCall checked the bedroom and saw that Lisa was still asleep. He used the second bathroom to shower and shave. By the time he finished and went back in the master bedroom to get some clothes from the closet, Lisa was taking a shower. He regretted that she had awakened, because he had planned to leave her sleeping while he did some solo investigating. He knew she would try to negate his plan, because she wanted to be involved.

After dressing, he returned to the kitchen and made himself another cup of coffee. He was reading the want ads when Lisa joined him. She had dressed.

"Looking for a new job?" she joked.

He gave her a light kiss on the lips and answered, "The idea has crossed my mind. Do you want some breakfast?"

"I can fix something," she responded.

"Naw, let's go out and get something?"

"You never let me cook. Are you afraid of my cooking?"

"Not really," he replied, "though I have to admit that I've never found a woman who could beat me cooking."

She laughed. "You amaze me. You never give a woman credit for being able to do anything better than you."

"I wouldn't say never," he teased. "I give women credit for being able to do some things better."

"Such as?"

"I'd rather not get into that."

"That's because you can't really think of anything," she argued.

He dismissed the subject with, "Forget it. Let's go get that breakfast."

They went to a *Denny's Restaurant,* and he became annoyed at the slowness of the service. "I didn't want to spend the day here," he complained.

"What do we do today?" she asked.

"Why don't you just take the day off?" he suggested. "You've already put in a tough week."

"Are you taking the day off?"

"No, but that doesn't mean you have to work."

"I'd like to."

He shrugged his shoulders. "It's up to you."

"Well, can I tag along with you?"

"If you want," he answered. "I'm just going to do a little more legwork."

"It's a chance for me to get some more experience."

"You're going to have to do a lot of that on your own."

"I know, but it can't hurt to watch experience at work."

"Meaning me?"

"Meaning you."

After they had finished a breakfast of scrambled eggs, bacon and orange juice, McCall drove them to the *Tribune* Building. There, they plotted their course for the day.

"I really want to talk to Dr. Summerfield," McCall told Lisa.

"I thought you were satisfied after what Bill Haloran told you about him."

"You've only known me a short time," he said, "but you should know me better than that. I like to go one-on-one with all the players."

She laughed. "You're right. I should have known. But I imagine it's going to be kind of hard for you to get in touch with the doctor. And I also doubt that he's going to want to talk to you."

He grinned. "Well, I doubt that I'm on his social calendar, but I plan to talk to him today anyway."

"You've made an appointment?" she quizzed.

"Not exactly, but I know where he is. Surprise is on my side."

"And just how do you know where he is?"

"I have a few contacts here and there."

"I'll just bet you do."

"Well, as an old cowboy said, we're burning daylight. Let's go talk to the good doctor."

"Do you know where he is right now?"

"You bet. Just follow my lead."

"I'm right behind you."

They left the *Tribune* Building and got back in McCall's car. He started it, accelerated through the quiet, almost empty-of-traffic streets, and was soon away from the city and in a more country setting.

Lisa broke the silence with, "May I ask where we're going?"

"You may."

"Well, where are we going?"

"I didn't say I was going to tell you."

Actually, he didn't have to expend the vocal energy. By then they were entering the grounds of one of the city's posh country clubs.

"I should have guessed that the doctor would be playing golf on Sunday," Lisa said.

"You could guess that almost any day, weekend or weekday," McCall said. "And you could guess it about most doctors."

"Anyone ever tell you how cynical you are?"

"Lots of people, and lots of times. And I thank you for thinking of me in that way."

She shook her head in mock resignation and smiled. "You're one of a kind."

McCall had found out that Summerfield had a ten o'clock tee-off time and that he was playing with his lawyer, Cameron Baxter. While the reporter was not a member of the club, he had a contact who did have membership. The contact had arranged for McCall to have guest privileges, so he had scheduled a tee time immediately after Summerfield and Baxter.

Of course, he had also planned to have a friend play with him. But when he saw that Lisa was going to tag along with him all day, he had called the friend and told him they would try another day.

"You do play golf?" he asked Lisa.

"I took a course in school, but I'm not very good," was the reply.

"Who cares," he said. "It's one of the world's most boring games anyway. We can have some fun driving the golf cart and drinking beer."

"You sure know how to treat a girl to a leisurely Sunday."

"Your sarcasm is noted. I told you that you didn't have to work today."

"You didn't say anything about golf, either. I'm not exactly dressed for the sport." She was wearing a sweater, jeans and running shoes.

"You look alright to me," he said. "Hell, you don't need any kind of special dress to play golf." He was dressed in casual fashion . . . jeans, sweater and penny loafers.

"What about golf shoes?"

"I've got a pair in the trunk."

"Well, I don't have a pair."

"Hell, if you need a pair, I'll get you some at the club's pro shop."

"That would be an unnecessary expense. I probably wouldn't wear them again."

"Who cares. I was planning on putting them on my expense report anyway."

She laughed. "Do you think you could get away with that?"

"It's a legitimate expense. We're working on a story."

"I can get by with my Nike's. I suppose you have golf clubs in the trunk, too."

"Yep, but you can't use my clubs. We'll rent you a set made for damsels."

"What I use isn't going to make any difference. I think you're going to be disappointed and upset with the way I play."

"Hey, we're here to pester Dr. Summerfield, not to really play golf. I'd just as soon pick up aluminum cans along the highway as play golf."

They picked up what they needed at the club's pro shop, then boarded a rented golf cart. They arrived at the first tee just as Summerfield was getting ready to drive. He gave them a cursory glance, then positioned himself and hit the ball. The ball went straight down the fairway, but low and without much distance. It landed in the middle of the open area, however, ideally located for an iron shot onto the green.

"Nice shot," McCall said.

The doctor looked over to where they were now standing and replied, "Thank you, Mr. McCall."

"You know me?" McCall asked.

"Even without your American Express card," Summerfield quipped.

McCall laughed and responded, "Good line, I'll have to use it some time." Dumb shit, he thought.

"I try," was the doctor's retort.

McCall waited to respond until Cameron Baxter, a short man with too much belly, teed up and hit his ball. His shot left much to be desired.

"Mind if I ask how you know me?"

"Ask away," the doctor said. "No, on second thought, it's probably best that you don't ask anything. I'll volunteer that I don't really know you, just the name and what you do. Which, I might add, I don't like. But I always make a habit of checking at the club to see who's playing in front of me and behind me."

"You're a careful man," McCall observed. And an arrogant bastard, he thought.

"You misunderstand my reason for checking," Summerfield said, "which isn't surprising. All you journalism types tend to misinterpret everything."

McCall laughed. "Everything, huh? Isn't that a bit all-encompassing?"

"Perhaps, but I doubt that I'm misinterpreting your reason for being here today. You're certainly not here to play golf, and I happen to know that you're not a member of this club. I doubt that you could afford it on a reporter's salary."

McCall wanted to smash the sonofabitch's nose, then pound his face until it was a bloody pulp. But he maintained his cool.

"I'm sure you make more checking snatches than I do cranking out words, but I get a lot of satisfaction bringing assholes like you to your knees."

McCall noted that Summerfield, who was casually leaning on his golf club, looked a helluva lot like Clark Ramsey. They were about the same size and build, though women would probably consider Summerfield the more handsome of the two.

"Come, come, Mr. McCall," the doctor cautioned. "Your language is embarrassing to your young lady friend. And I might add that you haven't introduced us."

McCall noticed that Lisa's face was a bit red, probably, he thought, because of his reference to *snatches*.

He coldly replied, "The lady's name is Lisa DiMaggio, and she's also one of those reporters you hold in such contempt."

Summerfield smiled. "I never hold a beautiful woman

in contempt."

"That's what I hear," McCall said. "And I also hear that all three of the women who were recently murdered were your patients."

For the first time Baxter piped in with, "You don't really have to talk to these people, Norris."

Summerfield dismissed his advice. "I don't mind, Cameron. I have nothing to hide. And I'm sure that Mr. McCall is not accusing me of anything by mentioning that all three were my patients. Am I right, Mr. McCall?"

"All I'm looking for is someone who can shed some light on the murders," McCall replied. "I thought you might be able to tell me something about the women that would give us a clue."

Summerfield sighed. "I've talked to the police, and I gave them all that I can give you, which is nothing. I'd have to say that you're wasting my time and yours, Mr. McCall."

The way he said *Mr. McCall* was sarcastic, irritating.

"I appreciate your candor, Dr. Summerfield, but I would appreciate it if you could answer one simple question for me."

"I would be delighted."

"Were you having affairs with Velda Rose Caldwell and Maggie Burleson, or just Colette Ramsey?"

He could see that the question caused fear to dart across the doctor's eyes, which was soon replaced with anger.

"I think enough has been said," Baxter warned. But Summerfield wouldn't let it die.

"You sonofabitch," he said in an almost controlled scream. "Who in the hell do you think you are that you can come out here and make that kind of accusation? I could sue your ass for libel."

"Slander," McCall corrected. "The spoken word is slander, the written word is libel. And if you want to, buddy boy, sue away.

"You're not going to sue, though, because I have proof positive that you were banging the late Mrs. Ramsey, and that's something you don't want your family or good friend Clark Ramsey to know."

"I think you'd better leave," Baxter told McCall. Summerfield was standing red-faced and speechless, but with a look that indicated that he wanted to use his golf club on McCall.

"I'm not going anywhere," McCall answered. "We're playing golf behind you and pretty boy here. I can't help it if he dallied here to carry on a conversation with me."

"You want to leave, Norris?" Baxter asked.

"Yeah," Summerfield said. "I want to leave." After they were seated in their golf cart, the doctor turned to McCall and warned, "If you write anything about this or say anything to . . ."

McCall interrupted with, "Hey, fuck you and the horse you rode in on, big shot."

"I was not having an affair with Colette Ramsey," Summerfield said.

"Okay, whatever you say."

"Don't be patronizing to me, McCall."

"Whatever happened to Mr. McCall? Does your respect come and go so quickly?"

"Nothing is being served by this," Baxter said. "Let's go, Norris." Summerfield was at the controls of the cart. It was like, however, that having been discovered, he was unable to move. And it seemed as though he really wanted to talk about it.

"Colette was a lovely woman, a special woman."

"I'm not arguing the point," McCall said. "I can't say as I blame you, or her, since she had to put up with Clark."

"Damn you, McCall, I'm not saying I had an affair with her. I'm just saying that she was a lovely woman. And Clark is my friend. In fact, by god, I'm going to have him nail your ass."

"He hasn't got the balls to do that, and you don't have the balls to tell him about our little conversation. You know that if he goes poking around, he's liable to find out what you did."

"What do you want, McCall? Why are you bringing all this up?"

"I just want some answers as to why three women were killed. And whether you like it or not, you're a link, because all three were your patients."

"I swear that I don't know anything. The Caldwell woman only came to see me once. Colette and Maggie Burleson were my patients for quite a while."

"I've got some questions I'd like to ask you privately," McCall said. "Can we get together soon?"

Baxter shook his head in the negative, but Summerfield answered, "Yes, I'll tell you whatever I can." His mood was subdued, far different than the earlier arrogance.

"I'll check with you later this week."

"McCall, I would appreciate it if you wouldn't broadcast the stuff you said here today. It's not true, of course, but someone might get the wrong idea."

"Don't worry, doctor. You're cooperating with me, I'm going to cooperate with you."

"Thanks."

As they drove off, Lisa said, "Well, you sure as hell ruined his golf game."

McCall laughed. "He'll be a better man for it. Golf destroys a man's sensitivity."

"Are we ready to go?"

"You don't want to play a few holes?"

"You've got to be kidding."

"Okay, but before we go, I want to get rid of this dozen new golf balls I bought."

"You mean that the company bought."

"Whatever."

He systematically set all twelve balls on tees and drove

each down the fairway with one of his woods. Then he said, “I’m ready to go.”

“You’re not going to pick up those balls?”

“You have to be kidding.”

Chapter 16

Monday, 2 p.m.

McCall entered a cold, modern-looking building located next to the hospital, found a button for elevator service on a lobby wall close to the entrance and pushed it. When one of the building's elevators reached the ground floor and opened its doors with the customary *ding,* he started to board. But that's when he recognized Carolyn Bell as one of the elevator's departing customers. She saw him about the same time.

"Mrs. Bell," he greeted.

"Mr. McCall," she responded.

He let the elevator depart without him and said, "I'm glad I ran into you, because I was planning to call you anyway."

"Really?" she stopped her trek toward the door and faced him.

"Yeah, I thought we could get together and talk about Maggie a little more."

"I'm not sure there's anything left to talk about," she said. "I've told you everything I know."

"Maybe, but perhaps there's something there in the subconscious that I can stimulate with a few more questions."

She laughed, and he couldn't help but think that it looked good on her. In fact, she looked good all over, not like the cold fish that he had talked to who was wearing a nurse's uniform. She was dressed in casual attire that accentuated every curve of her body. There was a sensuality to her whole being, especially the mouth and eyes, that would stimulate almost any man.

"If you think you can get something from me, I'm more than willing to talk to you," she agreed.

Her friendliness was disarming, so different from the woman he remembered questioning earlier. Of course, that had been shortly after Maggie Burleson's death. There had been reason for her to be in a dark mood.

"Any particular time and place when you'd like to get together?"

"You name it."

"I shouldn't be here long," he said. "How about meeting me at The Plum at three o'clock?"

"That's fine. There are a couple of shops near there that I want to check anyway."

On the elevator ride to the fourth floor and Dr. Norris Summerfield's office, McCall's mind kept comparing the two Carolyns he had met, the one at the hospital and the one leaving Summerfield's office. He knew that was where she had been. And her radiance caused him to wonder if Ol' Norris didn't have something going with her, too.

He had called Summerfield earlier that morning, and the doctor had agreed to meet with him a little after two o'clock. The morning had been spent chasing leads that all ended up in blind alleys, so he was hoping to get some decent information from Summerfield.

Not surprising was the doctor's receptionist, a good-looking young blonde with nice tits and a nice ass and legs to match. She was standing at a file cabinet when McCall entered the waiting room, which was empty.

"You must be Mr. McCall," she greeted with a smile that showed perfect white teeth."

"Guilty," he admitted, "but you probably knew my name only because I'm Dr. Summerfield's only male patient."

She laughed. "He's waiting to see you. Go right in."

When McCall entered the office, Summerfield looked up from some papers on his desk and motioned to a chair. The reporter plopped down and did a quick examination of the room. It was about what he expected of a country club doctor's private sanctuary, furnishings of rich-looking woods, leather, chrome and glass.

Summerfield's first words were, "That bitch Michelle told you, didn't she?"

"Told me what?"

"About me and Colette." Summerfield was much more composed than he had been on the golf course the previous day.

"Well, I'm not at liberty to tell you who told me anything," McCall said, "which should be some comfort to you. I'll consider what you tell me confidential, too."

"I understand that some of you newspaper types will go to jail rather than reveal your sources."

"That's right."

"I guess that's considered noble."

"I wouldn't know," McCall replied. "The person who wants to be protected might think it noble, but a person who wants information might have some other words for that type of reporter."

"And what kind of reporter are you, Mr. McCall?"

"The kind, doctor, who doesn't give a damn who you laid or who you're laying now. If you want some strange, that's fine with me. I'm not interested in broadcasting your fucking habits to the world. I'm just interested in finding out why three of your patients were murdered."

"I've already talked to the police about my whereabouts at the time of each murder."

"I have that information," McCall said, "and as far as the police are concerned, you're clear. But I'm looking for anything that can give me a lead on these murders, and the only common denominator that I can find between these women is that all were your patients."

Summerfield responded, "While that's true, I don't see how that has anything to do with the murders."

"Maybe it doesn't, but would you please just answer a few questions for me honestly? And I promise that what you say isn't going to leave this room."

"Ask your questions."

"Okay, Velda Rose Caldwell . . . what was your relationship with her?

"She was my patient."

"And how many times did she come to see you."

"Twice, I think."

"C'mon, you know how many times she was here."

"Alright, she was here twice."

"Did you ever put any moves on her?"

"What in the hell do you mean by that?"

"You know damn well what I mean. We're not going to get anywhere if you play games. You're a womanizer, Doc. You know it, and I know it. I know it because there's not a lot of difference between us."

Summerfield laughed. "I wish I got all people thought I got."

"I'm sure you get enough. Now, did you ever sleep with Velda Rose Caldwell?"

"No."

"Did you ever try?"

"Of course not. She was just a kid."

"What about Maggie Burleson?"

"I never slept with her, either."

"And I guess you're going to plead innocent to sleeping with Colette Ramsey?"

"Colette was a good friend, that's all. And anyone who says there was ever anything between us other than friendship is a liar."

"You're a real piece of work, Norris."

"Thank you, Mr. McCall."

"By the way, I met Carolyn Bell in the lobby. Would you like to tell me that you haven't slept with her, either?"

"I'll be glad to tell you that. In fact, I'll be glad to tell you that I don't sleep with any of my patients, only my wife. I happen to be a good family man."

"You're a helluva guy, Norris. But I'd really like to know why you allowed me to waste my time coming over here."

"You wanted to come, and it's your time."

McCall stood and said, "Don't bother to show me the door. I'll let myself out."

"Come see me anytime, Mr. McCall. You're always welcome."

While closing the door behind him, McCall wondered why the sonofabitch had suddenly returned to the arrogance that he had encountered the day before. His thoughts were interrupted by the mellow southern voice of the receptionist who invited him to "You come back to see us now."

He smiled. "That is a most pleasant invitation, but you know, it occurs to me that I don't even know your name."

"I'm LeAnne Bevins."

"And I'm Matt McCall."

"Oh, I know who you are, Mr. McCall. I know you work for the *Tribune*."

"Well, since you do know me, perhaps you won't think me too forward in asking you to have a drink with me after work."

"It's a nice offer."

"Does that mean you're accepting?"

"It does."

"What time do you get off?"

"Five o'clock."

"You know where the Cactus is located?"

"Yes."

"Good, let's meet there a little after five."

"I'll be there."

In the building's lobby, McCall found a pay phone and called the *Tribune*. The switchboard put him through to Lisa, who told him Clark Ramsey had called and wanted to talk to him right away.

"What time did he call?"

"Around two."

The timing made McCall think that Ramsey's call might in some way connect with Summerfield's display of arrogance. "Call Ramsey and tell him I'll get back to him after seven. And then find out everything you can for me about Dr. Summerfield's wife."

"Do you think she's involved in some way?"

"Frankly, I don't know what to think at this point. But right now Summerfield is all we've got."

"What are you going to do now?"

"I have a couple of people I have to meet."

"What about later?"

"What do you mean?"

"Do you want me to cook dinner for you or anything?"

"I don't think so. I'll call you when I'm free."

In closing the conversation, she made a couple of comments that indicated disappointment and hurt. Damn, all he needed now was a jealous, frustrated, clinging female. Things were complicated enough without a fucked-up love affair.

Carolyn Bell had already commandeered a table at *The Plum* and had a glass of white wine in front of her. He took a seat and ordered a scotch and water.

"I'm glad you were able to meet me," he said.

"Hey, I'm not working today, the husband's out of town, the maid's taking care of the kids and I didn't have anything to do but shop until five o'clock. And since I can't afford to buy everything I want, I might as well have a few drinks at your expense."

He laughed. "It sounds like you're a lady with a plan."

"Not really," she said. "Having something planned as far in advance as five o'clock is unusual for me."

The waitress brought his drink, and he tasted it. "And what are your plans at five o'clock?"

She smiled and put a hand on his. "I'm not saying," she teased.

McCall knew he wasn't seeing the real Carolyn Bell. The real Carolyn Bell was probably closer to that person he had first met at the hospital, a person who was a bit cynical and bitter about her lot in life. The person he was with now was on something, something that had probably been given to her by the notable Dr. Norris Summerfield.

"Well Carolyn . . . you don't mind if I call you Carolyn, do you?"

She pursed her lips, wrinkled her nose and replied, "It's okay, if I can call you Matt."

"I certainly have no objection to that, Carolyn, but since we're on a first name basis, do you think you should keep secrets from me?"

She laughed. "You're a very devious man, Matt. You're probably the kind of man who would get in my pants if I'd let you."

He teased her with, "You're right, of course, but the only time I have available is five o'clock, and you're already tied up for that time slot."

"Forget it," she soberly advised.

"Forget what?"

"Trying to get me to tell you what I'm going to be doing at

five o'clock. The truth is, I'm not going to be doing anything of interest to you."

He could see that her mood was unstable, so he figured that he should drop the questioning about her rendezvous at five.

"How about another glass of wine?" he asked. She agreed, and he motioned to the waitress.

He continued, "I guess you're still undergoing a little trauma about what happened to Maggie."

"I'm okay," she replied. "It's not like Maggie and I were real close or anything."

The statement contradicted what she had said in their earlier meeting, and things he had learned from other members of the hospital staff.

"I thought Maggie spent a lot of her time off with you and your family."

"Oh, she did, but we weren't all that close. She didn't discuss her personal life with me or anything of that nature. I really don't know what she did when she wasn't with me."

He wasn't sure why Carolyn was talking about Maggie as she was, but suspicioned that it had something to do with her afternoon visit to Summerfield's office. Everything was getting out of line. There were no ducks in a row. Everyone connected with the victims was taking on an air of mystery.

He was sure, however, that the wrong questions at this point could send Carolyn packing, so he broke the pattern and started asking her about her family. Though the wine and Dr. Summerfield's contribution had her in a good mood, she seemed eager to lament her fate, to complain about her husband, the children, Mexican help, financial burdens and unfulfilled ambition. It was easy to see that she thought that simply by being a woman she had gotten the short end of the stick in life.

For at least an hour he did nothing to discourage her

lamentations, but simply signaled the waitress for glass-after-glass of wine. Carolyn was a real motor mouth, and her engine was running full throttle. He caused that engine to sputter with one probing question.

"Tell me, Carolyn, was Maggie having an affair with Dr. Summerfield?"

The delay in answering, the rabbit-like fear in her eyes, told him that he had pricked a nerve.

"Why . . . why do you ask something like that?"

"It's just something I'd like to know, something that might help in the investigation of Maggie's death."

"No . . . Dr. Summerfield was never interested in Maggie."

"Was Maggie interested in him?"

"I have no way of knowing," she replied indignantly.

"Are you interested in Dr. Summerfield, Carolyn?"

She got up from her chair and icily replied, "Up until now, having a drink with you was pleasant, Matt. But it's obvious now that you're out to hurt a lot of people who don't deserve to be hurt."

"You're wrong. I'm just out to find the murderer of a woman who was your friend."

"You have a funny way of doing it."

"Maybe, but I will find the person responsible, Carolyn. And you might not like who it is."

"It won't be anyone I know," she said.

"I wouldn't bet on it if I were you." He glanced at his watch and continued, "You'd better get a move on anyway. You don't want to keep Norris waiting."

She didn't respond immediately, then said, "If you think . . ."

"It doesn't matter what I think," he interrupted. "This has been a day of pious platitudes by everyone I've talked to who knew any of the victims, but a day of reckoning is coming."

Before leaving she said in semi-cordial fashion, "Thanks

for the drinks anyway, Matt. And I really hope to see you again."

"You will."

She had been gone a couple of minutes before he got the check from the waitress. He paid it, laughed inwardly about the expense report he would soon be turning in to the paper, then headed for the *Cactus.*

LeAnne Bevins had not arrived. Annie Cossey was there, though, trying to handle her share of the happy-hour crowd. She was able to get in a few snatches of conversation with him between customers.

"Have you found out anything?" she asked.

"It sounds contradictory," he replied, "but mostly what I've found out is what I haven't been able to find out."

She laughed. "You're right, it sounds contradictory."

"It would help if you'd tell me that you'd seen Dr. Norris Summerfield in here molesting Velda Rose."

"Like I told you before, if he'd been in here, I would have known it. He's my doctor, too."

"And to your knowledge, he never put any moves on Velda Rose?"

"If he did, she didn't say. But a lot of guys put moves on Velda, and she just ignored them."

"Thanks, Annie, it seems that no one wants to make my day."

"Sorry," she said. Then, teased, "Did you come in here just to see me or are you meeting some other broad?"

"Dr. Summerfield's receptionist."

"It figures."

LeAnne looked good, a fact that didn't escape the many males and females who had converged at the *Cactus* for happy hour. She made her way through the throng to his table and said, "Sorry that I'm late, but the traffic was awful."

"No problem, except that I'm pretty well soused. So, it'll be easy for you to take advantage of me."

She laughed, giving him the chance again to admire her pretty white teeth. "That sounds promising, but maybe I'd better get to know you a little better first."

"Don't tell me you're one of those persons who believes in long, drawn-out foreplay."

"I can't believe you said that."

"Don't pay any attention to me, I'm liable to say anything."

"I believe it."

"Also try to understand that I just like to kid around."

"I'll try to understand that."

"Well, I do want to thank you for coming here to have a drink with me," he said.

"It's my pleasure."

"Are you from this area?"

"Born and raised right here in San Antonio."

"That's good. You don't find many natives. Most people find their way here because of the Air Force."

She laughed. "My parents are guilty of that. My dad's a retired Air Force officer."

He sighed. "I might have known. It seems that everyone who was in the Air Force ends up retiring here."

"Well, it is a nice place. I have to admit, though, that I'd like to live in Dallas or some other place for a while."

"What about Houston?"

"Ugh," she grimaced. "Too crowded. And the traffic here is a picnic compared to there."

"True, but Dallas is getting just as bad."

"Oh, do you go to Dallas much?"

"Fairly often. I have a few friends there."

"I have some friends there, too. Maybe I could ride up there with you sometime."

"It would be my pleasure."

The conversation went that way for the better part of an hour, until he had plied her with several glasses of wine. A half-hour into their conversation, she had told him that wine made her talkative and sometimes passionate, the latter if it was someone she liked.

"I hope you like me," he said.

"I wouldn't be here if I didn't," she answered.

He figured she was now mellowed out enough to answer some questions, to discuss something other than family, friends and what she liked to do for fun. He figured it was time to talk about Dr. Norris Summerfield.

"How do you like your job?" he asked.

"It sucks," she replied. "I know I can say that to you, because I know you're not a big buddy of Dr. Summerfield."

"You're right about that. I would have guessed, though, that you would call the good doctor by his first name."

"Oh, he'd like that. In fact, there are a lot of things he would like."

McCall laughed. "Now I'm going to guess. Has the doctor been putting some moves on you?"

"Ever since I've been there," she confirmed.

"And how long has that been?"

"Almost six months. And there's no way I'm going to last another six months. Probably not even another month."

"A lot of women obviously find Norris very attractive."

"He's disgusting."

"Why do you say that?"

"I just don't like a man who runs around on his wife."

"I didn't know Norris did that," he lied.

"Are you kidding? He's after everything in a skirt."

"Do you know Mrs. Summerfield?"

"Not really. She has come to the office a couple of times to have lunch with him. She's very nice. Pretty, too."

"Well, you'd expect Ol' Norris to have a good looking wife. What about the kids?"

"I've never met them," she answered. "I just know that he has a son in medical school and a daughter who's a registered nurse."

"I didn't realize the kids were following in their dad's footsteps."

"Oh, yes. Young Norris is at Baylor Med in Houston, and the daughter works right here in San Antonio."

"Is she married?"

"No," was the reply. "In fact, there's some talk about father and daughter."

"What kind of talk?"

She laughed. "Some people say that incest is best."

"You're kidding," he said. "I'd figure Ol' Norris is getting enough from some of his grateful patients so as not to have to tap his own daughter."

"I'm only repeating what I hear."

"Does the daughter live with her parents?"

"No, daddy's fixed her up with a nice townhome."

"And I guess mom doesn't suspect a thing?"

"That I don't know. But some of the nurses have told me that daughter is a whole lot more jealous of daddy's playing around than mama is."

"Do you think Mrs. Summerfield knows about her husband's chasing?"

"She's not blind, deaf and dumb. She's bound to know."

"Do you think she knew about Colette Ramsey?"

"Oh, you know about Colette, huh? There's been more gossip about that one than any other. She was a real nice lady. I don't know what she saw in the asshole."

"She probably wasn't comfortable with anyone other than an asshole. She was married to one."

"That's what I heard. I also heard that the Ramseys and Summerfields were good friends."

"I heard the same thing," he said. "But that obviously didn't keep Norris out of his friend's hen house."

"Like I said, he's a real turd."

McCall laughed. "I don't believe you used that word, but I like your description. You indicated that he had come on pretty strong with you. Do you want to tell me about it?"

"There's not much to tell. He's just asked me out several times. And he's grabbed me a few times and tried to kiss me when we've been alone in his office."

"Since you've resisted his charm, I'm surprised that he hasn't sent you packing."

"Believe me, it's just a matter of time. Right now I'm a challenge, and he doesn't want to admit there's someone he can't have."

"Does Norris get most of the women he wants?"

"Enough," she said. "The only setback I know of, other than myself, was with that first girl who was killed."

His attentiveness level went up several points. "Velda Rose Caldwell? Are you saying he tried to make out with her?"

"Tried is an understatement. When he met her, he was like a bore hog in heat. I don't know it to be a fact, but some of the nurses said he started hanging out here a lot when he was trying to get in her pants."

That Summerfield spent time in the *Cactus* didn't jibe with what Anne Cossey had told him. Maybe the nurses were just talking.

"Do you recognize the cocktail waitress on the other side of the room?" he asked.

"Sure, that's Anne Cossey. She's one of Dr. Summerfield's patients, and I understand she used to be one of his favorite punches."

LeAnne's statement bothered him, if for no other reason than that he had thought Annie too sharp to be conned by a clown like Summerfield. It also bothered him that Annie might have lied about Summerfield visiting the *Cactus*. If she had, he wondered why. He knew he was damn sure going to find out.

"Used to be?" he asked.

"Yeah," she replied. "He doesn't have anything to do with her now. Their affair was before my time. A few years ago, I think."

"But you're sure the doctor was unsuccessful with Velda Rose Caldwell?"

"Very sure. I thought he was going to go bananas because of her turn down. He took her death pretty hard, too, but I think it was only because it deprived him of the opportunity to get in her pants."

McCall laughed. "Was he upset at Maggie Burleson's death?"

She paused, then replied, "Oh, my god, I see what you're doing. Every one of the murdered women had something to do with Dr. Summerfield."

"That's right," he agreed. "Maybe it's just a coincidence, but it does make you wonder."

"Matt, I'd be the first to say that Dr. Summerfield is a no good sonofabitch, but I don't think he's a murderer."

"I'm not saying that he is, but right now the connection he had with all three women is all I've got. And from your reaction, I'm going to assume that he had something going with Maggie Burleson."

"Had," she said. "From what I've heard, he and Maggie had a mini-affair a couple of months ago, but she decided it wasn't for her. That didn't set any better with the doctor than Velda Rose's rejection."

"So, he had something going with Colette Ramsey, had been dropped by Maggie Burleson and had the hots for Velda Rose Caldwell. And reports are that he isn't beyond tapping his own daughter. Tell me, when does the good doctor have time to practice medicine?"

She laughed. "Believe me, he has a great practice and makes lots of money."

"As long as you're telling me about the doctor's conquests, what about Michelle Sharp?"

"Maybe, but if so it was a long time ago. I know that Mrs. Sharp didn't like her friend Mrs. Ramsey having an affair with Dr. Summerfield."

"And how about Carolyn Bell?"

"A regular. From what I've heard, that one's been going on for some time."

The news didn't surprise him.

"How about Katie Hussey?" he asked, jokingly.

"Who's that?"

"A bitch that works at the newspaper. She's probably never been to a gynecologist, probably goes to a vet."

She laughed. "Sounds as though she's not one of your favorites."

"That's an understatement. But I sure like you, LeAnne. Is this going to be all there is between us, a conversation in a bar about the love life of Dr. Norris Summerfield?"

"I'd say that was up to you."

"If it's up to me, I'd like to have you invite me to your place for a drink."

"Consider yourself invited."

"The problem is that I've got about three things to take care of before I can get there. But if you're agreeable, I can pick up a bucket of fried chicken and be there by eight."

"Sounds good to me."

"And please be nice and tell me that you like fried chicken and chili dogs."

She laughed. "I like fried chicken and chili dogs, and that's no lie."

LeAnne gave him her address and left. As soon as she was out the door he cornered Annie.

"Why?" he asked.

"She told you, huh?"

"Yeah, she told me."

"I dunno, Matt. I guess I just thought no good purpose could be served by telling you. And I'm also ashamed of what happened between Summerfield and me. I didn't want you to know, and I knew you'd find out if you started prying around. Hell, I guess I should have known you'd find out anyway."

"Hey," he said with irritation, "it was your friend who was murdered. I'd have thought you'd think enough of her to tell me."

"What was I going to say, that Summerfield wanted to make out with Velda Rose like he had once done with me?" she asked. "What difference does it really make? He never got what he wanted from her."

"The fact that he tried might have a tremendous bearing on this investigation," he said. "Is there anything else that you're keeping from me?"

"No, nothing."

"How often did Summerfield come in here?"

"A lot just before the murder."

"Did he come in the night Velda Rose was killed?"

"No."

"Do you know his wife?"

"No."

"Daughter?"

"No."

"Son?"

"No."

"Carolyn Bell?"

"Yes."

"How do you know her?"

"I've just seen her a few times. I know that Norris is having an affair with her."

"Has she been in here?"

"A few times."

"Was she here the night Velda Rose was killed?"

"No, I don't think so."

"Has she ever been in here with Summerfield?"

"Yes, but it was before he got interested in Velda Rose."

"Summerfield knew you worked here, so since you once had an affair with him, why would he bring another woman to the Cactus?"

She laughed. "I hope you don't think it's because he was trying to get me back, make me jealous or something like that. He likes jealousy, tries to make a woman jealous of his affection for another. But our deal has been over for a long time, and there's no way it's ever going to start up again. He doesn't want it, and god knows, I sure don't want it."

"That really doesn't answer the question."

"I'm sorry, but I don't know why the man acts the way he does. I just know he can be very childish at times."

"Do you think he's capable of murder?"

"Norris? No way. For all his big talk, he's really a coward."

"He must be a helluva lover."

She laughed. "No, he's really not that, either. He's big on talk, short on performance."

"So, how does he get so many chicks?"

"There's just a lot of chicks out there. With Norris, the only attraction is money and power," she said. "That's all I can figure. He's good-looking, of course, but I think the real infatuation is the fact that he's a doctor.

"Matt, I am sorry that you had to hear about me and Norris from somebody else. He came into my life at a time when I needed someone, and I wasn't too smart about who I chose."

"Hey, I'm not condemning you, Annie. Your life is your own private affair. I'm just trying to get to the bottom of three murders, and everyone keeps putting obstacles in my way."

"Well, I'm sorry."

"Forget it. I have to make a couple of phone calls. While I'm away, fix me a scotch and water, will you?"

"I'll take care of it."

He first called Clark Ramsey at his home number. When the district attorney answered, he said, "This is McCall. I understand you want to see me."

"That's right," the voice said. "Can you come out to the

house right away?"

The lord summoning one of his servants, McCall thought.

"No, I can't get out there, Clark. Meet me at the Cactus in about fifteen minutes and we can talk."

"I don't know if I can get there that quickly."

"Try."

He next called the *Tribune* and asked to speak to Lisa. When she got on the line, he said, "In addition to that check on Mrs. Summerfield, run checks on the two Summerfield offsprings."

"Are you on to something?" she asked.

"Your guess is as good as mine."

"When are you going to be home?"

"Your guess is as good as mine."

"Do you want me to go over and wait for you at your place?"

"Not tonight," he answered. "With all that I'm doing, there's no telling when I'll get in."

"I don't mind waiting."

He sighed. "Do whatever you like, but don't count on me being home until the wee hours. There's a key to the place in the upper right-hand drawer of my desk."

"I'll stop by my apartment first."

"Fine."

Damn, Lisa was going to be a problem. He could already tell she would do everything in her power to make him forget Cele. And she would get some support from Bill Haloran in her efforts. But the truth was that he didn't want to forget Cele. He might need the comfort of a warm bed from time to time, but he told himself Cele would always be his only true love.

Ramsey arrived at the *Cactus* a little later than the fifteen minutes McCall had suggested. He sat down at the table, ordered a drink, and immediately started a line of bullshit that McCall wasn't in the mood to hear.

"My good friend Norris Summerfield told me that you accosted him on the golf course yesterday."

"Did he also tell you that I accosted him in his office today?"

"No," Ramsey replied, "but he did tell me that yesterday you accused him of having an affair with Colette. That was way out of line, McCall, and you couldn't be more wrong. But be that as it may, I won't have you embarrassing my friends, even if I did ask for your help."

"Sorry, Clark, but when I'm investigating a murder, I tend to embarrass lots of people," he replied, sarcastically. "As for helping you, if what I do aids in finding your wife's killer, fine and dandy. But I'm not working for you, nor would I, so I'll accost anyone I choose. And if they don't like it, they can sue."

McCall was sure that Ramsey's face had turned beet-colored, but the light in the place was too dim for him to enjoy it.

"Think whatever you want of me, McCall," the district attorney said, "but there's no reason to drag a fine woman's name through the mud, even if she's dead."

"I haven't dragged anyone's name through the mud, and I don't intend to," he said. "I am surprised that Summerfield told you about our little meeting yesterday, but it does explain his arrogance at our meeting today. His only concern is that you not believe he was having an affair with your wife. And your only concern is that it not be made public, even if it's true. Do you think it would cost you some votes, Clark?"

"You're an insensitive bastard."

"Thanks, Clark. You're one of the few people I trust to tell me the truth."

"Damn it, McCall, I don't know why you have to be so fuckin' difficult."

"No particular reason. But to alleviate all your fears, you don't have to worry about me writing anything about

Colette and Summerfield. Hell, all I've got is hearsay, and that doesn't fly in my copy."

"That damn Michelle told you something, didn't she?"

Michelle had made two enemies, Ramsey and Summerfield, which made McCall like her even more. He didn't confirm Ramsey's allegation, just as he hadn't confirmed Summerfield's.

"Where I get my information is privileged, but I've already told you it doesn't matter. The secret is safe with me, unless, of course, it comes out as being important to the final judgment in this case. You should know, though, that the paper wouldn't allow even me to print hearsay that could be considered libelous."

"You do a lot through innuendo," Ramsey said. "But I'm here to tell you to not harrass my friends."

McCall sighed. "My suggestion is that you drop it, Clark. I've had about all the bullshit I can stand today."

"Okay, McCall, I'll drop it. But I'm going to be watching you."

"When have you ever stopped? You do need better people keeping tabs on me, though. The yoyos who work for you are too obvious."

"I haven't had anyone following you."

"Bullshit." McCall didn't know whether the district attorney was having him followed or not, and didn't really care. He just liked to keep Ramsey off-balance.

"Have you discovered anything new about the murders?" Ramsey asked.

"When I do, you'll be one of the first to know." Along with thousands of other *Tribune* readers, he thought.

"Well, do keep me posted."

"Count on it."

"And McCall."

"Yeah."

"I appreciate the fact that you aren't going to print any lies about Colette, even if you have someone to whom you could attribute them."

"I'm not into printing lies, Clark, even about you."

"Do you want another drink?"

"No, I have an invitation to eat some chicken."

Chapter 17

Melanie Summerfield had been a dutiful wife and mother for more than twenty-five years. She was born and raised in a small Texas town, the only daughter of a religious zealot mother and a father who was both pharmacist and owner of the local drug store. The father, now dead, had been known to partake of some of the drugs he was dispensing. He was, however, a deacon in the First Baptist Church and a strong voice against alcohol.

The mother, along with a Mexican maid, still lived in the white two-story house that had been Melanie's childhood home. She spent much of her time praying and getting ready to go to church. For Melanie's mother, there were never enough activities at the church. It was as though she had been called on to do penance for all the evil doers in the world. Television news broadcasts were, to her, religious experiences, because they supported her belief that the world was going to hell in a hand-basket.

In spite of her mother's fervor and her father's hypocrisy, Melanie had a relatively stable and happy childhood. She was popular in school, even nailed down a majorette spot with the high school band when only a sophomore. That might have been because the band's director had an eye for good legs and tits, and even then young Melanie was well-endowed.

After all the normal high school stuff, which didn't include getting laid, Melanie enrolled at Baylor University. It was there she came in contact with young Norris Summerfield, a pre-med student with considerable potential.

Norris, a senior, wasn't looking for marriage, but he was looking for love wherever he could find it. Melanie's virginity was soon in the past tense, and Norris was smitten with the idea that his new conquest would be the perfect mate for a doctor. It took no time at all for him to convince the naive young woman that instead of continuing college she should work and support him through medical school, which was probably what God wanted her to do. After all, he was going to be the great healer, the one for which the poor and downtrodden had been looking.

Melanie worked at a couple of secretarial positions, even had a stint at nursing, while Norris pursued his medical education. The children were born during this period, but Melanie never missed more than a month of work for either birth. And eventually when she didn't have to work, when the children were in elementary school, she obtained her nursing degree.

She envisioned the degree as a means of working by her husband's side, but soon discovered that he wasn't buying that type of arrangement. In fact, he preferred that she not work, so she honored his wish and allowed her training to lie dormant. She became what he wanted, which was a housewife and social butterfly, a country-club groupie and charity work volunteer.

Melanie was no dumbie, so it took her only a few months of marriage to realize that she was nothing more than a convenience to Norris. He made love to her regularly, but she knew he was not adverse to sleeping with almost any woman who was agreeable. She would have preferred that he be more cunning and secretive about his affairs, but even now his boyishness gave him away.

She could almost tolerate the strangers who shared his bed, but when he started tapping her friends, it was too much. And the fact that he was ignoble enough to have had an affair with Colette, her friend and the wife of his friend, almost pushed her over the edge. It was the closest she had ever come to leaving him. She had gone so far as to discuss divorcing him with Norris, Jr., their son and Meredith, their daughter.

The children had objected to the possible divorce. But it was not their objections that stopped her. It was the thought of having to face her mother. Anything was preferable to that.

What amazed Melanie was the fact that Norris didn't even realize that she and the children were aware of his indiscretions. He always thought himself too smart to be caught.

It also amazed her that Clark Ramsey didn't know about Colette and Norris. Just about everyone at the country club knew, but not Clark. It was as though Clark and Norris lived in different worlds.

Meredith, twenty-two and a registered nurse, wasn't surprised to learn about Colette and her father. She had, in fact, known about Colette for some time. She blamed her mother for the situation, thought Melanie incapable of giving her father what he needed.

From the time she was a teenager, Meredith had slept with her father. She knew the relationship was not something that would last forever, but she did want to be available when he needed her. Because of a number of factors, their lovemaking had become infrequent of late. But she knew that no matter who she married, if she did, she would always be daddy's girl.

Melanie knew about most of the women in her husband's life, but she didn't know that their daughter was one of them. She only knew her daughter developed severe emotional problems when a teenager, and that she was still a very disturbed young woman. Norris had tried to quiet her concern by telling her that Meredith was going through a phase. He claimed Meredith's malady was common.

Melanie didn't buy the diagnosis, but she admittedly didn't have the background and insight of her husband. She wanted psychological help for Meredith but, as usual, acquiesced to Norris.

She had found it strange that, when a teenager, Meredith had suddenly stopped dating boys. She worried that her daughter might be a lesbian, but the fear was dispelled by the fact that she withdrew from girls, too. Meredith became very much a loner, a very beautiful girl who seemingly found most people, male and female, distasteful. The one person whose company she craved was her father.

The closeness of father and daughter did not bother Melanie. She did not read anything into it, saw no problem with it. If anything, she was pleased that Meredith had not withdrawn from Norris.

As for Norris, he had watched his daughter grow into a beautiful woman. He had fondled her from the time she was small, never anything more. But in her teens, he became insanely jealous of her, couldn't bear the thought of another male touching her. So, one night when Melanie was occupied at the country club and Norris, Jr. was out with friends, he had sex with his daughter. She didn't resist, came into his arms willingly.

Being the first time, she cried some. But she was more

than willing to do it again and again with her daddy. It became a regular thing, almost as regular as the doctor's sex life with some of the disturbed women who visited his office.

Meredith saw no reason for Melanie to leave her father. For one thing, she was understanding about her father and another woman. For another, she didn't consider her mother a threat to her own relationship with Norris.

When his mother told him about Colette, Norris, Jr. reacted much differently than his sister. His anger was toward his father and the other woman.

"I'd tell you to leave the sonofabitch," he told Melanie, "but I'm afraid he'd beat you out of what's rightfully yours. He wouldn't have his lucrative practice if it wasn't for you."

Norris, Jr. was not close to his father. In fact, he detested the man from whose sperm he had been conceived. He hated what Norris stood for, the type of medicine his father practiced.

Norris, Jr., twenty-four and a student at Baylor Medical School at Houston, had many of the same characteristics as his maternal grandmother. That is, he was out to right all the wrongs in the world.

Not that he was religious, or anything like that. He was closer to being a bleeding-heart agnostic, one who was not adverse to discussions of socialized medicine. Such a philosophy did not make him popular with other medical students, most of whom tempered their caring for mankind with thoughts of eventually owning expensive cars, yachts and estates, of having the financial leverage to play golf instead of practice medicine.

Norris, Jr., was one of those types who, most colleagues thought, would devote his life to caring for some primitive people who didn't use toilet paper. He was totally unmaterialistic, which some said was easy because his father had already amassed a fortune.

No matter how strange some thought him, faculty and classmates had to respect Norris, Jr. He had an unbelievable mind, a step beyond genius. However, it was this step beyond that bothered many who knew him. He was sometimes considered irrational in what others deemed normal thought. For while there was compassion for the poor and downtrodden, there was within him anger and suspected latent violence toward the more fortunate. Some said he would travel to the end of the earth to aid the poor and helpless, but might be unwilling to provide an aspirin to one economically secure whose political and philosophical bent did not match his own.

But Norris, Jr., loved his mother. It was not a matter of sexual fantasy or anything of the sort, only a genuine caring for the woman who had brought him into the world, protected him and always had time for him. Time was something his father had never been willing to give.

Norris, Jr., had known of his father's womanizing from the time he was a small child. He wasn't sure how he knew, how he had first learned that the man was constantly betraying his mother, but he knew. And from the time he was a child, he wanted to smash the women who he thought were hurting his mother. And he wanted to destroy everything his father held so sacred.

Norris, Jr., was a dual personality. He had the sensitivity of the caring shepherd, along with the righteous indignation of the avenging angel.

What Lisa DiMaggio learned about these three persons was neatly typed and double-spaced on three sheets of paper. Her investigation into their lives turned up sanitized biographies, which was not the meat for which McCall was searching. He didn't belittle Lisa's effort. Instead, he took what she had and, through careful and thorough investigation, put meat on the bones.

It took him a week to put all the pieces together. When he had finished, he contemplated his discoveries and decided all three might possibly have been motivated to kill Colette Ramsey. As to whether any of the three actually committed the crime, that would be hard to determine. But he was sure that all three were smart enough, maybe even crazy enough, to kill Velda Rose Caldwell and Maggie Burleson, too. And for the same reason, which was a relationship, or suspected relationship, with Dr. Norris Summerfield.

Mrs. Summerfield, McCall thought, had more reason to blow away her fuckin' husband. But for some reason, he couldn't really see her as a murderer. Norris, Jr., and Meredith were better bets, both for different reasons.

For Norris, Jr., the murders would be, because he couldn't stand to see other women taking that which belonged to his mother, even though he considered his father as worthless as a piece of shit.

And for Meredith, the murders would be because she couldn't stand seeing, or believing, that her father could love anyone other than her. She might actually believe the three women were forcing their affections on Summerfield.

Over the course of the week, McCall had talked to at least a hundred people who knew the Summerfields in one capacity or another. He was sure that some of what he had learned was nothing more than gossip, possibly with no basis in fact. However, as the ol' coach had said, "You have to dance with what brung you." Therefore, he was going to have to dance with some hunches, because that was all he had.

When McCall met Bill Haloran at the diner for breakfast, the detective told him his hunches amounted to the same as nothing.

"Hell, I know it," McCall agreed, "but you have to admit that I'm right about some things in this case."

"Such as?"

"The fact that a couple of the murders may have been committed to cover up Colette Ramsey's murder."

"You're not still after Clark's ass, are you?"

"No," McCall answered, "and I've even refined my theory about why Velda Rose Caldwell and Maggie Burleson were killed."

"How's that?"

"I think they were all killed because of some connection with Dr. Norris Summerfield. After all, there have been no more murders."

"It's a good theory, McCall. I just wish we could nail it down. But we really can't prove Summerfield had anything to do with the three women except for being their doctor. We certainly can't prove he was banging any of them."

"I know we have nothing but hearsay there, Bill, but I really believe someone in the Summerfield family is the key."

"You like the son as a suspect, don't you?"

"Why not? He's in med school, so I'm pretty sure he knows how to carve up a body. But I'm sure not dismissing the daughter. She's a real head case."

Haloran laughed. "Have you talked to any of the Summerfields, other than the good doctor?"

"Not yet, but I expect to have conversations with all of them within the next few days."

Before stuffing his mouth with ham, the detective said, "I'll be interested in what you come up with."

Chapter 18

It had now been two weeks since Velda Rose Caldwell's body was discovered, and McCall was feeling the frustration of not being able to get a decent clue as to who killed the three women or why. In the newsroom, while downing his third cup of coffee of the morning, he pondered the situation with Lisa.

"I think Bill Haloran believes me now," he said.

"About what?" she asked.

"That the bathtub murders were not random killings, that there was a reason for each murder."

"I agree, but what makes you so sure?"

"If we were dealing with an indiscriminate killer, I think he would have struck again by now. But I've checked, and there hasn't been a similar murder anywhere in the country."

"Maybe the killer's taking a vacation," she said.

"You might be right, but I don't think so."

"Okay, so if you had to pick one of your suspects for the killer, who would it be?"

"That's a good question. And believe me, I've been giving it a lot of thought. But right now, I'm stumped."

"C'mon, you have a favorite."

He laughed. "My favorite choice would be Clark Ramsey, but based on the information I have, which I might add is limited, he's down at the bottom of the list. Clark's my favorite, because I hate the bastard's guts. Unfortunately, I don't think I can pin these murders on Clark."

She laughed, showing a sense of humor he had grown to appreciate in the brief time he had known her.

He continued, "Now, if it can't be Clark, I'd really like for it to be Dr. Norris Summerfield. He's a guy I've learned to dislike a lot in a very short time. But again, he's way down on my list. He has proven to me that you don't have to be smart to be a doctor. All you need is good bedside manner and greed. But when I eliminate Ramsey and Summerfield, there aren't many names left.

"Velda Rose didn't have any friends here, other than Annie Cossey. Any other semi-friendships were limited to where she worked, and none of those people figure in the killings. I'm not saying one of them couldn't have done it, but they've all checked out pretty clean. And we know it wasn't her ex-fiance, because he wasn't anywhere in the area.

"We also know that Velda turned thumbs down on all the men who showed interest in her, including Summerfield. He had the hots for her, but he seems to heat up over any good-looking woman with whom he has contact. We also know that in the past he had a brief fling with Annie, but it's unlikely that Annie killed Velda and the other two women because of jealousy. From what I can ascertain, if she was going to kill anyone, it would be Summerfield. But I did check her out, and there's nothing in her background that indicates she had medical training, which I think would be essential to carve up the victims as precisely as the killer did."

Lisa shuddered and said, "The killer also had to be strong enough to subdue each victim and put them in the bathtub."

He laughed. "Annie's a strong lady. Besides, as long as we're just speculating on who the killer is, I'm an equal opportunity speculator. I wouldn't want you to think I'm against women's lib and all that shit."

"Oh, I'd never think that," she said with mock seriousness.

"Back to what we were talking about, I have to believe that Velda Rose was killed because she knew Summerfield, and because he wanted her."

"That would indicate jealousy."

"Maybe, but maybe not the kind we normally think about."

"What do you mean?"

"Well, we've also got Maggie Burleson. She had a brief fling with Summerfield just like Annie did. The difference is that Annie's deal was back there in the past, whereas Maggie was more recent. And maybe the killer knew about Maggie, but doesn't know about Annie."

Lisa laughed. "I hope you're not saying Summerfield has a communications problem with his affairs."

"Very funny. No, what I'm saying is that maybe the killer took out only the women he knew, or thought, were having an affair with Summerfield.

"From what I've been able to find out, Maggie had come to her senses where the good doctor was concerned. But Colette Ramsey, that was a different matter. She posed a real threat, because she left her husband for the express purpose of being with Summerfield. The other women we know about didn't have husbands to leave. That is, none that we know of, except Carolyn Bell. And maybe the killer doesn't know about her."

"Wait a minute," Lisa said. "What about Carolyn Bell? She may be jealous."

"Right, and she was a friend of Maggie's. But being a friend, she probably knew that it was over between Summerfield and Maggie. The real killer might not know."

"But you said yourself that two of the women might have been killed to set up Colette Ramsey's murder."

He laughed. "You've got me there. That's what I get for theorizing. But you wanted to know who I would choose as a prime suspect, and I'm about to give you the answer."

She smiled and said, "It's about time."

"My hunch, and I'm making it with benefit of very limited information, is Norris, Jr."

"Why?"

"Maybe it's because he's just there," McCall replied. "He loves his mother, knows his father's an asshole, and he's in medical school. I'm sure he knows how to carve up a body in a very precise way, the way the victims were carved up."

"Do you have anything other than just a hunch?"

"Not really. I just know the boy's kind of strange, lives alone, and just might have the kind of mentality to take out his father's mistress if he thought she posed a threat to his mother."

"All that's pure speculation."

"That's right, but it's what you asked for," McCall said. "You wanted to know who on my list I thought was the best suspect, so I'm telling you."

"But he lives in Houston."

"So what? He has a nice sports car, and the drive from Houston to San Antonio isn't that far."

"If, as you say, Norris, Jr., is a loner, it will be difficult to find out if he was in San Antonio when the murders were committed."

"No one said it would be easy," McCall affirmed. "But one way to check would be to see if he bought gas in San Antonio on the dates when the women were killed."

"And how would you go about doing that?"

"If he paid cash, it might be next to impossible. But if he used a credit card, we'd have a chance. Unfortunately, he didn't use a credit card."

"How do you know that?"

"I've checked. Norris, Jr., has Gulf, Exxon and Texaco gasoline credit cards. He also has American Express, MasterCard and VISA. I obtained records of his most recent purchases, and he didn't charge any gasoline in San Antonio over the past month. But he did fill his tank in Houston on the day prior to each murder."

"My god," Lisa exclaimed. "Big Brother is watching."

He laughed. "Norris, Jr., also makes regular calls to his mother, but there were no calls from Houston to San Antonio on the dates when he would have had to be here to commit the murders. Of course, that could just be a coincidence, since he doesn't call his mother every day."

"Anything else?"

"Yes," McCall replied. "Norris, Jr., eats out a lot, and usually charges it to one of his credit cards. On the days when he would have had to be here, there were no charges."

"Again, that could be a coincidence," Lisa said.

"True," he agreed. "But on the Monday prior to Velda Rose's murder, Norris, Jr., cashed a five hundred dollar check on his personal account in Houston."

"Well, you've certainly put together a wealth of circumstantial evidence that Norris, Jr., might have been in San Antonio on the dates when the murders occurred, but I don't think he would have thought things through so carefully. You have a truly devious mind."

"Hey, don't let the fact that Norris, Jr., is only twenty-four fool you," he said. "From what I've been able to find out, the boy is a step over the genius line, which, I might add, must come from his mother."

"Still, I can't believe Norris, Jr., would be so careful as not to use a credit card when in San Antonio," she said. "He probably wouldn't even think about the police checking such things."

"Maybe he reads a lot of mystery novels."

"From what you've said, I'd think they would be a little light for him."

He feigned hurt. "That's a cut. I read mystery novels."

She laughed. "Maybe that's why you're so weird."

He laughed with her, appreciated the fact that she liked playing the role of the devil's advocate. "Okay, I know it's thin, but we don't have anything better."

"Have you talked to Norris, Jr.,'s professors?"

You know I haven't been to Houston."

"I don't know anything. I just know that I haven't seen you much for the past week, except for a few minutes at work every day."

He knew it was just a matter of time until she confronted him about what she considered neglect, but he wasn't ready to deal with it now.

"I'm going to Houston tonight," he said. "And if I'm lucky, I'll talk to Norris, Jr., and his professors."

"Can I go with you?"

"You'd better stay here. Someone has to mind the fort."

The hurt was obvious in her eyes, but she articulated it with, "Okay, I know when I'm not wanted."

Damn women, he thought. They always try to fuck you over with a sorrowful routine.

"Look, Lisa, we have a job to do. After it's done, maybe we can talk about us. But for now, let's concentrate on getting the real story of the bathtub murders, who the killer is and why he did what he did."

"You're right," she said, then with a tinge of sarcasm

added, "We must not let personal feelings get in the way of our professional integrity."

He ignored the remark and continued with, "Bill Haloran is just as dubious as you are about Norris, Jr., being a suspect. And I'm not all that convinced. All I know is that Summerfield has to be the key."

"What about Mrs. Summerfield? Or Meredith?"

"I haven't forgotten about them," he said. "After Norris, Jr., I'd say that Meredith is the best prospect. If what we hear is true, that she and her father are engaged in an incestuous affair, then her jealousy could have prompted the murders."

"With the kind of strangeness that's here, Matt, shouldn't we get some input from a psychiatrist?"

"Why? Psychiatrists don't know shit."

"One might give you some insight into the Summerfields."

"I know as much about human nature as any psychiatrist," he insisted. "All a psychiatrist would do would be to ask us what we thought."

"You're stubborn, you know that? I'll bet you didn't even read the psychological profile of the killer that the police psychiatrist put together."

"You're right," he admitted, "and there's another little verse right under that. Hell, Lisa, I've read those things over the years until I was blue in the face. They all contain about the same stuff, some of which will fit just about anyone that's caught. Psychological profiles of unknown killers are about like the horoscope that the *Tribune* prints every day. They achieve about the same vagueness."

"Okay, okay, have it your way," she said. "I just thought we might get a little professional help."

"Bullshit isn't professional," he said. "However, I've told my theories to Bill Haloran. He agrees that Summerfield is the key to the murders, so if he wants to bring in the police quack, it's up to him."

"Have you talked to Mrs. Summerfield or Meredith?"

He sighed. "No, I haven't talked to them. I'm sure they're not just chompin' at the bit to converse with me. But I have a contact that may be able to get me a hearing with Mrs. Summerfield."

"Have you checked as closely on Mrs. Summerfield's and Meredith's activities at the time of the murders as you did on Norris, Jr.'s."

"I certainly have."

She seemed surprised. "I'm sorry I haven't been much help."

"You've helped a great deal."

"I don't feel like I have. I have the feeling that you prefer working alone."

"I'm used to working alone, so I probably have shut you out of some things. If so, I'm sorry. And again, you have been a big help."

"You want a cup of coffee?" she asked. "I can at least do that for you."

"Oh, brother," he said with a laugh. "Don't try that poor female bullshit on me, Lisa."

She laughed. "Doesn't work, huh?"

"You know damn well it doesn't."

"I'll still get you a cup of coffee."

"I'll let you."

She took his cup and left. For a minute or two he wondered what he was going to do with Lisa, how their relationship would end. But his thoughts were soon on the Summerfields. He had a lot of work to do. And though he didn't have a concrete lead, he felt that he was very close to the killer.

Chapter 19

Though the weather was quite pleasant, Houston always reminded McCall of a continuous humid summer. He found the city oppressive, especially its traffic, which seemed a never-ending stream. He thought it would be nice, however, to live in a smaller city that had Houston's vitality, without, of course, the humidity or hellish traffic.

The professors at Baylor Medical School were not all that enlightening about Norris, Jr. He thought that overall there was an underlying tone of dislike for young Summerfield, but what came out of professorial mouths were statements like *brilliant student* and *great potential.* It was what McCall expected, especially since he was working through the school's public relations director. He had contacted the p.r. director under the guise of doing a feature on the medical school, using a San Antonio student named Norris Summerfield, Jr., as an integral part of the story. The features editor at the *Tribune* was backing his play.

But even though his questions were guarded, McCall was able to find out about Norris, Jr.,'s class attendance. He had never missed a class, was always prepared and alert. Questions of a seemingly joking nature about Norris, Jr., possibly sleeping in class on occasion, after a long night of study, were met with responses that such was never the case.

Some of Norris, Jr.,'s classmates, those the p.r. director rounded up to talk to him, told McCall pretty much the same thing he learned from his professors. They also said young Summerfield was brilliant, that he was potentially a great doctor. However, they all said he was a loner, that they never spent time with him socially.

So, after he had questioned everyone at the school who had any association with the young man, it was time to question Norris, Jr., himself. At the time, however, Norris, Jr., was in class. The p.r. director told McCall he would have young Summerfield call him at the hotel where he was staying, that it would be up to Norris, Jr., as to when they could get together.

Since Norris, Jr., was going to be in class all afternoon, McCall decided to spend his afternoon in the hotel's dimly-lit bar. It was a good plan, but about mid-afternoon the young housewife for whom he was buying drinks decided she would like to see his room. He had room service bring up a bottle, then he and the young woman spent a couple of hours getting to know each other better. She had to leave about five in order to beat her husband home, but only after soliciting a promise that he would call her when he was in Houston again.

The woman had been a good diversion, but she had caused him to think about Lisa. He worried about how he was going to handle that situation, because he knew she wasn't interested in something temporary. But as long as Cele continued to live so vividly in his memory, he knew his romantic attention span was going to be very short.

He dozed off and slept for about an hour, only to be awakened by the ringing of the telephone. When he answered, an amused voice said, "I understand you want to interview me."

McCall grunted sleepily, "It depends on who you are."

"Sorry that I didn't identify myself," the voice said. "I'm Norris Summerfield, Jr."

"Well, you're the guy I want to interview, if it's agreeable."

"Sure."

"Where do you want to meet? And when?"

"Have you eaten?"

"Not yet."

"Do you like seafood?"

"It's okay."

"I take it you're not crazy about it."

"My preference is steak, chili dogs or fried chicken, but I'm not adverse to a few fried oysters on occasion."

"I need to prescribe a better diet for you."

"I'm sickeningly healthy."

"I know a place where you can satisfy at least one of your likes."

"Fine. Where and when?"

"Why don't I just pick you up in front of your hotel in fifteen minutes?"

"I'm ready, so that's no problem."

"I'm driving a black Three Hundred ZX."

McCall wanted to say, "I know." Instead, he said, "I'll be watching for you."

Norris, Jr., was right on time, which McCall appreciated. It required a major catastrophe for McCall to be late for an appointment, so he liked punctuality in others. He considered it a virtue.

After they had exchanged greetings, the younger Summerfield hit the accelerator and started weaving through the city's traffic.

"Where are we going?" McCall asked.

"The San Jacinto Inn. Have you ever been there?"

"Yeah. It's one of my favorite places here in Houston."

Actually, the *Inn* is not in Houston. It is outside the city and near the historic *San Jacinto Battlefield,* where General Sam Houston led the Texas Army to a victory over the Mexican Army and gave the state its independence. The *Inn,* a huge barn-like structure, is also adjacent to where the battleship *Texas* is docked. There is no menu. A variety of seafood is served, along with fried chicken and biscuits.

"I was hoping to take you to a place you didn't know," Norris, Jr., said.

"I've eaten at most of the better places in this area."

"Oh, did you work in Houston at one time?"

"No, just visit here occasionally." It was semi-truth. He had done a lot of stuff for the *Company* in Houston, but had never considered himself on permanent assignment in the city.

"You must have an interesting job, Mr. McCall. I mean, heck, getting to go around and do feature stories in different cities."

"It's okay."

He thought the kid seemed amused by the whole thing. Maybe he knew the feature story thing was a ploy. It didn't matter whether he knew or not. He planned to tell him when he was questioning him.

Norris, Jr., was about what he expected physically. He was slightly under six feet, his hair a bit too long and uncombed. The face had a seriousness to it, but there was also humor evident in piercing brown eyes. The clothes were expensive, but he didn't wear them well. The starch had gone out of the oxford shirt, which he wore tieless, and the English tweed sport coat hadn't been cleaned for some time.

McCall figured Norris, Jr., liked playing the role of the brilliant eccentric to the hilt.

At the restaurant McCall ordered a scotch and water, Norris, Jr., a Dr. Pepper. The drink seemed fitting.

They were immediately served all the seafood of the day, boiled peeled shrimp with cocktail sauce, oysters on the half shell, fried oysters, fried redfish, and crab. They also received a platter of fried chicken, biscuits and jam. There's one price at the *San Jacinto Inn*, no limit on how much a person eats.

Norris, Jr., was into the shrimp, crab and oysters on the half shell. McCall ate a few shrimp, but primarily the fried chicken.

"Do you want another drink, Mr. McCall?" young Summerfield asked.

"Yeah," he replied nonchalantly, "but I think I can get the waiter's attention. And by the way, is Dr. Pepper about the extent of your drinking?"

Norris, Jr., laughed. "I'm not adverse to a little wine occasionally, but I thought I'd have that after the meal, while you're interviewing me for the story that's going to be in the *San Antonio Tribune*."

"From the way you said that, you obviously think there isn't going to be a story."

"Let's just say that I doubt if that's the reason you're here."

"Doubt if you like," McCall said, "but there will be a story on the medical school and, if you're agreeable, some stuff on you."

"I'm quite agreeable, but I don't think that's the real reason you're here."

"Really. Just why do you think I'm here?"

"You want to talk to me about those three women who were murdered in San Antonio."

"And how do you know that?"

"My dear father told me," Norris, Jr., said. "You see, when I was told that I was going to be an integral part of a feature about the medical school, I called my mother. She called dad, and he called me."

"And what did he tell you?"

"He told me not to talk to you."

"So, you're talking to me. Anyone ever tell you that you're a naughty boy?"

Summerfield laughed. "People tell me that all the time."

McCall was impressed with the young man. He was a cool customer, no doubt about it, the kind the *Company* liked to use in Vietnam. "Why do you think I want to talk to you, Norris?"

"I know why."

"Then why don't you tell me?"

"All the women were my father's patients, which means you suspect a member of the family is in some way linked to the killings. I'm a good choice as the murderer because . . . well, you met my father. You probably saw right through his mediocrity, saw that he didn't have the intelligence or balls to think through and commit a murder."

"But you do?"

"Most assuredly. And you obviously know it."

"Well, in a way I hate to get right to the climax of what is a stimulating conversation but . . . did you murder the three women?"

Summerfield laughed. "I didn't even have the satisfaction of murdering one of them. Not that I wouldn't have enjoyed doing one of them in."

"Which one?"

"You already know the answer."

"I prefer that you tell me."

"Okay, that Colette Ramsey slut."

"Why?"

"You know the answer to that, too, but I suppose you want me to tell you."

McCall nodded agreement.

"My mother was hurt very badly by the fact that she was having an affair with my father."

"Did your mother tell you this?"

"Yes."

"But your mother must know that your father hasn't been celibate with a lot of his patients."

"She didn't know any of the others. She wasn't friends with them."

"And she was a friend of Mrs. Ramsey, huh?"

"She thought so."

"I wonder why she told you about it?"

"What do you mean by that?" Summerfield asked. "Besides, who else was she going to tell? It's not the kind of thing she wanted to share with her friends."

"I'm wondering why she felt the need to share it with anyone. Did she tell your sister, too?"

"I can't answer that."

"Can't, or won't?"

There was annoyance in the reply. "Either way. Read into it whatever you will."

"Look, I want you to know that you don't have to talk to me, especially if you think you might say something that would be harmful to your mother, sister or yourself." He knew how Summerfield would react to the statement. He knew the kid thought himself too brilliant to make a mistake in an exchange of verbage.

"No problem, Mr. McCall. I can answer any and all of your questions."

The little bastard, McCall thought. It's all a game to him, and he's enjoying every second of it.

"Do you know if your father was screwing around with Velda Rose Caldwell and Maggie Burleson?"

"I have no idea, but he'll screw anything in a skirt. I'm

sure they were not exceptions, if they were willing."

"Has it occurred to you that the killer may have selected only those with whom your father had affairs?"

Summerfield laughed. "If that was the case, half of San Antonio's female population might be murdered."

"How does your sister feel about your father's womanizing?"

"Hell, she doesn't believe he does anything wrong. If you believe what she says about him, you'll come away thinking he's a saint."

"How do you feel about your sister?"

Summerfield shrugged his shoulders. "She's okay, but she's not the brightest female I've ever known."

"I'm sure you have trouble finding people bright enough to converse with you."

There was a pause, then the response. "Was that a cut?"

"If you spent more time talking to common folk, maybe you'd know."

McCall ascertained that what he was seeing was a lonely young man, one who was so eaten up with his own intelligence that he had cut himself off from most human companionship. It was not pseudo-intellectualism on Norris, Jr.,'s part, but rather a narrow-mindedness that kept him from accepting anyone else as an equal. McCall didn't know whether to feel sorry for or to detest the type person Summerfield had allowed himself to become. He decided that there was no excuse for idiocy. And that summed up Norris, Jr., an idiot genius.

"You take a lot for granted, Mr. McCall."

"Do I?"

"Yes, you do. I knew why you were here and was still willing to talk to you. You don't seem very appreciative of that fact."

"Frankly, Norris, I know that the only reason you're talking to me is because it's against your father's wishes. If your mother had told you not to talk to me, we wouldn't be here."

"Are you saying I'm queer for my mother?"

"No, I'm not accusing you of being queer for your mother. I can't blame you for preferring her to your father. But you have to admit that your father has given you quite a bit."

"Material things."

"And you're not into the material?"

"Not at all."

"Oh, that's right," McCall said, "you plan to devote your life to the poor and helpless."

Summerfield shrugged his shoulders. "Anything wrong with that?"

"Not at all. In fact, it's very noble. It's also easier to do when you have a fat bank account." He recalled the bleeding heart liberals of the sixties and seventies, youths who spoke out against materialism, dressed in ragged clothes, smoked pot and lived in squalor. But a lot of them drove Porsches, paid for their gasoline, booze, dope, food and rent with daddy's money. It was easy enough to be against something if you didn't have to do without it. Maybe Norris, Jr., wasn't that way, but he doubted it.

"Do you resent my having money?"

"I only resent the fact that you act like it's not important."

"It's not. It means absolutely nothing to me."

"I guess you just give it away, huh?"

"Sometimes."

"Okay, Norris, we've gone far afield from why I came here, so let's get back on track. Now, you're obviously a smart man, so I want to ask you a question."

"Ask."

"Well, you've obviously read the newspaper accounts of the murders, and you know that all three women were your father's patients. Knowing the limited amount that you do, who would be your choice as the killer?

McCall had used the word *limited* purposefully, because he knew it would bother Summerfield.

"If I were you, I'd probably think that Norris Summerfield, Jr., was a good candidate to be the murderer. I've heard the women were mutilated in the same way, all very precisely. So I'm sure you've concluded, Mr. McCall, that the killer is knowledgeable about anatomy. And I daresay that I'm already a better surgeon than my father.

"Of course, he's never been much but a pill-pusher. Anyone who would trust him with a knife is a fool."

"Okay, Norris, you've made a good point for yourself. We might be able to convict you of these murders yet."

Summerfield laughed. "Not in a million years. Even if I'd committed them, there would be no way to prove it."

"Everybody slips up, my friend."

"I wouldn't."

"What if I told you that your car was seen in San Antonio the morning Velda Rose Caldwell was killed?"

"I'd tell you that you were mistaken."

"What if I told you I'd checked with one of your credit card companies and found that you'd purchased gasoline at a San Antonio service station the night before she was killed? What if I told you that another of your credit card companies showed a charge for a meal in San Antonio that night?"

Summerfield laughed again. "The coroner thinks she was killed in early morning, right?"

That's right."

"If I'm not mistaken, the coroner thinks she was killed shortly after getting home from work, three to four a.m., right?"

"You're doing very well."

"Well, if I'm correct, this all happened early one Tuesday morning, and that's the day I have a seven a.m. class. Don't you think I'd be cutting it close to kill a woman in

San Antonio at three or four o'clock, then make it to a seven o'clock class? And I'm sure my professors told you that I've never been absent from a class. I haven't been tardy, either."

"I admit that it would be a tough drive, but it could be done."

"Only if all the highway patrolmen were asleep. And I'm sure you've checked to see if I got a speeding ticket on the night in question."

"You're right."

"As for the hypothetical credit card charges, you know that if I'm smart enough to plan three fiendish murders, I'm not going to be stupid enough to charge anything on a credit card in the city where I commit the murders. At least, if my alibi is that I'm in another city."

"Is that your alibi, that you were in Houston when all three murders were committed?"

"It is if I need an alibi."

"Whether you need one or not isn't up to me."

"I think it is. If the police had any suspicions, they, not you, would be questioning me."

"I'm certainly not here to accuse you of anything, Norris. I'm just here to get information."

"Bullshit, Mr. McCall. You came down here to check me out, because I'm your best suspect. I know you'd rather it be my dad, but I'm the member of the family most likely to be the killer. I'm not pissed, just glad I've had the opportunity to meet someone as insightful as you. I like bright people."

"I appreciate being put in the *bright* category, Norris. But in the brief time I've known you, you've become almost as obnoxious to me as your father. I know you think you're intelligent enough to commit murder and get away with it, but if you did kill these women, I'll get you. If you're the murderer, you fucked up somewhere along the way, and I'll find where.

"I'm going to get the killer. My only regret is that we have become so humane that we now inject murderers and let them die peacefully and painlessly. If I had my way, we'd still have the electric chair. That way, if you're guilty, I'd have the pleasure of watching you get your ass fried."

Summerfield laughed. "I'd certainly rather have you as a friend than an enemy."

"You can't have me as a friend, so the best way you can have me is disinterested in you. What I'd like you to do is give me an accounting of your time during the general time frames in which all the women were killed."

Norris, Jr., had turned suddenly sober, as if realizing for the first time that McCall was not a man with whom he could play games. "I'll tell you as best I can."

Over the next quarter hour, Summerfield gave McCall a fairly thorough accounting of his whereabouts for the time frames in question. McCall wasn't sure he believed what Norris, Jr., told him, but it gave him something to check.

After he was sure he had all the information he was going to get from Summerfield, McCall got up from his chair.

"Are you ready to leave, McCall?"

"No, I'm going to the john. But you go right ahead and leave, Norris."

"Don't you want me to give you a ride back to your hotel?"

"Don't take this personal, Norris, but I think I'd prefer to catch a cab."

As it was, he was able to catch a ride with one of the pretty hostesses. They had a few drinks at the hotel bar, then she made him think that Houston was a pretty good place to visit.

The next day he did a little more checking on Norris, Jr., He couldn't get a handle on anything, so about mid-afternoon he headed back to San Antonio.

Chapter 20

McCall arrived back in San Antonio in early evening, so he didn't think it too late to call Michelle Sharp. When she answered, he identified himself and asked her to meet him at *The Plum* for a drink. He didn't have to explain to Michelle that it wasn't social.

He was the first to arrive at the establishment, secured a table in the bar and ordered a drink. The waitress hadn't even brought it by the time Michelle arrived.

She had told him she wasn't prepared to be seen in public, that she needed to fix her hair and put on makeup. He convinced her to come as she was and, as he expected, she looked like she was modeling. She possessed that cool, mysterious beauty that defies description, that never needs touching up.

Michelle ordered a glass of white wine and then said,

"Well, Matt, what have you been up to?"

"I just got back from Houston, had a long talk last night with Norris Summerfield, Jr."

If she was surprised, it didn't show. But then, he figured it would take a lot to surprise Michelle.

"Any particular reason you were talking with Norris, Jr.?"

"You already know." Michelle had provided him with much of the information he had about the Summerfield family.

"You obviously suspect him of the murders," she said. "And I have to say that I think you're way off-base."

"Why?"

"I don't know. Maybe it's because I've known him ever since he was an adolescent hanging around the country club swimming pool."

"He's not an adolescent now," McCall reminded. "He's a grown man. And, I think, a very disturbed one."

"I agree he's different, but that doesn't make him a murderer."

"I've never figured out what makes someone a murderer," he replied. "But Norris, Jr., is not why I called you."

"Oh," she teased. "Don't tell me you suddenly realized that I'm the woman of your dreams?"

"You might be. God knows, you're the classiest, nicest lady I know. Which makes what I'm going to ask very difficult."

"Hey, ask. I know how to say no."

"Do you think you could wrangle me a meeting with Mrs. Summerfield and Meredith?"

She sighed. "You don't want much, do you?"

"C'mon, Michelle, it's important."

"I'm sure it is, but I told you I wanted to be left out of this mess. I told you about Colette and Dr. Summerfield. That's enough."

"You told me you wanted to help find Colette's killer."

"I do, but after you talked to Norris he called and chewed my ass. He told me that you identified me as your source for what you said about him and Colette."

"And you believed him?"

"Of course not. I knew he was fishing. I know a good reporter never reveals his sources."

He laughed. "Maybe I'm not a good reporter."

She smiled. "Anyway, I know you didn't betray me. But I still think you're off base about Norris, Jr."

"That's your right, and maybe I am. But you still haven't told me if you'll set up a meeting with Mrs. Summerfield and Meredith."

"I can trick Melanie into a meeting, but I don't know about Meredith. I really don't have much association with her."

"When do you think I can meet with Mrs. Summer . . . Melanie?"

"Well, I'm obviously not going to tell her that I want her to meet with a man who thinks her son is a killer. We're going to have to be a little more devious than that."

"What do you suggest?"

"I'll invite her to lunch, you can just happen by, and I'll have no choice but to ask you to join us."

He smiled. "That's nice and devious."

She returned the smile and said, "Now, tell me about your visit with Norris, Jr."

"There's not much to tell."

"I'll be the judge of that."

So, over a few more drinks he told her about the time he spent with young Summerfield. Then said, "But you haven't told me how I'm going to get with Meredith."

She sighed. "Don't you ever give up?"

"Of course not."

"I'll need a little more time to think about it."

"Take a few minutes," he said. "I'm sure you'll think of

something. By the way, have you eaten?"

"No, but I'm not all that hungry."

"If you won't think it forward of me, I'll invite you over to my place for a steak."

"Now, that's disappointing."

"What?"

"That you're not being forward."

"Okay, I lied. I was being forward as hell."

She laughed. "That's better. But instead of me going to your place, why don't you come to mine? I could fix you some eggs, something like that."

"Ugh," he groaned. "I don't really care for eggs. How about some chili dogs?"

"Those things are disgusting."

"Hey, I can't help it. I obviously have some sort of genetic imbalance."

"Haven't you ever heard that you are what you eat?"

"Are you calling me a weenie?"

The alcohol had loosened her up, made her more relaxed than she was or normally appeared. As for McCall, he was in a constant state of loose. The only time it wasn't apparent was when he was angry. Anyway, he had a hand on one of her legs and she wasn't protesting. In fact, she seemed just as interested as he was in some sort of physical contact.

They left the bar, got in their respective cars, and he followed her home. They stopped at a store on the way and picked up the ingredients for chili dogs.

McCall was glad she had suggested her place, because he thought Lisa might be at the condo. Or she might just happen to be in the neighborhood and drop in while Michelle was there.

When they arrived at Michelle's address, she pushed the remote control for her garage door, and it opened smoothly. There was room enough in the garage for him to park his car beside hers.

He kissed her in the doorway entering the house, kept on kissing her as she closed the door. She responded willingly enough, so he swooped her up in his arms and carried her to the master bedroom. He had never been in her house, but he had a sixth sense about where bedrooms were located.

Chapter 21

Friday, June 19, 11:45 a.m.

"Well, hello Mrs. Sharp. Nice to see you again."

The prearranged greeting by Matt McCall was in a restaurant where Michelle was having lunch with Melanie Summerfield.

Michelle returned his greeting with, "Nice to see you again. Do you know Mrs. Summerfield?"

"I haven't had the pleasure."

Melanie Summerfield smiled, extended a hand and said, "Just call me Melanie."

He took her hand and said, "Matt McCall. And you can just call me Matt."

"I know who you are, and I want to tell you that my son thinks you're wonderful."

He feigned mild surprise. "You know, I didn't make the connection for a minute there, but you're Norris' mother."

"That's right."

If he read her reaction correctly, Norris, Jr., had reported favorably on their meeting. Actually, there was little else he could do. He was not likely to tell his mother that a reporter from the hometown paper suspected him of killing three women. And as for Dr. Summerfield, he probably hadn't said anything to his wife. He certainly wouldn't tell her that he was a suspect, that he had been confronted about having an affair with Colette Ramsey. McCall was pleased. The fact that father and son had something to hide from Melanie Summerfield was working in his favor.

"Are you alone?" Michelle asked.

"Yes."

"Why don't you join us?"

"I don't want to intrude."

Melanie joined in with, "Oh, you won't be intruding. And it can only enhance our luncheon, being seen with a good-looking man."

He laughed and looked over his shoulder. "For a minute there, I thought you were talking to me. Must be someone standing behind me."

Melanie laughed. "Don't be so modest."

Taking a chair, McCall said, "I'll join you, but only on the condition that I get the check."

"That's not fair," Melanie replied.

"My intense commitment to male chauvenism won't allow me to do otherwise."

"Oh, let him, Melanie," Michelle said. "We need our money for important things, like buying new clothes."

"I see you ladies already have a drink. Have you ordered yet?"

"No," Michelle said, "we were hoping to pick up some guy who would buy our lunch."

McCall signaled the waiter and told him Michelle and Melanie needed a refill. He ordered a scotch and water.

"When is the paper going to print the story about my son and Baylor Medical School?" Melanie asked.

"It will be in Sunday's paper," he answered. He had knocked out a comprehensive story on the medical school, featuring Norris, Jr., and the paper had sent a photographer to Houston to secure the necessary pictures. It was not the type of story he liked doing, but it was necessary to support his alleged reason for visiting Norris, Jr.

"That's great," Melanie said. "I can hardly wait to tell Norris, Sr., because he said the paper probably wouldn't print the story."

"Why would he say that?"

"If you knew him, you'd understand," she said. "He's pretty negative."

He's also probably scared shitless, McCall thought, because he thinks his stink is going to be aired publicly. Maybe not, though. To be a doctor, Norris, Sr., isn't the brightest guy around.

"You don't know my husband, do you?" she continued.

"Mostly, I just know of him," he lied.

She laughed. "Well, he doesn't like you, but he doesn't have to know someone to dislike them."

He smiled. "What does he have against me?"

"I don't know, but at breakfast the other morning he was reading the paper and complaining about something you wrote. And he didn't seem too pleased when I told him you were doing the story on Norris, Jr. Are you sure you don't know him?"

"I'm sure we've met," he admitted, "but I didn't realize I had created such a negative impression."

She laughed. "That's it. I'll bet you've written something negative about the American Medical Association."

He smiled. "Well, if I wrote anything about the AMA, it was probably negative," he said.

Michelle interrupted with, "Why don't we order?"

"Good idea," he agreed, "and let's get these glasses

refilled again."

There was more casual conversation, then the waiter brought their food. During the meal, Melanie said, "I believe I told you earlier that my son was quite impressed with you."

"I'm glad," he replied. Then, hoping lightning wouldn't strike him, he continued, "He's a fine young man."

"He's a very committed young man," she said. "I may be wrong, but I see him as an Albert Schwitzer. I think he will spend his life providing medical care to the indigent."

"You have worthy aspirations for your son."

"They're his aspirations, not mine."

"Do you think his inspiration comes from his father?"

She laughed. "Hardly. If it comes from anyone, it's from my mother."

"Your mother?"

"Oh, yes. She's one of the *most Christian* people I know."

"And you think she had a profound effect on Norris, Jr.?"

"Yes," she replied. "When he was a child, he loved to visit her. And he still goes and visits her quite often."

Melanie was anxious to talk about her son, which caused McCall to be irritated at himself. He thought that if he had read the situation properly, he would have realized that Dr. Summerfield and his son would not have thrown up any roadblocks to him visiting with Melanie. The doctor was afraid because he knew about Colette. And Norris, Jr., well ... he just wouldn't do anything to hurt mommy dearest. He could easily have arranged to meet with Melanie under the guise of doing a story on her son. He would not have had to drag Michelle into it. Now, he wondered if Melanie wouldn't think it unusual that he did a story on Norris, Jr., without talking to his folks.

He covered with, "You know, I had planned to talk to you and your husband about Norris, Jr., but with what I got from him and his professors, I had more material than I could use."

She laughed. "Don't worry about it. I figured the story was more about the medical school than Norris, Jr."

"That's true, but he's important to the story, too."

Michelle piped in, "I believe Mr. McCall . . . I mean Matt . . . is the one who's been writing the stories about Colette's murder."

Melanie's mood changed. "That's right, you are. Terrible, terrible thing. Do the police have any idea who did it?"

"If they do, they haven't told me," he said. "Were you a friend of Mrs. Ramsey?"

"They were very close," Michelle injected.

"Yes," Melanie acknowledged. "My husband and I spent quite a bit of time with Clark and Colette." She proceeded to tell him pretty much what he already knew about the Ramsey/Summerfield relationship. While she was speaking, he signaled for more drinks. He hoped her talkativeness would eventually shed a ray of light on Colette's murder.

He ventured, "I guess Clark and Colette were pretty close to the children, too."

"Norris, Jr., adored Clark," she replied. "Now, I do think some of his concern for mankind might come from talking with Clark."

Why? McCall thought. That sonofabitch has never had one second of concern for anyone other than himself.

"And Meredith loves Clark, too," Melanie continued.

No mention of Colette, he thought. Of course, the bitch knows that her husband was tapping Clark's wife. She probably has great empathy for Clark.

"When was the last time you saw Colette?" he asked.

"It was some time ago," she replied. "After she and Clark separated, we didn't see her much. Oh, I saw her at the country club a couple of times, even had drinks with her there, but she didn't come over to the house."

"But Clark came."

"Yes, but we didn't see him as often as when he and Colette were together. He's always come over a lot on Saturday and Sunday mornings, had breakfast with us before he and Norris played golf."

"They play golf a lot together?"

"Oh, yes. Until Colette's death, they rarely missed a Saturday or Sunday. In fact, they're playing tomorrow and Sunday."

"Have you talked to Clark since Colette's death?"

"A few times."

"How's he doing?"

"Not all that well. I think he's still in shock from it. He loved her very much."

"So, he wasn't responsible for the separation?"

"Not at all," she replied with emphasis. "Colette wanted it, not him."

"I guess he was hoping for a reconciliation?"

"That's what he wanted more than anything."

"He told you that?"

"Yes."

He didn't know how she would react, but he had to ask, "Do you have any idea why Colette left Clark?"

"I haven't the foggiest," she lied. Then, she continued, "Do you have any idea, Michelle?"

Michelle calmly replied, "I sure don't."

"It's my understanding that Colette was not only your friend, but that she was also your husband's patient."

"That's true," Melanie said.

"Did you know the other two murdered women were also patients of your husband?"

She seemed startled. "No, I didn't know."

"I'm surprised that he didn't tell you."

"Norris is a firm believer in patient/doctor confidentiality. He's never told me anything about any of his patients."

I don't doubt that, McCall thought, but said, "I just thought he might mention it, because it's unusual that three patients of the same doctor are murdered in the same way."

She was now visibly disturbed. "You think there's some connection, don't you?"

He attempted to calm her with, "If there were some connection, the police would have already found it. It's just kind of a strange coincidence."

"Norris never mentioned that the police had even talked to him."

"And probably with good cause," McCall said. "He probably didn't want to upset you with something that didn't amount to a hill of beans. And here I am, I've upset you."

"No, I'm glad you told me," she responded.

"Well, do me a favor," he said.

"What?"

"When you talk to your husband, don't mention that I even brought this up."

"I doubt that I'll even tell him I talked to you," she said. "But I'll have to admit all this is upsetting. Are you sure all three women were patients of Norris?"

"I'm sure."

"I knew about Colette, of course, but I didn't know about the other two."

He was sure she was computing the situation, pondering in her mind the possibility that her husband had also been having affairs with Velda Rose Caldwell and Maggie Burleson, that the affairs had in some way caused their deaths.

McCall tried to reassure her, "Hey, we're talking strange coincidence here, that's all. In covering homicides over the years, I've run into all kinds of strange stuff like this."

She smiled and replied, "It's strange alright."

"Let's get on a more pleasant subject," McCall said. "Let's retire to the bar, have a few more drinks and talk about something totally unrelated to Colette Ramsey's murder. You have another child, don't you? A daughter? Tell me about her."

Michelle, out of Melanie's line of vision, rolled her eyes for McCall's benefit.

They retired to the restaurant's bar and spent another two hours drinking and talking. Melanie got more than a little bit drunk, insisted that McCall meet her daughter Meredith.

"You're just the kind of man she needs," Melanie said.

"I'd think I would be a little old for her."

"Nonsense," Melanie replied. "I think she's looking for a father image anyway. She adores her father."

Chapter 22

Dr. Norris Summerfield found out about McCall's meeting with his wife. The source was Norris, Jr., who had been filled in about the chance encounter by his mother. He had told his father for the express purpose of upsetting him. But neither man had the nerve to tell Melanie she had been duped. To tell her would have possibly required answering some unpleasant questions, something for which neither was prepared.

Norris, Sr., telephoned Michelle and cursed her for the part she had played in the scenario. Of course, she denied having any part in it, told Summerfield that the meeting was accidental. He did not believe her, which caused her to get angry and throw a few barbs his way. The end result, she later told McCall, was that she was going to have to find another doctor.

Melanie, in the meantime, was unaware of anything that was going on behind the scenes. She went merrily on her way, trying to arrange a meeting between her daughter and McCall, one that would not agitate the high-strung Meredith. She was even more a McCall fan after the Sunday paper came out, complete with photos of and quotes from her son.

She telephoned McCall and lauded his writing, for what he considered an average story. The story did not, as she thought, profile her son as a great humanitarian. The article contained a number of subtleties about Norris, Jr., that Melanie did not catch.

McCall was pleased with Melanie's perception of the story, because he didn't think he compromised himself in writing it. It was straightforward, unopinionated, with the only opinions coming from the quotes of Norris, Jr., and others interviewed. But he figured if Melanie wanted to canonize him for his efforts, fine. At the moment, his primary concern was in talking to Meredith, and he was counting on mom's help.

McCall's primary concern was in finding a killer and converting the discovery into a story, but his concentration was being interrupted by a lot of nagging problems, some of which he had created. Lisa, for example, had become a serious problem. She was obviously interested in a long-term monogamous relationship, something he could not abide.

He had difficulty understanding Lisa. She was, after all, much too young to think of him as a permanent mate. From the beginning, he had never thought of her as anything more than a temporary bed partner. And he figured she was smart enough to realize that.

But now she was in the possessive *you belong to me* syndrome, which always turned him off. He had tolerated it in Cele, but had never accepted it. And Cele was different. He had been in love with her.

Or, at least, he thought he had been in love with her. The memories were still there, but lately he had begun to wonder if, because she had died so tragically, he had not created an illusion. He wanted to remember her forever, but maybe it was not because of love. Maybe it was because she had died as a result of a bomb meant for him.

Whatever, he was now confronted with women-problems, seemingly on all fronts. There was Lisa, Michelle, LeAnne, even Annie Cossey to some extent. Of course, Annie and Michelle didn't put any pressure on him, something that couldn't be said for Lisa or LeAnne. Maybe it was their ages, or maybe it had something to do with their first names starting with *L*.

The deal with age, though, it had never mattered with Cele. Nor had he given much thought to it with anyone else. With Lisa, maybe he was just using it as an excuse. Anyway, he wanted no family ties. Not now, not ever.

At times he could admit to himself that he had a weakness where women were concerned. And he often thought he was never the best he could be because of that weakness. Maybe with one woman he could overcome his need for continual sexual gratification, but Lisa was not that woman. He had not yet met that woman.

He had explained to Lisa that theirs could be nothing more than a casual relationship, but she remained unconvinced. He thought it strange that when they had first met she showed dislike and actual hostility toward him. Now, she wanted to talk about eternal love.

And though he had known LeAnne Bevins for even less time than he had known Lisa, she was talking the same way. What was it with these bimbos in their twenties? For that matter, McCall wondered what was with him.

He didn't like the pressure that Lisa and LeAnne put on him, but he really didn't want to give them up, either. He wanted Lisa, LeAnne, Michelle, Annie and Debbie. And he already knew he was going to want some others that he did not yet know.

Helluva note.

While waiting for Melanie to set up a meeting with Meredith, McCall started going back over the same old ground. He again questioned everyone known to have had contact with Velda Rose Caldwell, Maggie Burleson or Colette Ramsey. Except, of course, Dr. Norris Summerfield, who wouldn't talk to him. Summerfield, in fact, contacted his good friend Clark Ramsey about McCall's harrassment, which led to another confrontation between the reporter and district attorney.

The parents of the three slain women still proved to be of no help in providing even the slightest clue, which was also the case with friends and coworkers of the victims. In terms of clues, there seemed to be no light at the end of the tunnel. But McCall knew from experience that if he turned over enough rocks, he would find something under one of them.

An indication that he was causing someone discomfort came the following Wednesday, at ten p.m. He and Lisa had just left the *Tribune* Building enroute to their cars when they were confronted by three tough-looking Mexicans.

"Hey, baby, you want some fun?" one asked Lisa. "The three of us want to give you a fuck you will never forget."

While the one was talking, the other two were trying to flank McCall. It seemed obvious to him that there was no way to avoid a fight. So, he drop kicked one in the groin and smashed the other in the face with a fist.

The one he kicked was on his knees groaning, the other on his back with blood all over his face. The talker then turned combatant, pulling a long, ugly-looking knife and going into a crouch position.

McCall couldn't help it. He looked at the man and laughed.

His laughter startled the knife-wielding attacker, who

backed up to better survey his opponent. In the meantime, McCall saw that the man he had kicked had also pulled a knife. He kicked him again, this time in the face. The knife flew from his hand, and McCall quickly picked it up.

"Okay, mother fucker, let's see how you like cold steel," he said to the other attacker.

The man looked at his two companions and acted as though he wanted to run, but the building was to his back, and he couldn't count on his opponent allowing him to run to the right or left. He did the only thing he thought he could do, which was to slash at the man coming toward him.

McCall easily avoided the man's wild attempts to cut him, grabbed the wrist of the hand holding the knife, then swept the blade of his recently acquired weapon across the man's throat. As the blood spurted, Lisa, who had moved away from the action and was frozen against the building, screamed.

The attacker dropped his knife, slumped to his knees while grasping his throat in his hands. But there was no way he was going to stop the blood. A few onlookers, including the paper's unarmed guard, had arrived by this time, and they watched him die. While the action was going on, the other two attackers made their escape.

"Damn," McCall said to no one in particular, when looking at all the blood on his jacket. Then he asked the guard, "Charley, would you mind getting me a wet towel? And call the police. See that Bill Haloran knows what happened."

"What about that guy?" Charley asked, referring to the body lying in a puddle of blood. "Do you want me to call an ambulance?"

"Tell the police to send the meat wagon," McCall answered. "He's past medical help."

While the guard was gone to take care of his assigned duties, and while onlookers continued to mill around the scene, McCall went to where Lisa was supporting herself against the building and asked, "Are you okay?"

She had vomited.

"Helluva question, Matt."

He put his arm around her. "Well, it's kind of hard to come up with something clever at a time like this."

"I can't believe this," she said. "I just can't believe it."

He laughed. "If we had gone to prayer meeting tonight, it probably wouldn't have happened."

She gave her incredulous look and said, "How can you say something like that? You just killed a man."

Her statement angered him. "Would you feel better if he had killed me? I'll tell you this, if I hadn't killed him, we'd both be dead."

"We should have just given them our money," she replied.

"Money, hell. They didn't want money. They had already been paid money to kill me."

She again looked shocked. "Why would anyone want to kill you?"

He started to jokingly bring up the fact that she had probably wanted to kill him on occasion, but instead answered, "Because I'm making someone nervous. Maybe I'm getting close to the bathtub murderer."

That he might be right caused her to shudder.

"Why don't you go inside?" he asked. "It's going to take a while to get this cleaned up."

"Why can't I just go home?"

"The police are going to want to ask you some questions."

When the guard returned with a wet towel, McCall said, "Charley, take Lisa inside and get her some ice water or something. In fact, make her a stiff drink. She can use it."

"You know we aren't allowed to have liquor in the building," Charley said.

McCall handed him a key and replied, "Look in my desk. There's a bottle of Chivas in there. And pour one for yourself, Charley."

The guard grinned. "I hope that's an order, McCall."

"Consider it such."

After what seemed an hour, but was only five minutes, the police arrived. They cordoned off the area and began their usual procedures. An officer took McCall's statement, along with that of a couple of witnesses who happened on the scenario near its conclusion. Another officer took Lisa's statement.

Haloran arrived about fifteen minutes after the uniforms and immediately quipped, "McCall, when in the hell are you going to leave town and make my life a little easier?"

"Sorry, Bill, but I thought I was making life easier for you. If these clowns had jumped a normal citizen, you'd be investigating a murder."

"By normal, you mean someone who isn't crazy as a fuckin' loon?"

"Hey, it's a shame you've discouraged me from carrying a gun," McCall said. "If I'd had a piece, you could have hauled three sacks of shit to the morgue."

Haloran laughed. "Any idea why three guys jumped you?"

"I imagine they were just competing to see who was going to take me to the senior prom. Hell, Bill, you know damn well it's probably because I'm getting close to the bathtub murderer."

"Meaning, you think the killer hired three guys to give you a good ass-kicking?"

"William, my man, your idea of ass kicking and mine are different. I didn't know you used knives to kick ass."

"Well, McCall, you're not exactly without enemies. And who's to say they weren't just after your wallet?"

"They sure as hell didn't say anything about a wallet."

"From what I've heard, they didn't have much chance to

say anything."

"Okay, Bill, I confess. Lisa and I left the building, I saw these three guys coming down the sidewalk, so I attacked them. My motive, of course, was to impress Lisa."

Haloran laughed again. "I think you impressed her alright. I have a feeling you gave the girl a night to remember."

McCall sighed. "Yeah, I'm a real bundle of laughs and good times. But c'mon, Bill, you know there's validity to what I say about the killer sending these guys after me."

"I'd think the killer would come after you himself."

"He's a woman killer. He's not going to face up to a man."

"That's your psychological profile of him, huh?"

"Oh, shit. Take your fuckin' psychological profile and shove it up your ass."

"Whoa," Haloran replied with a laugh. "I'm not discounting anything. Maybe the killer hired your would-be assassins, or maybe they were hired by someone you miffed."

Now it was McCall's turn to laugh. "Miffed. Where in the hell did you come up with that word? And who in the hell would be that miffed at San Antonio's most beloved reporter?"

"Offhand, I can't think of more than a hundred people," Haloran said. "Hell, there are times when I'm tempted to send someone after you."

McCall shook his head with mock hopelessness. "It's hard for me to believe that you've ever felt that way."

They bantered back and forth a while, then McCall said, "I'll take Lisa home, then we can meet at the diner, and you can fill me in on the clown that I took out tonight."

"We might not have anything for a few hours," the detective said. "Besides, don't you think Lisa's going to need some consoling?"

"You have a dirty mind, Bill. I just want to get out of these bloody clothes and take a shower. I'll meet you at the diner at about one o'clock."

"Maybe I want to go home and go to bed," Haloran complained.

"Bullshit. If you go home and go to bed, your ol' lady's going to want you to perform. At your age and weight, that's not easy. Besides, I'm buying."

"I'll be there, asshole," Haloran said, "but I'm not guaranteeing that I'll have any information."

After Haloran had left, McCall went back to the newsroom and found Lisa. She and Charley had taken a pretty good bite out of the scotch.

"If you can wait about thirty minutes, I'll take you home," he told her.

"Why do we have to wait thirty minutes?"

"I've got to write the story."

"About what just happened?"

"Yeah."

"You're unbelievable. Someone else can write it. After all, you just killed a man."

He grunted. "It's my story. I'll be damned if someone else writes it."

Chapter 23

Thursday, June 25, 1:30 p.m.

McCall and Michelle had finished their lunch, were in the bar having a drink and discussing the meeting he would have the following day with Meredith Summerfield. Meredith, of course, did not know about the meeting. It was being orchestrated by her mother, who would be bringing her to the restaurant for lunch.

"I can't imagine what you hope to gain by meeting with Meredith," Michelle said.

"I don't either," he admitted. "I'm just looking for that one thread that will lead me to the murderer."

"My guess is that you won't find it with Meredith."

"Maybe not, but I've just about exhausted my list of potentials."

"Have you given up on Norris, Jr.?"

"Not really, but I sure can't prove anything. I've checked

him out forwards and backwards, and can't place him in San Antonio at the time of any of the murders. That doesn't mean he's not guilty, though."

She laughed. "No one can accuse you of giving up easy."

"For someone who doesn't give up easy, I'm sure not getting anywhere."

"What about last night, Matt? Why do you think those men attacked you?"

"What I think and what the police think are two different things."

"What do you mean?"

"Well, they're going to call it attempted robbery, but I honestly think the killer sent them."

"Why wouldn't the killer come himself?"

It was a good question, the same one Bill Haloran asked. He answered the same way. "Because he only kills women. He's probably afraid to face up to a man, which makes young Norris an even better suspect."

"Did the police find out anything about the man you killed?"

"Only that he was an illegal alien. His name was Juan Sanchez. His wallet contained a bogus social security card and half of a hundred dollar bill. You know what that says, don't you?"

"My god. He was going to get the other half when the job was done."

He laughed. "My guess is that the other two each had half a hundred dollar bill, too."

"Three hundred dollars," she mused. "That's not much to pay to get someone killed."

"If the killer had checked with me, I could have got him someone for fifty bucks. And he would have done a better job."

"I don't know how you can joke about something like that, Matt."

"Who's joking. In this town, you really can get someone hit for fifty dollars."

"That's not what I mean. I'm talking about your casualness regarding someone trying to kill you."

"Sorry, Michelle, it's not that I'm blase about it. People with guns and knives do make me nervous."

"How's your little friend, Lisa?" The cattiness was there, which he thought she was beyond. She was a woman, though, so he should have known better.

"She'll survive, but I think she'll have a little trouble putting the incident out of her mind. She's probably never seen anyone killed before."

"Neither have I, and I hope I never do."

"I'm sorry I didn't get over to your place last night," he said, "but after this happened, I was pretty well tied up until the wee hours."

She put a hand on his. "You know you're welcome at any hour."

"I appreciate it, but after putting up with Bill Haloran until three a.m., I was bushed."

"That's understandable."

"By the way, has Summerfield called to curse you out again?"

"I haven't heard from him," she said, "and I haven't missed his wonderful voice."

"You know, Michelle, I'm beginning to believe that you're one of the doctor's few good-looking patients that he didn't bang."

"Former patient," she corrected. "Norris has made it clear that he doesn't want to see me ever again. And he didn't *bang* me, as you call it, because I wasn't buying his garbage. And while I don't condone the good doctor's actions, it takes two to tango. I don't think he forces women to sleep with him."

"That's a good point," he said, "and one that certainly hasn't escaped me. I just wonder if he really sleeps with his daughter."

She laughed. "Why don't you ask her tomorrow?"

"Maybe I will."

"Don't you dare."

"Why not?"

"Because Melanie will never speak to you or me again."

"Would that be so bad?"

She pondered the question for a moment, then answered, "Maybe not."

"Well, don't worry. I'm crass, but not that crass."

"You can be crass with me," she said. "I like it when you're crass in bed."

"Really? You know, I'm pretty well rested now and not in any hurry to get to the office. Maybe we could go over to your place and catch a nap."

"Sounds good to me."

He paid the check, and they went to Michelle's place. He stayed most of the afternoon, then went by the police station to see Haloran. The police had no leads on the other two attackers, which didn't surprise McCall. He arrived at the newsroom about six-thirty p.m., to be greeted by Lisa's unhappy mouth. He invited her to dinner, which caused the corners of her mouth to turn up a bit. It wasn't quite a smile, but he figured a smile was too much to expect anyway.

Of course, she didn't help matters by asking, "Where have you been?"

He ignored the question, asked her if she had come up with additional information from those with whom the victims were known to have had contact. She hadn't, which didn't surprise him. He had already decided that she didn't have the tenacity necessary to be a good investigative reporter. He planned to cover the same persons assigned to her, because he feared she had missed something. Her reports were neat, but with a lot of holes.

Lisa wanted Mexican food for dinner. He wasn't fond of

it, but he deferred to her on this occasion.

Drinking margaritas in the courtyard of a small Mexican cafe, he suggested that she might do well to disassociate herself from him, that the previous night's episode could happen again.

"Is that the real reason?" she asked. "Or is it just that you don't find me sexually appealing?"

"Why would you say something like that?"

"Since our first few times, you haven't seemed all that excited about making love to me," she answered. "I've certainly been available to you more than you wanted."

He shrugged his shoulders. "I'm sorry, but I'm not inclined to settle for one woman. And I haven't asked you to settle for just me. You need to find a decent young guy who'll make you a good husband."

"I'm not interested in a decent young guy. I'm interested in you."

"That I can't help," he said. "I care a lot about you, but I'm not interested in any family ties."

"And I'm not asking for any," she replied. "I would like a little faithfulness, though."

"I can't give you that. In fact, I can't promise you anything."

Sarcasm was obvious in her voice. "Is it because of Cele?"

"Let's not get into that."

She expressed exasperation. "My god, she's dead, Matt."

He controlled his anger and coldly replied, "I'm quite aware she's dead."

"I don't think you are. You're still letting her memory affect how you think and feel."

"That's not true."

"Deny it all you want, it's the truth."

"You don't know anything about Cele, and you don't know anything about my feelings for her."

They both knew they should drop the subject, that too many margaritas could make them say things they would regret. But she persisted with, "Maybe you ought to tell me about Cele and your feelings for her."

"Why?"

"You should talk with someone. You shouldn't go through the rest of your life idolizing a dead girl that you probably really didn't care that much about."

He replied angrily, "You don't know anything about my feelings, my caring. Cele was special, very special, and if I want to spend the rest of my life loving someone who's dead, it's my business."

She sighed. "You're right. It's just that I think you feel so guilty about her death that you can't be objective about caring for someone else right now."

Her sudden mellowness cooled him. "I don't think there's anything objective about love. And you might be right that I'm guilt-ridden. But that's something I have to discover for myself. And I certainly can't tell you that I love you, Lisa."

She protected her feelings with the statement, "I don't know for sure if I love you, Matt. I just know I miss you when you're not there."

"Well, you can't count on me being there. Cele couldn't even count on it, and I cared more about her than anyone I've ever known. Maybe I'm just not capable of love."

"I don't believe that," she said. "You can be the most gentle, the tenderest man I've ever known."

"Let's face it, Lisa, your range of experience isn't that great. I'm sure there are a lot of guys out there who can fill your needs better than I can."

"Just having a man isn't the answer. Just any little bimbo may satisfy your needs, but just any man doesn't satisfy mine. What's amazing to me is that I think you're a romantic, but won't admit it."

He laughed. "Any little bimbo, huh? I'm glad you think so

highly of my selections."

"Well, I certainly don't like to have myself categorized with some of the women you sleep with."

"How in the hell do you know who I sleep with?"

"Pardon me," she answered. "I should have said with whom I think you sleep."

"This conversation is going nowhere, Lisa. I'm going to do what I want, when I want, and that's all there is to it. I care for you, but you're probably too young and family-oriented to be messing around with someone like me. Besides, being with me isn't all that healthy. Cele died because of it, and you could have suffered the same fate last night. If you're as smart as you think you are, you need to stay away from me."

"You're right," she agreed, "but I seem to be a real dumb-ass where you're concerned."

"Do yourself a favor and use that brain of yours," he suggested.

"I will," she said.

They had a few more margaritas and went to his place for the night. They both knew it wouldn't be the last time.

Chapter 24

Friday, June 26, 11:30 a.m.

When McCall arrived at the restaurant, he immediately went to the bar. Melanie and Meredith Summerfield were not scheduled to be there until noon, so he figured on having a scotch and water while waiting.

Melanie had chosen the place, because it was the site of their accidental meeting. She suggested that McCall walk by their table and speak to her, at which time she would introduce her daughter and invite him to join them. McCall had to laugh privately at the intrigue of the scheme, since it was the same one he and Michelle had used on Melanie.

He was surprised to find Carolyn Bell in the bar. She was perched on a stool having a glass of white wine.

"Do you mind if I join you?" he asked.

"Not at all," she invited.

He took the stool next to her, ordered a scotch and water,

and with a laugh asked, "You weren't waiting for me, were you?"

She smiled. "Hardly. A friend is joining me for lunch."

"I hope it's not Dr. Summerfield."

She seemed amused by the suggestion. "No, it's not Dr. Summerfield. I don't guess it would do any good to tell you that I have nothing to do with the man?"

"You're right, it wouldn't do any good." McCall's assessment was that Carolyn really wanted him to know that she and Summerfield had a thing going.

"Well, I hate to disappoint you, but the friend who's joining me for lunch is female."

"Is she one of Summerfield's patients, too?"

She laughed. "You're a persistent sonofabitch."

"Yeah, I need to do something about that." He thought Carolyn seemed even more self-assured than when they last talked, and it bothered him.

"If I didn't know better," she said, "I'd think you were jealous of Dr. Summerfield."

"Why would I be jealous of him?"

"You obviously think he has all these women, including me."

"Well, no offense, Carolyn, but I'm certainly not jealous of him. And I'd think all his women would be a little nervous, since three he allegedly had got their throats cut."

She laughed, then in a more serious tone asked, "Have the police found out anything yet?"

"If they have, they haven't told me."

"What about you? Have you found anything new about the murders?

"I'm afraid not."

She sighed. "It looks like Maggie is going to go in the books as another unsolved crime."

"The case is still young," he said. "I don't think the police have dismissed it just yet."

"I have the feeling that even if they had, you wouldn't."

He smiled. "I might not have any choice. You can ram your head against only so many stone walls."

She laughed. "Your head looks in pretty good shape. I'm sure you'll turn up something eventually."

"Sure," he agreed, "my head is bloody but unbowed."

She laughed again. "So, why are you here?"

"I came here for lunch. It's one of my favorite places."

"This is my first time here. What do you recommend?"

"I don't recommend the food. I just come here to look at the beautiful women."

"You can't eat beautiful . . . forget I said that."

He laughed. "Just about anything on the menu is okay, though there is one notable absence."

"What's that?"

"They don't serve chili dogs."

"You don't eat those things do you?"

"For me, a chili dog is a staple."

"Keep eating those things, and they'll be wheeling you into the emergency room some night."

"Well, I'm sure you would give me some excellent care. Maybe you'd even give me some information about Dr. Summerfield."

She laughed. "You have a one-track mind. Norris Summerfield is my doctor, that's all."

"Did he tell you to say that?"

"Why would he tell me to say anything?"

"Maybe he's afraid the police are closing in on him for the murders of three of his patients."

"Oh, c'mon, Matt, you can't believe Norris is a murderer."

"Oh, now it's Norris."

She sighed. "Be that as it may, be honest. You don't believe Norris is a killer, do you?"

"Not really, but I do think he could be more helpful."

"In what way?"

"He could come clean about his relationship with the

three victims."

"And how would that help?"

"It might give us a clue. In addition, it might show that he cares. That would be worth something."

"I don't know why you can't accept the fact that the killer was probably just some psycho who was passing through town."

"No way, baby. The killer may be a psycho, but there's reason for these murders. They weren't just wanton killings. And they have something to do with Norris Summerfield."

"If the police thought that, I'm sure they would have questioned Norris."

"They have questioned him, at least two or three times."

The news seemed to startle her. "I guess that shouldn't surprise me. They've questioned me a couple of times, too. But I guess they've questioned everyone who had contact with the women who were killed."

"Everyone they know who had contact," he corrected.

"So, they questioned Norris just like they questioned everyone else."

"That's right, in the sense that they haven't accused him of having affairs with the women, which isn't a crime anyway. The subject has been touched on, but he denies anything other than professional contact with the victims."

"If the police are satisfied, why can't you be?"

"I didn't say they were satisfied. But, as for me, I'm not going to rest until I know it all, including all about his sick relationship with his daughter."

His statement shocked her. "What relationship?"

"Surely, you've heard that the good Dr.Summerfield has more than a fatherly interest in his daughter?"

She had recovered enough to emit an uneasy laugh. "Matt, you'll lie, do anything to shock people and try to get information."

"I have pretty good sources."

"Well, your sources are wrong. Norris isn't that kind of man."

"Defending him the way you do, you'd think that there's more than a doctor/patient relationship between you and Summerfield," he teased.

There was anger in her response. "You really think you know it all, don't you? There's a helluva lot that you don't know, Matt. But maybe someday you will."

"Are we talking romance here, or just plain old passion?"

"As far as you're concerned, we're not talking anything right now. And I haven't admitted a damn thing."

"That's true, but I think there are some things you'd like to tell me."

"Not really. In fact, I can't think of a single thing."

"Tell me, Carolyn, did it bother you that Summerfield had slept with your good friend Maggie Burleson?"

She stared at him, a combination of anger and hurt in her eyes. Then she smiled, the eyes brightened and she said, "Hi, Betty. I'd just about given up on you."

McCall turned to see a smiling, dumpy woman that he guessed to be several years older than Carolyn. There was evidence in the face that she had been attractive at one time, but that she had now given up on diet and life in general.

Carolyn continued, "Betty, I'd like for you to meet Matt McCall. Matt, this is Betty Murphy."

He shook hands with the woman and exchanged pleasantries, then Carolyn asked, "Would you like to like to join us?"

"I appreciate it," McCall said, "but I'm expecting someone."

After Carolyn and Betty left the bar, he ordered another scotch and water, then let his mind wander. Among other things, he wondered if the bass were hitting in the Brazos

River. He loved the river, loved its changing moods.

From the bar, he could observe everyone entering the restaurant. He picked out some of the more interesting looking patrons and wrote descriptions of them on napkins.

Finally, Melanie and Meredith Summerfield came through the door. After a brief conversation with the hostess, they were ushered out of McCall's sight by a swarthy-looking character carrying a couple of menus. McCall gave them a few minutes to get settled, then wandered into the restaurant, drink in hand.

At Melanie's table, he stopped and said, "Mrs. Summerfield, I saw you come in the door and thought I'd say hello."

"Mr. McCall," Melanie chirped, "this is a pleasure. I don't believe you've met my daughter Meredith."

He took the extended hand of the younger woman and said, "My pleasure. You're as beautiful as your mother."

Meredith, unsmiling, responded with a "Thank you."

"Won't you join us, Mr. McCall?" Melanie asked.

"Mother, I'm sure Mr. McCall isn't interested in joining us," Meredith said.

"If I'm not interrupting anything, I'll be glad to join you," he replied.

"Oh, you're not interrupting a thing," Melanie assured.

Meredith didn't say anything, but McCall thought she looked a bit pissed.

"Matt's the one who wrote the story about Norris, Jr.," Melanie said to her daughter.

"Yes, I know," was the cool reply.

"I understand that you're a nurse," McCall said.

"That's right. Other than mother, the entire family is in the medical profession."

"Did you ever consider being a doctor, like your father and brother?"

"Not really," she replied. "I don't like the feel of surgical instruments, and I can't stand the sight of blood. What I know about anatomy, Mr. McCall, could all be written on the head of a pin."

Her response indicated that she had been warned about him by her father.

"That's a strange thing to say, Meredith," her mother observed.

McCall laughed. "With micro chips, what could be written on something the size of the head of a pin could be quite a lot."

The waiter arrived, took their orders for drinks and lunch.

"I read the other day where you were attacked by some hoodlums," Melanie said.

"Yeah, nothing serious." The fact that Melanie had mentioned the attack, and Carolyn hadn't, made him wonder. But he had, perhaps, controlled the conversation too much with Carolyn. Maybe she hadn't really had the opportunity to mention it. Or maybe she didn't read the paper.

"Since someone was killed, I would hardly call it nothing serious," Meredith said.

Though she was somewhat sullen, McCall liked what he saw in Meredith. She had inherited her mother's beauty, had an excellent figure and carried herself well.

He laughed. "If I had been the one killed, then it would have been serious."

"You've obviously been around so much death, Mr. McCall, that it doesn't bother you," Meredith responded.

Melanie said, "Meredith, you shouldn't say . . . "

McCall interrupted. "Death bothers me, especially the deaths of innocents. But when it comes to murderers, or those who attempt it, I'm not adverse to an eye for an eye. For example, whoever it was that murdered the three women who were patients of your father, I would have no qualms about the same type justice being meted out to him."

Meredith showed no surprise at his mention of the three victims being patients of her father, which indicted that Summerfield, or Melanie, had told her. She certainly hadn't read it in the paper. Haloran had asked him to keep it under wraps, so he hadn't reported it.

"I had no doubts that you were an advocate of capital punishment," she said.

"I've never tried to hide it," he said.

"Do you really think executing a murderer keeps someone else from committing murder?" she asked.

"Yeah, I think the threat of capital punishment keeps some criminals from killing," he said. "And it sure as hell keeps those who are executed from committing more murders."

She finally smiled. "Well, there's no arguing with that logic."

"Crimes of passion, though, are different," he admitted. "I don't think those who kill out of passion give any thought to whether we have capital punishment. But the criminal who robs a store or bank, I really believe that he might hesitate to pull the trigger if he knows he's likely to be caught and executed."

"So, you think the person who kills in a fit of passion ought to receive more leniency from the court than someone who kills in the act of committing another crime?" she asked.

"Not at all," he answered. "You asked if I thought capital punishment was a deterrent to murder. I just told you the conditions under which it might be. Personally, I'm an advocate of fitting the punishment to the crime."

"Which gets back to an eye for an eye," she said.

"That's right," he agreed. "If someone steals something, they can give it back, pay it back, whatever. But if someone takes a life, that's something that can't be given back. There's a big difference between material possessions and human life."

"You took a life the other night."

"In self defense."

"If you had wanted, couldn't you have subdued that man without killing him?"

"I don't know. It was a risk I wasn't willing to take."

"My, my," Melanie said, "this conversation is getting too serious. Can't we talk about something more pleasant?"

"This is the kind of stuff Mr. McCall knows about," Meredith replied. "I'm sure he doesn't object to talking about it."

He laughed. "I know a little about a few other subjects, too, but the conversation's fine with me."

"Have you found out anything more about Colette's murder?" Melanie asked.

"There's been no progress to speak of," he answered.

"Maybe there's been no progress, because you're looking in the wrong places," Meredith said.

"Obviously," he replied. "I'd welcome any suggestions as to the right places. Where do you think I should look?"

His reply caught her off guard. "I have no idea," she stammered.

He pressed on, "I'm not so sure it's a matter of looking in the wrong places. I think it's a matter of getting more cooperation from the persons who knew the victims."

"Speaking for myself," Melanie said, "there's nothing I know that I haven't told you about Colette."

Oh, yes there is, he thought. You haven't told me that you know she was having an affair with your husband. But I can't really blame you for that.

"How about you?" he asked Meredith. "Is there anything you could tell me about Colette Ramsey? Anything about her friends?"

"I'm sure my mother has told you everything I would know," was the reply. "I don't think I ever really knew Colette. I felt much closer to Clark."

"Any reason for you to think that Ramsey would want his wife out of the way?"

"That's ridiculous. Clark couldn't kill anyone."

"Maybe he was jealous," McCall said. "Maybe Colette had another man in her life."

McCall could see the fear his statement brought to Melanie's eyes. But Meredith's eyes were expressionless, like a shark's. In the short time he had observed her, McCall got the idea that she was much like her brother, with the cold ability to do whatever necessary to achieve her own ends.

"If Colette was running around, I don't think Clark knew it," Meredith said. "But if he had found out that she was, he's too kind a man to have hurt her."

McCall wondered if this was the same Clark Ramsey he knew. It certainly didn't sound like him.

"But to your knowledge, Colette was not running around? Is that right?"

"I hardly ever saw the woman," Meredith answered. "After she and Clark separated, I saw her only at the country club."

The waiter brought their food and they ate, abandoning the more serious conversation for talk about the weather and some of San Antonio's upcoming events. They were almost finished when he saw that Carolyn and Betty were making their way from the back of the restaurant. When the two women were even with their table, he stopped them.

"Carolyn, I don't know whether you know Dr. Summerfield's wife and daughter."

Carolyn, shocked and ashen-faced, said she had not had the pleasure. After introductions all around, Carolyn and Betty left.

"She's a pretty lady," Melanie said, referring to Carolyn. "Is she one of your lady friends, Matt?"

"She's married."

"Oh, do you have an aversion to married women?"

Meredith asked.

"No, I just have an aversion to their husbands."

After lunch, he suggested they retire to the bar for a couple of drinks. Melanie's willingness overcame Meredith's objections.

As soon as they had given their drink orders, Melanie said, "I have to go to the ladies room. Do you want to go with me, Meredith?"

The younger woman answered in the negative, and Melanie left.

"I think your mother is interested in us getting together," McCall said.

"She's a real looney-tunes if she thinks I could get interested in you," Meredith replied.

He laughed. "I'm that bad, huh?"

"Mr. McCall, you're the biggest piece of shit I know."

"Has daddy been telling you lies about me?"

"Daddy has told me about your harrassment," she replied.

"Well, if daddy's against me, I guess that shoots me down as far as you're concerned."

"You would have been shot down even if daddy hadn't said anything."

"Why's that?"

"You just would have been, that's all."

"You know, Meredith, there's a lot of talk about you and daddy. With the attitude you have toward me, I might start believing it."

"I don't give a damn what you believe," she said. Then she added something that shocked even him. "I will fuck you, if you'll leave daddy alone."

"I don't need any that bad," he said. "I guess you'd do just about anything for daddy, though. Even kill."

"I do love my father," she replied, "but I didn't kill that bitch, or the others. I'm glad she's dead, though."

"I assume you're talking about Colette Ramsey?"

She nodded her head in the affirmative. "I know about my father's women, and I can forgive him because of my mother. She's too busy being a social butterfly to give him what he needs."

"If you don't care about your father's women, what's with this hatred for Colette Ramsey?"

She laughed. "I love Clark, stupid. There's never been anyone but Clark for me. Now that she's dead, Clark can marry me."

Chapter 25

With Meredith's revelation that Clark Ramsey was her lover, McCall was forced to go back to square one in his quest to identify the bathtub murderer. The new information called for reevaluating some of the players.

Meredith, herself, became an even more viable suspect. Her unsolicited comments about not being able to stand the sight of blood, and knowing nothing about anatomy, were the result of a conversation with her father regarding McCall. There was good reason to suspect the truth of those statements.

But if she wanted Ramsey, what better way to get him than to kill his wife? Which still left some big questions. Such as, why she would feel the need to also kill Velda Rose Caldwell and Maggie Burleson? Was Meredith capable of planning such a scheme, the killing of two innocents in order to cover the real motive for murder? And if so, why Maggie and Velda Rose?

The more he thought about it, the more convinced McCall became that Meredith could not be the killer. Had there been only the murder of Colette Ramsey, yes, she would be a prime suspect. But the murders of the other two women made her only a remote possibility.

Unless, of course, she had help. What if Clark had planned the whole thing? Perhaps there were two murderers, not just one. That would explain how the victims had been overpowered, seemingly without struggle, and placed in their bathtubs.

But there still remained the question, why Maggie and Velda Rose? If two women were going to be killed to cover the real motive behind Colette Ramsey's death, why, of all the women in San Antonio who could have been selected, these two?

No matter how he analyzed it, it kept coming back to Norris Summerfield. The primary victim may have been Colette Ramsey, but the deaths of two, possibly all three, was the result of a connection with Summerfield.

Which certainly didn't rule out Meredith and Ramsey.

In spite of Meredith's declaration that she didn't blame Summerfield for his womanizing, McCall had, with further questioning, discovered that an unhealthy relationship existed between father and daughter. Meredith had, in fact, been quite blatant in telling him that she had slept with her father, that she still did on occasion.

Meredith also told McCall that her father was aware of her relationship with Ramsey, that he had encouraged it. She said Ramsey did not know about the sexual relationship she had with her father, a relationship that would continue even when she and Clark married.

If daddy needed her, she wasn't going to cut him off.

McCall figured that, in spite of statements to the contrary, Meredith's jealousy for her father's affection could be the reason Velda Rose and Maggie had been selected to die. That is, if Meredith had anything to do with the murders. Her sexual strangeness didn't necessarily make her a killer.

And what about Ramsey? McCall had never doubted that the man was capable of planning and carrying out the murder of his wife. But why would he have chosen Maggie and Velda Rose to cover the real motive for Colette's murder? The only explanation was that Meredith was his accomplice, that she had selected them because of their suspected relationship with her father.

But what if the killer wanted to throw suspicion on Summerfield for the murders? That wouldn't be Meredith, of course, but what better way to direct suspicion than for all three victims to be patients of Summerfield?

Norris, Jr., wouldn't be beyond framing his father for murder. He was as strange as his sister, and he had given every indication that he would like to avenge his father's treatment of his mother. McCall's problem with Norris, Jr., was that he hadn't been able to find evidence to put the younger Summerfield in San Antonio at the time of any of the murders.

As for Dr Summerfield, himself, he wasn't the brightest guy around. But he probably considered himself brilliant enough to commit murder and get away with it. But McCall figured the doctor's self-image and arrogance made him a prime suspect.

But he couldn't really see Summerfield killing a beautiful woman. For him, they were collector items.

As for Melanie, there was no way she was going to kill anyone without help. He couldn't definitely say that she hadn't gotten that help, but from whom? Maybe Norris, Jr.? Mother and son would make a good murder duo. The paper's management would love it if Melanie and Norris, Jr., were in cahoots. Talk about some banner headlines.

He kept remembering snatches of his conversation with

Meredith. Melanie had returned from the ladies room to interrupt some of their more serious dialogue, but had stayed at the bar for only one drink. She had then excused herself, and asked McCall if he would mind giving Meredith a ride to her townhouse. He agreed to do so and was surprised that Meredith didn't object to the arrangement.

He and Meredith had a few more drinks, talked some more about her relationship with her father and Ramsey, then he took her home.

Maybe it was the drinks, maybe it was the fact that she'd had the opportunity to talk about her situation; whatever, her attitude toward him had warmed considerably. She invited him in for a drink.

As much as anything else, he was attracted to what he considered her *strangeness.* He had never been that familiar with products of incest, and especially with one who seemed to enjoy it so much. She was quite open and descriptive about sexual encounters with her father, a fact that he found both disgusting and fascinating.

She also told him about her sexual relationship with Ramsey, which she indicated wasn't on par with what she enjoyed with her father. However, she said her father had told her it was time that she married and got on with her life. And Clark, her father said, was a good man, one who could provide her with all the creature comforts she desired. As for Colette, Ramsey was going to divorce her anyway.

As he was about to leave, she told him to wait for just a few minutes. She went into what he assumed was the bedroom, while he stood impatiently at the small bar just off the kitchen. When she returned, she was wearing only a pair of bikini panties.

She was beautiful and desirable. The dress she had been wearing had been hiding a goddess-like figure, perfectly shaped tits and legs.

He was the first to admit that he liked a little *strange* stuff now and then, and there Meredith was for the taking. But this chick was *too* strange for him.

He had left her standing there.

Chapter 26

Saturday, June 27, 10 a.m.

McCall didn't figure Clark Ramsey was going to enjoy talking about his relationship with Meredith Summerfield. He certainly couldn't expect the same candor from Ramsey that he had gotten from Meredith.

However, when he called Ramsey for an appointment, the district attorney was cordial enough. Of course, McCall didn't reveal that he knew about Meredith, only that he had uncovered some new information that possibly related to the murders.

And since Ramsey was cordial, McCall surmised that Meredith had not told her lover that she had spilled her guts to a reporter, especially one the D.A. considered an enemy. But then, McCall figured there was a lot Meredith did not tell Ramsey.

He was greeted at the door of the Ramsey home by a

Mexican maid, who escorted him through lavish furnishings to the patio and swimming area. Ramsey was sitting at a table near the pool, a cup of coffee in front of him, thumbing through the newspaper.

He motioned for McCall to sit and said, "It's such a beautiful day, I thought we might talk out here. Would you like a cup of coffee?"

McCall nodded in the affirmative, Ramsey gave the maid some unspoken signal, and another cup of coffee was quickly on the table. There was even a package of Sweet 'n Low, a subtle reminder that Ramsey knew his adversary well.

McCall doctored his coffee and thought Ramsey's observation about the day could not be disputed. The sun was shining brightly, the temperature was just a notch above eighty, and there was a slight breeze from the south. It was a perfect day.

"You said you had some information that might relate to the murders," the D.A. began.

Usually, McCall didn't like to meet an adversary on his own turf, but on this occasion he had actually suggested Ramsey's home as a site for their meeting. He hoped familiar surroundings would put the D.A. at ease, make him more susceptible to a verbal mistake.

"Well, the information I have isn't going to be all that much of a surprise to you," McCall said.

Ramsey tensed up. "Why's that?"

McCall didn't answer directly. "You know, Clark, when you asked me to work with you on these murders, I agreed to cooperate if you'd be straight with me. Now I find you haven't been, so I'm thinking you've tried to play some bullshit game with me."

"I don't know what you're talking about, McCall, but I was being honest in asking for your help."

McCall laughed. "I have a little trouble believing that you're capable of honesty, but, be that as it may, when I asked you about your relationship with your wife, you indicated that you were interested in a reconcilation. I now find that you've been playing house with Meredith Summerfield and that you were anxious to get a divorce from Colette."

"That's not true," he stammered.

"What's not true?"

"None of it's true."

"Oh, c'mon, Clark. Meredith unloaded on me. I know all about you and Dr. Summerfield's daughter."

It was not the summer morning that brought the pink to Ramsey's face. "Damn it, McCall. I'm telling you there's nothing to your accusation."

"For god's sake, Clark, are you going to sit there and lie to me about tapping Meredith Summerfield? She looks like pretty damn good stuff to me. I'd think you'd be proud that she'd fuck an old fart like you."

"You have a disgusting mouth and mind, McCall."

"Maybe so, but I'm wise to you, asshole. Meredith told me all the sordid details, so do you want me to go back and tell her that you said it's all a lie?"

"The bitch," Ramsey rasped.

"Look, Clark, I don't care who you fuck, just so it's not me. Level with me and everything's going to be okay between us. But if you try to fuck me around, you've got more trouble than you bargained for."

"One of your famous threats, McCall?"

He sighed. "You're always accusing me of making threats. I don't make threats. When I tell you something, it's gospel."

Ramsey shrugged his shoulders. "Whatever's between Meredith and me has nothing to do with the murders. And I was trying to reconcile things with Colette. I wanted her back."

"Funny, Meredith thinks you two are on the verge of sharing wedded bliss."

This time Ramsey sighed. "I know. But I swear to you, McCall, I've never mentioned marriage to Meredith."

"She got the idea somewhere."

Ramsey tried to defend himself. "You know how it is McCall. When you're making love to a woman, you can say a lot of things that she might misunderstand."

"Yeah, it's tough to be honest when all you want is a piece of ass," McCall sarcastically replied.

"There's no point in me lying about seeing Meredith once in a while," Ramsey crawfished, "but I can assure you that if Colette had come back, the situation with Meredith would have ended. I certainly had no intention of divorcing Colette to marry Meredith. If anyone wanted a divorce, it was Colette."

"What about now?"

"You mean in terms of marrying Meredith?"

"That's what I mean."

"It's not going to happen," Ramsey said. "You've been with Meredith and she obviously told you a lot more than she should. A marriage to Meredith would probably destroy any chance I have for political office."

"Oh, I doubt that it would destroy your chances, Clark. With the Democratic Party behind you, you always have a chance in Texas. Of course, that's the real rub, isn't it? Colette's father is one of the real powers in the Party. And he probably wouldn't think it wise for you to marry a woman as young as Meredith."

"You underestimate me, McCall. If I wanted to marry Meredith, I'd do it, Party be damned."

"Well, it's probably fortunate for you that you don't want to marry her. Of course, I think it's fortunate for her, too."

"Always have to get in a shot, don't you?"

McCall laughed. "You're lucky I'm so tactful, Clark. I also appreciate the information that you aspire to higher political office."

"I didn't say that."

"C'mon, damn it. You know you want to be governor. And if you didn't, I think you might be more interested in Meredith. Boy, I can see the both of you in Austin. What a pair."

Ramsey grunted disgustedly. "You can twist damn near anything to meet your own needs."

"It's not me who *needs* something."

"Maybe I don't have the right to ask this, McCall, but I'm going to ask it anyway. I would appreciate it if Melanie and Norris Summerfield didn't hear about Meredith and me from you."

McCall laughed. "Hear it from me? Hell, Summerfield knows about you and his daughter. From what Meredith told me, he has encouraged her to become the new Mrs. Ramsey. Of course, Melanie doesn't know, and I'm sure as hell not going to tell her."

McCall thought Ramsey looked a bit disturbed at the news that his golfing buddy knew he had been banging his daughter. But McCall wasn't about to let up. He teased, "Hey, don't take it so hard, Clark. You should be pleased Norris wants you for a son-in-law.

"By the way, which of you is oldest? I hope it's not you, because it wouldn't be right for you to be older than your father-in-law."

McCall's taunting infuriated Ramsey, but he showed surprising control.

"I know you're trying to rile me, but you might as well forget it," the D.A. said. "Besides, I don't know why in the hell you think this alleged situation between Meredith and me might have something to do with the murders."

McCall looked incredulous. "You have to be kidding, Clark. If you and Meredith have something hot and heavy going, it's motive for murder. Maybe Meredith didn't want to wait to see if Colette was going to divorce you. Maybe she took matters into her own hands."

Now Ramsey laughed. "You can't possibly believe that, not after having met Meredith."

"Okay, maybe I don't believe it," he agreed, "but I can't discount it as a possibility. And you wouldn't either, if you were being objective about your wife's murder."

"I'm being objective," Ramsey argued. "But I've been a student of human nature long enough to know that Meredith isn't capable of murder. And she's certainly not capable of three murders."

"Maybe not by herself."

"What does that mean?"

"It means you could have been her accomplice, Clark."

"Let's not get so far afield, McCall. You obviously don't have anything, so you're just wasting my time."

"Alright, Clark, let's just suppose that you're lying to me about Meredith, that you wanted to marry her and couldn't with Colette in the way."

"If that was the case, I probably wouldn't have had any trouble getting a divorce from Colette. So, why would I need to kill her?"

"I dunno, except that you're kind of strange. In fact, you might be as strange as Meredith, only it doesn't show as much. My guess would be, though, that you might think Colette's being murdered would help your politcal career. Whereas, a divorce might sound a death knell for it."

"That makes no sense," Ramsey said.

"Oh, yes, it does. If Colette is murdered, Colette's father is going to be a lot more sympathetic to you than if you divorce her. And since he's the big gun in the Democratic Party, you need his sympathy and support. And you can't tell me you haven't thought of that."

"It wouldn't do any good to tell you, but Colette's father's attitude toward me is the farthest thing from my mind. I told you I loved Colette, so don't try to make me an accomplice to her murder."

"I'm only being hypothetical," McCall pleaded with

mock earnestness. "I'm saying that you could have been the brains behind the slayings, making it look as though some maniac was out killing women indiscriminately."

"You can't believe that."

"I didn't say I did, only that it was a possibility. And right now I'm not ruling out any possibility."

"So, why couldn't Meredith have an accomplice other than me?" Ramsey asked.

"I was about to bring that up," McCall replied. "She could have solicited the help of her brother, father or mother. For that matter, all three."

Ramsey laughed. "What an imagination."

McCall grinned. "Hey, I admit that I'm tossing out some far-out stuff, but my imagination is eventually going to find the one little thing that leads to the killer. Sure, I play a lot of mental games, whereas you obviously only play with yourself. If you weren't playing with yourself, you would at least have run some of these things through your mind."

"My mind's too logical for the kind of bullshit you're tossing out, McCall."

"Sometimes I think your brain cells have turned to shit, Clark. For instance, a minute or two ago you said you were a student of human nature, so you know Meredith couldn't be the murderer. If you think you're smart enough to determine who is and isn't capable of murder, your elevator isn't running all the way to the top."

"Maybe you misunderstood me, which you often do. When I said Meredith couldn't be the murderer, I was taking a lot of factors into consideration."

"I can accept that," McCall said, "if you were with her during the time any of the murders were committed. Because there's absolutely no doubt the same person murdered all three victims."

"Oh, I see," Ramsey said. "You want me to give her an alibi. But if I say I was with her, then you'll try to connect the two of us as being accomplices in the murders."

"I'm beginning to like the way you think, Clark. If you could help me pin these murders on you, I'd certainly appreciate it. It would be the only decent thing you'd ever done for the public."

Ramsey laughed. "Your biggest problem, McCall, is that you don't know how much power I've got. If I was guilty of something, do you think the police or sheriff's department would come after me? There's really not anyone in law enforcement here who has the balls to take me on."

"That's sad, but true," McCall admitted. "But if you're guilty of something, and I can prove it, I have a vehicle that's not afraid to take you on."

Ramsey nodded agreement. "I know, which is why I'm trying to be straight with you. I know I can never get your political support, but I can get the support of some people who work for the paper. And that kind of support is important to me."

"Do you want me to tell some of your supporters at the paper that you plan to run for governor?"

"If you tell anyone, I'll deny it."

"You're good at denying damn near everything."

"At least we understand each other, McCall."

McCall laughed. "I'll not argue that."

"Obviously, your only purpose in coming here today was to make me aware that you know about me and Meredith," Ramsey said. "The girl didn't use good judgment in talking to you, which I'll try to get across to her. I doubt that there'll be any reason for you to see her again."

"I'd think that will be up to her."

Ramsey smiled. "Not really. I'm sure she'll listen to my reasoning and do exactly as I say."

"If that's the case, I wish I'd met her before she met you. I've never met a woman who could follow directions."

"Maybe you don't give good directions."

"Maybe all the women I know are headstrong."

"Anyway," Ramsey said, "I hope I've satisfied your

curiosity, and that you'll spend your time and thought on something more productive than trying to tie Meredith and me . . . any of the Summerfields for that matter . . . into the murders."

"Of course, you know that I'm going to do whatever you say, Clark, because my whole purpose in life is to please you."

Ramsey laughed. "I'm just trying to keep you from wasting your time."

"I enjoy wasting time, especially if there's a chance in hell of nailing you on something. As for the Summerfields, it's kind of hard to ignore that your wife and the other two victims were patients of Dr. Summerfield."

"That was one of the first things Norris told me," Ramsey said.

"Funny that you didn't bother to tell the police what he told you."

"It didn't seem important, and I didn't want Norris bothered."

"The one consistent thing about you, Clark, is that you think the law applies to everyone other than you and your friends. If some doctor you didn't know told you three murder victims had been his patients, you'd have been on that information like ugly on an ape. You'd have probably called a press conference to tell everyone what you'd discovered."

"Only if I thought it had some direct bearing on the case," Ramsey argued.

"Bullshit. With you, the law has never applied equally to everyone."

"Think what you will, McCall, but if you're through playing your little game, I have a lot to do today."

McCall got up from his chair and said, "Thanks for the coffee. I'm sure if you come across any worthwhile information, you'll call me."

Ramsey answered, "Just like you'll call me."

The maid reappeared, seemingly from out of nowhere. She led McCall back through the house to the front door.

Driving away from Ramsey's place, Willie Nelson whining from the radio, his mind recycled the meeting with the D.A. It was not so much what was said that bothered him, but what was left unsaid. McCall wondered why the attack on he and Lisa hadn't been mentioned. Certainly, Ramsey was aware of it. He probably read the newspaper account and the police report.

Maybe I didn't give him a chance to bring it up, McCall thought. Or, maybe he's the one who sent the assassins. The police still hadn't been able to come up with identities on the two assailants who escaped the scene, and McCall doubted that they ever would. He and Lisa had poured over mug books without success, and so had a couple of witnesses to the attack. The Mexican authorities had also been contacted, but McCall figured that was really pissing into the wind.

McCall also figured Ramsey was now on the phone to Meredith, and that she was catching a lot of hell from her lover. He had already decided, though, that she was flaky enough to handle anything Ramsey could dish out.

He laughed to himself. He had dished out a lot of misery for Ramsey, but thought his effort was probably minor compared to what Meredith was capable of doing to the D.A.'s psyche. She had the temperment of a hurricane unsure of its direction.

And though he had known her for only a short period of time, McCall would not have been surprised to discover that she, not Summerfield, was initially responsible for the incestuous father/daughter relationship.

He suddenly realized that he was tired, that his mind needed some time off to get a different perspective. He wanted to get away from any thoughts of the persons he considered murder suspects, and from everyone he knew.

So, when he came to the Interstate, he headed the car north toward San Marcos. From there, he would drive west to a small cabin he owned near Wimberly, a cabin located on the bank of the river. He figured he could fish, enjoy the solitude, and be back at work on Monday in a different frame of mind.

It was worth a shot.

Chapter 27

Monday, June 29, 11:56 p.m.

Cathy Morris was feeling mellow, very relaxed, when she left the *Cactus Bar and Restaurant.* Overall, it had been a very good day.

At three-forty p.m., her divorce was finalized, and, at five-fifteen p.m., she had joined some friends at the *Cactus* to celebrate her freedom. The party lasted until eleven-thirty, with everyone finally leaving the bar on the tipsy side.

Cathy had been one of the last to leave, escorted to her car by a married male co-worker with one thing on his mind. In her car, she had half-heartedly resisted his efforts to remove her pantyhose and panties, then struggled a bit harder when he tried to penetrate her. When she did give in, he had been so excited that he was unable to control himself. The sexual act had lasted less than a minute.

Now, after a night of drinking and nothing to eat but

munchies, she was hungry. She thought about going to a restaurant for bacon and eggs, but instead decided to pick something up at a Seven-Eleven. She thought she might like a pizza, which would take very little time to fix in the microwave.

By the time she finished shopping, it was half past midnight, and she was dreading the thought of getting up at six-thirty to get ready for work. She felt somewhat amused that the divorce had been finalized, then became melancholy about her ex-husband Dave.

It wasn't that Dave was a bad man that had caused their differences. In truth, she doubted that she could find a better, more understanding husband. But there wasn't any romance in him. He was content with a life of dull sameness, and she didn't want to squander all her youth doing nothing.

Cathy had married Dave when she was twenty-one and he was twenty-seven. Now she had crossed the thirty mark, they had no children, and Dave was mired in the same thankless county job in which there was no future. She had become a secretary, a title and position she detested, in order for them to acquire some of the better things in life.

And they had lived well enough, nice house and two nice cars. For Dave, that was enough, but she wanted more. She wanted to travel, but he hated spending money, especially if it meant going in debt.

So their incompatability grew, and she finally just walked out, got herself an apartment and started enjoying life, making the clubs and meeting new and exciting people.

Of course, there was a man, too. If it hadn't been for him, she realized she probably wouldn't have had the courage to walk out on Dave.

Her lover had been good to her, provided enough money to help her over the rough spots. And she liked the fact that he wasn't demanding.

Of course, when he wanted her, he wanted her. But when he couldn't be around, he didn't object to her seeing other men. She liked that kind of freedom, the freedom to make it with someone as she had after the party.

However, thinking about her most recent experience annoyed her. The guy had dumped his sperm in her without providing a bit of satisfaction. When he looks at me in the morning, he'll be redfaced, she thought. What an asshole.

A lot was going on in Cathy's head while she loaded the groceries in her car, and while she was driving to her apartment.

After parking in her assigned place, she put the strap of her purse over her shoulder and hoisted a sack of groceries in each arm. She shook her blonde hair as she went up the stairs, enjoying the exhiliration of her newfound freedom.

She had no remembrance of not locking the window adjacent to the front door, so there was no thought that an intruder might have entered the apartment. Cathy, in fact, felt so good that she could hardly contain herself. Life was just beginning.

It ended when she undressed and walked into the bathroom.

Chapter 28

The jangling of the telephone interrupted McCall's dream about a gently moving stream and a bass the size of a locomotive that was about to attack his lure. The caller was Bill Haloran.

"I knew that you'd want to know that the killer struck again," the detective said.

McCall looked at the clock radio beside his bed. It was three-forty a.m. "When did it happen?" he asked.

"No more than a couple of hours ago. We got an anonymous call."

"Man or woman?"

"The guy who took the call couldn't tell."

"Everything the same?"

"Carbon copy."

"I thought it was over."

"So did I," Haloran said, "but I guess that's what I get for thinking."

"Are you at the victim's house?"

"Yeah, only it's an apartment."

"Single woman?"

"Yep, a divorcee. And here's the ironic part, she had her divorce papers in her purse. She got her divorce yesterday."

"Are you going to question the ex-husband?"

"Of course. Under any other circumstances, he'd be a prime suspect, but you and I already know it's not him."

"You know what I'm going to ask, don't you?"

"I sure do. And yes, she was one of Summerfield's patients. Going through her papers, we found where her insurance company had made payments to him."

"I knew it."

"We gotta get some help from this guy," Haloran said. "Even if he's not guilty of anything, he has to know something that will help us."

"My guess is that he was seeing this chick, which is why she's dead. But you know he's going to deny it. He's never admitted to a relationship with Colette Ramsey or Maggie Burleson."

"And he didn't have one with Velda Rose Caldwell," Haloran injected.

"But the killer didn't know that. The killer thought he was popping Velda."

"What I hate about this is that we're going to have to go over all the same ground again. Same old people, same old questions."

"Yeah, but the first time we missed something along the way. Maybe we'll be lucky this time."

"I hope so. I don't know why, but I have a bad feeling the killer has cranked up again, that this isn't the only homicide we're going to be investigating over the next few days."

"I wish I could say you're wrong, Bill, but chances are

pretty good that you're right. Do you want to meet at the diner and get a little breakfast?"

"Sure, but you'll have to give me about an hour and a half."

"Done. Why don't we make it about five-thirty?"

After Haloran got off the phone, McCall rang Lisa's number. There was no answer. Strange, he thought. Maybe she's found someone else's bed. He didn't believe it, though.

He called again following a shower and shave. This time she answered.

"I called about thirty minutes ago and didn't get an answer," he informed her.

"I wasn't home, she replied.

"Well, there's been another murder, and I was going to suggest that you join Haloran and me at the diner, but I suppose you're pretty tired."

"Not at all. What time do you want me there?"

"I could come by and pick you up."

"That's not necessary," she said. "I'll need my own car, so I can drive down and meet you."

"Suit yourself. We're going to meet at five-thirty."

McCall arrived at the diner at five-ten, scanned the newspaper and had two cups of coffee while waiting. He agreed with a sportswriter on the pennant chances of the Houston Astros, which the scribe forcasted as "slim to none."

He mentally lamented the lack of commitment of modern major leaguers, wondered if there would ever again be players like Ted Williams, Stan Musial, Joe DiMaggio, Mickey Mantle and Willie Mays. And would there ever again be a team to compare with any of the great Yankee clubs?

Haloran arrived first, Lisa no more than a minute behind him. As soon as they all ordered breakfast, McCall said, "Okay, Bill, details."

"The gal's name is Cathy Morris," Haloran began. "She's thirty, divorced yesterday. Like I told you, we found the papers in her purse. She works for a computer company.

"Even while we're sitting here, her ex-husband is making a statement down at the station. But from what little I know at this point, he hadn't even seen her for four months. And since this one is identical to the other three, I don't think there's a chance in hell that he killed his wife."

"No medical background, huh?" McCall asked.

"The man's a county auditor. I doubt that he knows anything about the medical profession, but you never know. With these murders, I'm not taking anything for granted."

"You said, Bill, that the killer called the station and reported the murder."

"I said someone called," the detective corrected. "I assume it was the killer. But again, you never know."

"I'd think it was the killer, too," McCall reasoned. "But I am curious as to why the killer wanted you to find the body so quickly. There were no calls about Velda Rose Caldwell and Maggie Burleson, but the killer was so anxious for you to find Colette Ramsey's body that he called. And now, he calls about Cathy Morris."

"Don't ask me to explain the criminal mind, especially on so little sleep," Haloran pleaded.

"How did the killer get in the victim's apartment?"

"An open window. We think the killer was in the apartment when the victim got home. The way it looks, Mrs. Morris came in and set some groceries on the kitchen table, put a pizza in the microwave, then went to her bedroom and undressed. When she walked in the bathroom, the killer was waiting."

"I don't suppose she was raped, either?"

"I dunno," Haloran said. "We haven't gotten anything from the medical examiner yet."

"And of course, you haven't had a chance to question any

of her co-workers?"

"When they get to work this morning, my men will be waiting," Haloran assured.

Breakfast arrived, and they began eating. It was Haloran who said, "You're awful quiet this morning, Lisa."

"There's not much to say," she replied. "I'm just taking in all the questions and answers."

"She's tired," McCall said. "She's been up all night."

She didn't respond, just acted as though she was totally occupied with her breakfast. McCall couldn't figure what was wrong, but decided he wouldn't let it worry him. If she wanted to tell him something, she would.

"What about Summerfield?"

"I'm having his ass hauled down before he has his breakfast," Haloran replied.

"Good for you, Bill. You know, though, that he's going to call his good friend Clark Ramsey."

"I don't give a shit. The man's got to be questioned and that's that."

"Cathy Morris was one of Dr. Summerfield's patients?" Lisa asked.

"Yep, just like the other three victims," Haloran confirmed.

"I hope you get more out of him than you did last time," McCall said.

"I intend to," was the response.

After breakfast, McCall and Lisa went to the *Tribune* newsroom to plan editorial coverage of the murder, and Haloran went back to the police station.

It didn't take McCall long to decide on an editorial strategy. Once that was done, there was the usual detail work about the victim, crime scene and so on. Lisa had, in a short time, become very proficient in obtaining details, so he left a lot of the work to her.

Haloran called at eight-ten and told McCall that Summerfield had been uncooperative, that he had learned absolutely nothing from the doctor. Summerfield had denied any kind of personal relationship with Cathy Morris.

McCall got pissed off just thinking about the pompous Summerfield, so he called the doctor's office and got LeAnne Bevins on the line. "I can't talk now," she whispered.

"Lunch?" he asked.

"Lunch," she agreed.

They set up their rendezvous for eleven-thirty at a small Mexican cafe two blocks from the doctor's office.

At ten-thirty, Haloran called again. "The coroner found evidence of sperm," he said.

"That doesn't sound right," McCall responded. "I don't peg our killer as a rapist. If he was, he'd have done the other three victims, too."

Haloran laughed. "Just testing you. We've already found out that Cathy had a little after leaving the Cactus Bar last night."

"Not Summerfield?"

"No, one of her married co-workers," the detective answered. "He didn't want to tell, but we damn near scared the shit out of him."

"So, Cathy wasn't adverse to spreading her ass around a little bit," McCall said. "That still doesn't mean Summerfield wasn't tapping her."

"No," Haloran agreed, "but at least this guy has admitted to having sex with her. Summerfield hasn't."

"Where did this lovemaking take place?"

"In her car."

"Hey, what are we dealing with here, high school stuff?"

"Seems that Cathy and a bunch of her co-workers and friends were having a party to celebrate her divorce. They all got pretty drunk, and, after the party, this guy walked her to the car."

"Why is it I never meet any easy women?" McCall jokingly asked.

"I thought they were all easy for you."

"Dream on."

"Anyway," Haloran continued, "this guy's a classic case of being in the wrong place at the wrong time. I imagine it will be a cold day in hell before he cheats on his wife again. Do you want his name?"

"Sure, but I'm not going to use it. Just give me all the poop you got on Cathy's co-workers for my file."

Haloran gave him a brief summation of the persons who had seen Cathy the evening prior to her death. The police had done a good job of piecing together her activities for the entire day.

As soon as Haloran got off the phone, he called Annie Cossey. After he told her about the murder, she told him as many details as she rememberd about the party at the *Cactus* the night before.

No, Summerfield did not show up. Bill Harrison, the guy who had taken Cathy to her car, was a regular at the bar. He was harmless, always trying to make it with some single chick. Most laughed at him, told him to go home to his wife.

Annie's information pretty well substantiated what he had gotten from Bill.

At eleven-thirty he met LeAnne for lunch.

"I know this has to be business," she said. "Otherwise, you wouldn't call."

"C'mon, LeAnne, that's not true. You act like I don't enjoy being with you."

"Well, if you enjoy it so much, why don't we spend more time together?"

"Hell, I've been snowed under lately."

She laughed. "Maybe with other women, not with work."

"I didn't realize we were going steady."

"I don't ask for steady," she said, "just a little steadier."

He laughed. "To tell the truth, I was going to ask you to spend next weekend with me at my cabin in Wimberly."

"You've got a deal. Now, no more bullshit. What do you want?"

"I want to know if Summerfield has been shacking with a woman named Cathy Morris."

She laughed. "I knew it, I knew damn well that's why you called me. The minute I heard on the radio that Cathy Morris had been murdered, I knew you'd be calling."

"That not the only reason," he pleaded. "Aren't you enjoying your lunch?"

"Of course, I'm enjoying my lunch. But what's that have to do with anything?"

"Maybe I did want some information, but I wanted to have lunch with you, too."

She sighed. "You're no damn good, you know that?"

"Yeah," he drawled with a smile. "But isn't that why you like me?"

She shook her head in resignation. "The way I hear it, Norris helped finance Cathy Morris' divorce."

"He gave her money?"

"Oh, he gave her money okay, but it didn't come out of his pocket. He just billed her insurance company for a lot of medical treatment that she didn't get. She got enough money from the scam for an apartment, new clothes, legal fees and I don't know what else. And Dr. Summerfield made a little, too."

"You're wonderful," McCall said. "Even if Summerfield's not guilty of murder, I can get him on insurance fraud."

She moaned. "He's not stupid, Matt. He covered his tracks pretty well."

"With your help, baby, we can get him."

"My help," she exclaimed. "Don't drag my ass into

this mess."

"Damn, here's your chance to be a celebrity, and you're crawfishing on me."

She laughed. "I don't want to be a celebrity."

"Suit yourself. But anyway, you think Cathy Morris and Summerfield had something going?"

"The way I understand it," LeAnne replied, "she was Colette Ramsey's replacement."

Chapter 29

The more McCall thought about Dr. Norris Summerfield, the more angry he became. He was angered by the man's insensitivity, by his unwillingness to cooperate in the effort to find a killer.

From the time LeAnne had told him that Cathy Morris was the doctor's replacement for Colette Ramsey, McCall had been seething. Then, when he got back to the *Tribune,* Arturo Garza told him something that further intensified his rage.

Garza was a young reporter who often penetrated the illegal alien network, passed himself off as being fresh from Mexico. McCall had asked him to investigate the recent attack on Lisa and himself. He was not so interested in who the attackers were, but in who had sent them.

Garza had done his work well. He had located the two

remaining attackers, both of whom were now back in Mexico. Attempting to detain them for the police could have put Garza's cover and life in jeopardy, so he was forced to play a different game.

He befriended the attackers, gained their confidence. They told him about the man who paid them to kill the gringo reporter. They didn't know the man's name, of course, but the description given to Garza matched that of Dr. Norris Summerfield.

McCall knew that without the testimony of the two assailants, Summerfield would forever remain in the clear. And the chance of the police eventually getting the two was unlikely. But it really didn't matter. This was something he wanted to handle himself.

By the time he reached Summerfield's office, he was under control. He was cool, dispassionate.

He didn't allow LeAnne to announce him, but walked right into an examining room where Summerfield was checking a woman, a nurse looking on. Summerfield tried to utter a protest, but was interrupted by McCall's, "I've got to talk to you, doctor. Now."

Summerfield didn't really offer much resistance as McCall pushed him into an adjacent room and closed the door. He was, perhaps, too surprised by the sudden intrusion.

Once he had regained his composure, however, he started back out the door with the threat, "This time you've gone too far, McCall. This time you go to jail."

"If you touch that doorknob, sonofabitch, I'll castrate you."

Summerfield paused, reading in McCall's face that he meant what he said. "You can't get away with this type thing," the doctor said. "The newspaper can't protect you from the law when you practice this type of intimidation."

"Listen, asshole, and listen good," McCall said. "I'm sure your nurse is calling the police right now. But you might want to tell her to stop, so we can discuss the three guys you paid to kill me."

"I didn't . . ."

"Listen," McCall interrupted. "We don't have a lot of time, so if you want to stop her from making the call, do it now."

McCall stepped away from the door. Summerfield hesitated, then opened the door and went through. He was back in less than a minute.

"McCall, if you think I had anything to do with the attack on you . . ."

"Can the bullshit, Norris. We have the two guys who got away."

Summerfield's face whitened. "Who has them, the police?"

"If the police had them, they would be visiting you, not me."

"Who has them then?"

"The paper."

"I don't believe you. Not that it makes any difference to me, since I don't know anything about the situation."

McCall laughed. "Good try, Norris, but these guys have given us a positive identification of their employer. You should know better. None of the three had a legitimate Social Security card."

"I don't know what you're talking about."

"You know, I really would like to do some serious ass-kicking here, but I'd rather have some information from you."

"What kind of information?"

"Information on the women who were murdered."

"There's nothing I can tell you."

McCall acted as though he was leaving. "Okay, we turn the two Mexicans over to the authorities, and you can explain attempted murder."

Summerfield sighed. "Damn it, McCall, I had nothing to

do with hiring three Mexicans to kill you, but I'm willing to give you any information I can about my patients who were murdered."

"Amazing that you suddenly became cooperative."

"It's just that I don't need any scandals or allegations against me," Summerfield said, "even if they're false. Besides, if you really thought I was guilty of trying to have you killed, you wouldn't let me off so easy."

"Oh, you're guilty alright. It's just that I'm in a benevolent mood. And I'd rather have the killer of the four women than you. I'd rather have you knowing that I'm always going to be looking over your shoulder."

Summerfield emitted an uneasy laugh. "Look all you want. I've got nothing to hide."

"That's good, Norris. Then you've got nothing to worry about."

"Why would I try to have you killed?"

"Now, that's something you might want to talk to your psychiatrist about. Maybe it was because of fear of what I already know and of what I might learn."

"You don't know anything about me."

"I know a lot about you. I know about your sexual relationships with Colette Ramsey, Maggie Burleson and Cathy Morris. I know you wanted a relationship with Velda Rose Caldwell, but were rejected. I even know about your sexual relationship with your own daughter."

"That's not true."

"Which one?"

"None of it's true."

McCall acted as though he was leaving again. "Okay, Norris, if you're not going to be straight with me, we don't have a deal."

"Wait a minute," the doctor said. He sat down in a chair, put his head in his hands and asked, "What do you want?"

"I want to hear you say that you had a relationship with

Colette Ramsey."

"I thought you already knew that."

"I need verification."

"This is off the record, right?"

"Right," McCall answered. "None of this is going to get into print. I'm not interested in hurting the families of any of the victims."

"Okay, I was seeing Colette."

"What about Maggie Burleson?"

"We had something once, but it was over."

"And Cathy Morris?"

"Yeah."

"Velda Rose Caldwell?"

"Nothing," Summerfield replied. "But you're right about me trying."

"Your daughter?"

"That I won't admit, no matter what you do."

"You don't have to. She's already told me."

"She what?"

"Hey, your secret's safe with me, Norris."

"It's not as bad as you think," he said.

"It couldn't be," McCall agreed.

"I guess you no longer consider me a murder suspect?"

"After I met you, found out a few things about you, you were never a serious suspect."

Summerfield indicated surprise, then said, "I'll be honest, McCall. I just don't know what to make of the fact that all the women who have been killed were my patients."

"Don't forget that they were also your lovers. That is, with exception of Velda Rose."

"I'm not forgetting," the doctor growled.

"I don't think all your patients are in danger, Norris, but the ones who sleep with you sure as hell are."

"Okay, McCall, I've told you what you wanted to know. Can I get back to work now?"

McCall gave his incredulous look. "You think that's all I

want, just your verification about your relationship to the victims?"

"I thought that's what you wanted."

"Sure, but I also want you to tell me all you can about each victim."

Summerfield sighed. "I don't know all that much."

"Just tell me what you know, beginning with Velda Rose Caldwell."

For the next half hour, they discussed the four victims and, except for Colette Ramsey, McCall was ready to admit that Summerfield knew very little. He claimed that his only interest in any of the women was sexual, though from some things said, McCall ascertained that he did have deeper feelings for Colette.

As the conversation was coming to a close, McCall said, "Now I want a list, names and addresses, of all your women patients with whom you have had sex, past and current."

"You have to be crazy to think that I'd give you a list like that."

"Grow up, Norris. Every one of those women are in danger of being murdered, which is the only reason I want the list. If we put police protection on all of them, we have a chance to catch the murderer.

"And don't worry about your wife and kids finding out about your womanizing. I'm not going to tell them, and the police won't tell them. If you had any sense, you'd realize that they already know."

"What do you mean?"

"Do you think Melanie's stupid? She knows about your women. She knew about Colette. She hasn't confronted you because . . . well, maybe it didn't matter. Or worse still, maybe she loves you too much."

Summerfield seemed staggered by the news that his family knew about his affairs, so McCall continued.

"A lot of people, not just your family, have your number, Norris. Upstairs, you're not the swiftest guy I've ever known. And over the years, you haven't fooled a fuckin' soul."

Summerfield didn't respond, just picked up a nearby pad and started writing down some names.

"Make two lists," McCall ordered. "One current, one past. And try not to forget anyone."

McCall knew that Summerfield wouldn't, because women he had slept with were to him like a treasured hole-in-one to a golfer, something never to be forgotten. He even figured the doctor for the kind of guy who would have some type of token from each of the women he had seduced; a pair of panties, lock of hair, something.

When he finished writing, Summerfield handed McCall three sheets from the pad. One had six names with the word *current* above them. There were fifteen names on the other two pieces of paper.

"Miss Bevins will give you the addresses," Summerfield said.

"Are you sure this is it?"

"I'm sure. The six on the *current* list I've had sex with over the past three months. The rest spread over a period of three months to two years."

"Fine," McCall said. "This will give me a start, but before the day's over, I want you to prepare me a list that goes back at least five years."

"You have to be kidding."

"No, I'm very serious. Will you be here until six o'clock?"

"Yes," Summerfield answered with a moan.

"Then I'll be here to pick up the rest of the list about six o'clock." He knew Summerfield would have it ready. He had already committed himself too much to back out now.

LeAnne gave him the addresses for the names Summerfield had jotted down. With the list and Haloran's help he could, perhaps, prevent another murder. But the names were also a pretty good suspect list.

Maybe the killer was a jealous woman. Or maybe it was a husband wanting to make Summerfield a patsy for what had been done to his wife. He still hadn't ruled out any of the old players, but the list gave him something new to pursue.

He was fairly certain of one thing. The killer probably had at least part of the same list.

Chapter 30

Tuesday, June 30, 8:20 p.m.

McCall was in the diner with Haloran, the first time he had been able to get with the detective since the confrontation with Summerfield. He had returned to Summerfield's office at six o'clock, picked up the remainder of the list. The doctor wasn't in, but had instructed LeAnne to give McCall a packet.

"I can't believe what's in there," LeAnne had said.

He had grinned and replied, "Why not?"

"Because I just can't believe anyone could intimidate the doctor into providing this kind of information."

"Now, what kind of information are you talking about?" he had asked.

She had sighed with resignation. "You should know by now that you can't hide anything from me. Besides, it's all over the office."

"Damn," he had responded. "There's no point in putting something in the paper. I'll just turn it over to you women."

She had laughed. "That wouldn't be a bad idea. Am I going to see you before you pick me up Friday night?"

"I don't know. Things are beginning to break."

"We are still going away for the weekend, aren't we?"

"Count on it."

"I am."

Haloran was as astonished as LeAnne had been by the list McCall provided him.

"How in the hell did you get him to . . . never mind, I don't want to know."

They were each working on a couple of chili dogs with potato chips, washing the food down with cold milk.

"Do you think you can provide protection for these ladies, Bill?"

"I don't have enough people to protect all of them," he replied. "Maybe we can cover the six most recent ones, but that's going to be tough. I'm going to have to get an okay from the Chief."

"Think there'll be any problem?"

"I don't think so, but it will probably be tomorrow before we can get all of them covered."

"I hope that's not too late."

"So do I," Haloran said. The detective paused for a few moments, then continued, "C'mon, McCall, tell me how you got Summerfield to cough up this list."

"Can't do it, Bill."

Haloran laughed. "Is the man alive?"

McCall grinned. "Of course, he's alive. You act like I'm violent or something."

"You've been known to do a little ass-kicking in your time."

"All that's behind me," McCall deadpanned. "From now on, you can count on me to be a model citizen."

"Bullshit," Haloran replied. "The day you become a model citizen, I get elected to sainthood."

"Bill, with all your sterling qualities, that wouldn't surprise me a bit."

Chapter 31

Tuesday, 11:46 p.m.

Meredith Summerfield was having drinks in the *Cactus Bar* with Renee Coleman. Renee was a lesbian, but that didn't bother Meredith. She had, after all, made love to Renee on occasions when she was bored with men. But on this particular night, her interest in Renee was strictly conversation.

As they talked of former days in high school and college, Meredith couldn't help but be struck by the fact that Renee didn't look any different than most young women, except she was prettier. You would think, she thought, that a lesbian would look different. She mentally chuckled at the observation, realizing that a person looking at her wouldn't know that she had sex with her father, his best friend, and Renee.

Her only criticism of Renee was that she always seemed

too stiff, almost formal. There was such a properness to the business suits she wore, to the way she seemingly tried to hide the curves of her body. There were times that Meredith wished her body looked as good as Renee's.

The hair she could do without. Renee had it cut much too short, which overly accentuated her pixie-like face.

One reason Meredith had suggested Renee meet her for drinks was that she was still smarting from Clark Ramsey's verbal tongue-lashing regarding her conversation with Matt McCall. He had made it known in no uncertain terms that she was never again to discuss their relationship with the reporter, or for that matter, with anyone.

Her initial reaction had been to tell him to go fuck himself, but she didn't verbalize the thought. Instead, she had quietly endured his tirade, then took the matter to her father.

She had talked to her father on Sunday, and she was totally unprepared for his reaction. He had been sympathetic to Clark, had actually suggested that she heed Clark's advice. He, too, said Matt McCall was dangerous.

As for Clark's anger, her father said it was because of the terrible strain he had been under, Colette's death and all.

She had argued, "If the man loves me, why is he embarrassed to say so?"

"Timing," her father had replied. "Timing is everything. When the time is right, he will announce it to the world. But for now, it's best to wait."

Wait, she thought, I don't give a shit one way or the other as to whether Clark announces it. I don't give a shit whether I'm Mrs. Clark Ramsey or not.

The more she had thought about it, the more pissed off she was at Ramsey, the more she thought he wasn't the man for her.

"You certainly are drinking a lot tonight," Renee observed.

"This is just my third drink," Meredith said. "Besides, who's counting?"

Renee laughed. "I'm not nagging, just thought I'd mention it."

Meredith smiled. "Your concern is appreciated, but you know the one thing I can do is hold my liquor."

"I can hold it, too," Renee said, "but it does some funny things to my head."

"You don't have to try to keep up with me, Renee."

"I'm not trying. I couldn't if I wanted to."

Meredith pondered her drink for a moment, then said, "You know, Renee, I'm beginning to believe that all men are assholes."

"You're not going to get any argument from me."

"Tell me, Renee, have you ever slept with a man?"

The woman shuddered. "Not really. I was raped by one, though, when I was fifteen."

"And you've never had any since then?"

"I've never had a man, no."

"Of course, you know I go both ways," Meredith said, "and I can honestly say that I enjoy sex with a man or woman. I don't think I could do without a man all the time, though. I mean I couldn't just be content having sex with another woman."

"That's just the way you're made," her friend reassured.

Meredith sighed. "I've often wondered just how I'm made. For instance, now, I'm really in the mood to screw some guy. But it sure as hell isn't going to be Clark. I don't care how horny he gets, he gets nothing."

"You could come over to my place," Renee invited.

"No, that's what I'm trying to explain to you. I really want a man."

"Well, I can't help you on that score."

Meredith laughed. "Did you know a guy turned me down the other day?"

"He must have been queer."

"Not this one. He's the kind who undresses every woman with his eyes and takes you to bed mentally."

"What was the problem then?"

She pondered the question, then answered, "Timing, I guess. My father says everything is a matter of timing."

"I suppose it is."

"Anyway, I get this guy over to my apartment, we have a couple of drinks, then I go into the bedroom and come out a little later with just my panties on."

"And what did he do?"

She laughed. "He just left. He just looked at me and walked out the door. You know, that kind of rejection isn't good for a girl's ego."

Renee smiled. "Well, that's something I never have to worry about."

"Maybe you're better off."

"I'm happy with myself."

"I know, which is why I wanted you to have some drinks with me tonight. I needed to be with someone who is happy with themself."

"You know I'm always available to you."

"I know, and I appreciate it."

They talked past midnight. Meredith had four more drinks and announced, "I think I'm ready for beddy-bye. I'm even past the horny stage."

"The invitation is still open to come over to my place," Renee said.

"Not tonight, Renee. Tonight I'm going to plop my head down on the pillow and forget everything."

Meredith was somewhat fuzzy-headed as she drove home, the result of too much alcohol. However, she made the trip without incident, fumbled with her keys in trying to find the right one to her apartment, then had difficulty fitting the key into the lock.

When she finally got into the apartment, she went immediately to the bedroom, took her clothes off and dropped them on the floor, went into the bathroom, turned on the shower and got in. The shower was pleasant, but made her even groggier.

She toweled herself off in the shower and stepped out. The killer was waiting.

Chapter 32

Wednesday, July 1, 3:49 a.m.

McCall was startled out of a deep sleep by the ringing of the telephone. Through half-open eyes, he checked the time on the clock radio while picking up the receiver. It was Bill Haloran.

"Another one," the detective said. "And another anonymous call to tell us about it. Everything's the same, but you're going to be surprised at the identity of the victim."

"Well, tell me. Don't keep me in suspense."

"Summerfield's daughter."

"Meredith Summerfield?" McCall was shocked by the news. "Does he know?"

"Not unless he did it. You're the first person I've called."

"Well, you'll need to call the Summerfields and Clark

Ramsey."

"I'll let the Summerfields tell Clark," the detective said.

"I can't believe it," McCall said. "She's one of the women I didn't even think about giving protection."

"Well, her dad didn't put her on his current list. In fact, he didn't put her on either list."

"I know, but I should have known she was a potential victim."

"McCall, you can't know everything. And you can't protect everyone."

"Damn," McCall said. "I should have known."

"If you want to meet down at the diner in an hour or so, I'll give you what I have on this one. It isn't any more than I've had on the other four victims."

"Well, I'm awake, so we might as well go over this one like we have the others. Say five-thirty?"

"That sounds good to me."

For a few minutes, McCall laid there thinking about Meredith Summerfield. She was a strange chick, but she didn't deserve to cash in this way. Being born the daughter of Norris Summerfield was a bad break, but this was the cruelest break of all.

He decided to call Lisa, to see if she wanted to join them at the diner. There was no answer.

To hell with it, he thought. He showered, shaved, and went to the diner alone.

Chapter 33

Monday, July 6, 9:30 a.m.

McCall had spent an enjoyable but restless weekend with LeAnne. His body had been with her, but his mind kept wandering to the bathtub murders. He kept thinking about the lives of the victims and the lives of the players with whom they had contact.

It was late Sunday afternoon when he decided he knew the identity of the murderer. The only problem was finding proof that the person was the killer.

But late Sunday night, while driving from Wimberly to San Antonio, he concocted a plan to catch the killer. Early Monday morning he had outlined that plan to Bill Haloran, who said, "You're crazy, McCall. You can't go risking people's lives on some half-baked idea."

"Do you have a better plan?"

"No, but this is a job for a professional. If I go along with it, we use a policewoman."

"The killer might smell a cop."

"And the killer might murder a civilian."

"She's willing to take the risk."

"Well, I'm not willing for her to take it. Besides, you haven't got Summerfield's cooperation yet."

"I'll get it."

"I don't know. Even that sonofabitch could get killed."

McCall laughed. "That's a chance I'll have to take."

Haloran told him the police were attempting to protect all the women on Summerfield's list who lived alone, which McCall thought was adequate. The killer's modus operandi had been to strike Summerfield's single, divorced or separated women. And the killer was unlikely to change procedure.

Now, McCall was in Summerfield's office, explaining the plan to him.

"It's crazy," the doctor said.

"Maybe. But if it gets Meredith's killer, isn't it worth it?"

"When you put it like that, I don't really have a choice, do I?"

"You always have a choice, Norris."

"I'll do it," he agreed. "But it's for Meredith, not for you."

"I don't expect you to do anything for me. Just remember that you're not to tell anyone what you're doing. That means your wife, your son, and especially your lovers."

Summerfield snarled, "I can be discreet, McCall."

"Well, you'd better. A lot depends on this."

After leaving Summerfield's office, McCall went back to the *Tribune.* Lisa was there, got him a cup of coffee and asked if he had made any progress on the case.

"Nope," he replied. "Finding a clue is like looking for a needle in a haystack."

"I'd have thought something would have broken by now."

"Well, you'd think so, but we've evidently got ourselves a real smart murderer here."

"I guess you think he's going to kill again?"

"Oh yeah. This is just vacation time. We might have another killing tonight, tomorrow, next week. This killer is driven by passion, emotion. That accounts for the unpredictability, though I'm not sure I've ever really come across a predictable killer."

"You certainly are smug," she observed. "Are you sure you don't know something that you're not telling me?"

"I didn't know I was smug. If I am, it's not because I know anything about the murders."

"Well, you've kind of cut me out lately."

"Lisa, I haven't had anything to cut you in on."

She was in a pouting mood. "I just want you to know that I'd like to have a little part in covering these murders."

"Damn, Lisa, you do have a part. You've provided me with a lot of information."

"Most of which you double-checked."

He sighed. "There wasn't much else to do, and I'm always careful."

"I really don't think you have all that much confidence in me."

"I really don't have all that much confidence in anyone other than myself. If you become an investigative reporter, spend enough time on the job, you'll understand."

"Frankly, Matt, I think you resent me because I'm a woman. You don't think a woman can do anything as good as a man."

"Wrong, baby, I think some women can perform better professionally than some men. But I think there are places where a woman doesn't belong."

"You just can't accept the fact that a woman can do anything a man can do," she taunted.

It riled him that she hadn't understood a thing he said, which he figured he should have expected.

"When she's not having a period," he angrily replied. "Or when she isn't too busy making sure her makeup is on right. Or when she isn't all fucked up emotionally about some sin she thinks a man perpetrated against her."

Her face reddened at his outburst. "I really can't work with you."

"Then don't. Who needs you?"

He was sorry after he had said it, but too proud to do anything other than call Parkham and have Lisa reassigned. On the personal front, they'd had some magic together, but now it was gone. In terms of a professional working relationship, though, there had never been that much. He had always figured Lisa would dump pure journalism for something more glamorous, like advertising or public relations.

Lisa kept her distance for the rest of the day, a day made busy by numerous phone calls to contacts of the five victims. None could shed any light.

At four-thirty, LeAnne called. "Someone came in here a few minutes ago and picked up the doctor for a few drinks. Want to guess who it was?"

"I don't have any idea."

"Michelle Sharp."

"You're kidding."

"No, I'm not. I just thought you'd want to know."

"Looks like I owe you dinner."

"Sounds good to me. Just say when."

"I'll let you know."

After closing out the conversation with LeAnne, McCall put his feet on the desk and leaned back in his chair. He was pleased. Everything was going according to plan.

Chapter 34

Another week passed with no new developments regarding the murders. But in the case of Dr. Norris Summerfield, a lot was happening. All his friends and acquaintances were buzzing about his new relationship with Michelle Sharp.

If there was more speculation about the relationship than any in his past, it was because he was more open about this one. He and Michelle had drinks at the *Cactus* every afternoon, then dinner every evening at one of San Antonio's better restaurants.

And his car was usually parked at her house until the early morning hours.

If Melanie Summerfield knew about the relationship, she ignored it. She was still feeling the pain of Meredith's death, trying to find comfort by drinking too much with her country club friends. None of them dared mention what was going on between Norris and Michelle Sharp. But they did consider Norris a cad for deserting his wife in her time of need.

As for Summerfield, if he felt any remorse for his actions, it did not show. He was seemingly having the time of his life.

But it was not just Melanie Summerfield who had been deserted. The doctor had parted company with all women except Michelle. And some of those left out in the cold did not take kindly to his fascination with a new love.

Chapter 35

Thursday, July 16, 1:45 a.m.

Dr. Norris Summerfield and Michelle Sharp embraced in the doorway of her house, lamplight from the hallway silhouetting their bodies. They held each other for a few seconds, then he pecked her on the cheek and went to his car.

Michelle watched from the doorway until he was in the car, then closed the door.

The killer, crouched in some shrubbery at the end of the house, observed the scene between Michelle and Summerfield, and also noticed that a screened window near the front door was open.

I must wait, the killer thought, wait until the time is right. She'll be going to bed soon. Then I can move.

Lights in the house began to go out until there was only a glimmer coming from one room.

She's in her bedroom, the killer thought. She's probably going to bathe. The slut needs to take a bath, needs to clean his filth off her.

The anger began to intensify, and with it the need to kill this woman who had made such a mess of things. Uncontrollable rage put the killer's legs in motion, guided the knife as it cut the screen.

Then the killer was inside the house, moving ever so cautiously toward the bedroom. There was a pause at the bedroom door, then a smile at the sound of the shower. The feet began to move again, this time stopping at the bathroom door. It was also open.

The killer looked inside the room, saw the heavy blue shower curtain that ran the length of the bathtub, a barrier to the area where the water was cascading.

I'll wait, the killer thought. I'll wait until she steps out of the shower.

But after a minute went by, then two, the killer could no longer control the desire to murder. A hand reached for the one end of the curtain and flung it open.

"Hello, Carolyn."

Matt McCall was standing in the shower, fully clothed, water spattering his body. In one hand was an ugly nine millimeter automatic.

Carolyn Bell was so shaken that her body went into a convulsive reverse, slamming against the wall on the far side of the bathroom.

"I assume you weren't expecting me?" McCall deadpanned.

Carolyn was dressed in a black karate outfit, a gleaming surgical knife in her hand. There was a wildness in her eyes that McCall didn't figure he had time to interpret.

He stepped out of the tub and said, "Put the knife down, Carolyn."

She didn't obey. She looked at the knife as though she didn't know why it was in her hand. Then she shrieked and went into a crouch.

McCall had always figured most women who took up karate did it because they thought the outfits were cute, but not this chick. She had, after all, killed five people. He didn't want to be number six.

Crazy thoughts raced through his mind. After all that time in Vietnam, wouldn't it be the pits to get snuffed by a woman in a bathroom?

"Carolyn, you've got five seconds to put that knife down. Otherwise, I'm going to blow your fuckin' brains out."

But even as he said it, he knew she didn't hear him. She was in a trance-like state, intent on only one thing.

Killing.

He thought the best thing he could do for her would be to blow her away, save the state some time and money. As his trigger finger tightened, she lunged at him, slashing with the knife.

"Oh, shit," he hollered while avoiding the gleaming blade. Then with controlled resignation he kicked her in the stomach and followed up by cracking her across the head with the gun.

She slumped to the floor, a frighteningly small package for someone who had brought so much sorrow and death to the world.

Chapter 36

"Congratulations," Lisa said.

"Thanks," McCall replied.

"It must be very satisfying to be in on the close of a case like that."

"It's satisfying to see a murderer put away."

"I wish I had been more a part of it."

"Believe me, Lisa, you played a very important part."

"I don't feel that I did."

"Well, you did."

"Did you know I was leaving?" she asked.

"No, I didn't. Where are you going?"

"Back to Arkansas."

"Are you going to work for a paper there?"

"I don't have anything lined up yet, but I'm sure I'll find something."

"I'm sure you will.

"You know, I really thought we had something special."

"Maybe we did. Maybe it was just a matter of timing."

She sighed. "I guess that excuse is just as good as any."

"I think everything's going to turn out fine for you."

"You know, I could have done what Michelle Sharp did," she said. "I could have played that role."

"Carolyn Bell might have smelled a rat, you being a reporter and all."

"You could at least have told me what you were doing."

"I thought the fewer people who knew, the better," he responded. Then with a laugh he added, "Besides, maybe I considered you a suspect."

She smiled. "That I don't doubt."

"When are you leaving?"

"Tomorrow."

"That's fast. When you make up your mind, you don't waste any time."

"I've been thinking about it for quite a while."

"Well, all I can say is good luck."

"Maybe, when you've had time to think about it, you'll come visit me."

"There's always that possibility."

"I'm counting on it," she said. "Any possibility that we could have dinner tonight?"

He had been considering asking Michelle Sharp to dinner, but said, "Sure, I don't see why not. This last night, you get the best of San Antonio."

Just before noon, he met Haloran at the diner. The detective was in good spirits.

"I can't believe it all worked out, McCall. Of course, I wasn't real sure Carolyn Bell was the killer."

"Neither was I. It was pretty much gut feeling after I remembered that she told me she was into karate. Of course, I also recalled telling her about Meredith and Summerfield's relationship, which I don't think she knew about at the time. I remember she was really surprised by what I said."

"I guess we have to give Summerfield some credit," Haloran said. "He played his role pretty well."

McCall showed disgust. "Give him credit, hell. He's the one who created Carolyn Bell. We can give him credit for that."

"Well, it's all behind us now," Haloran responded. "Maybe we can get back to our fishing trip."

"Sounds good. But there's something I've got to do first."

"What?"

"I've got to run down to Mexico for a few days with Arturo Garza."

"What in the hell are you going to do there?"

"We're picking up a couple of illegals and bringing them back. We just want to make sure they get proper medical attention."

"McCall, half the stuff you say doesn't make a damn bit of sense. But I don't even want to know why you're going to Mexico. If I don't know, maybe I won't get involved."

McCall laughed. "You act as though I'm always dragging you into something. If it wasn't for me, your life would be pretty dull."

"I could stand a little dullness."

McCall thought, so could Dr. Norris Summerfield. The good doctor was now riding high on the part he had in capturing Carolyn Bell, but he was in for a low period. It would begin when McCall brought back the two illegals who Summerfield had hired to kill him. With the two illegals for witnesses, even Clark Ramsey couldn't save his golfing buddy.

McCall smiled when the waitress arrived. "How about a couple of chili dogs? Just what the doctor ordered."